The
Shining Fragments

ESSENTIAL PROSE SERIES 151

Canada Council **Conseil des Arts**
for the Arts **du Canada**

ONTARIO ARTS COUNCIL
CONSEIL DES ARTS DE L'ONTARIO

an Ontario government agency
un organisme du gouvernement de l'Ontario

Canadä

Guernica Editions Inc. acknowledges the support of the Canada Council
for the Arts and the Ontario Arts Council. The Ontario Arts Council
is an agency of the Government of Ontario.

We acknowledge the financial support of the Government of Canada.
Nous reconnaissons l'appui financier du gouvernement du Canada.

The Shining Fragments

—— a novel ——

Robin Blackburn McBride

GUERNICA
EDITIONS
TORONTO · BUFFALO · LANCASTER (U.K.)
2018

Julie Roorda, editor
Michael Mirolla, general editor
David Moratto, interior and cover design
Guernica Editions Inc.
1569 Heritage Way, Oakville, (ON), Canada L6M 2Z7
2250 Military Road, Tonawanda, N.Y. 14150-6000 U.S.A.
www.guernicaeditions.com

Distributors:
University of Toronto Press Distribution,
5201 Dufferin Street, Toronto (ON), Canada M3H 5T8
Gazelle Book Services, White Cross Mills
High Town, Lancaster LA1 4XS U.K.

First edition.
Printed in Canada.

Legal Deposit—Third Quarter
Library of Congress Catalog Card Number: 2017964543
Library and Archives Canada Cataloguing in Publication
McBride, Robin Blackburn, author
The shining fragments / Robin Blackburn McBride. -- First edition.

(Essential prose series ; 151)
Issued in print and electronic formats.
ISBN 978-1-77183-266-3 (softcover).--ISBN 978-1-77183-267-0 (EPUB).
--ISBN 978-1-77183-268-7 (Kindle)

I. Title. II. Series: Essential prose series ; 151

PS8625.B73S55 2018   C813'.6   C2018-900144-5   C2018-900145-3

Contents

For Hugh

Prologue

The boy waited alone on a cold bench beneath a sign's gold letters. People checked the posters nailed on wood, dragged cases across cobble, and called to one another, waving. The day went down; still the boy sat. He'd stopped speaking hours ago.

The boy's trousers were damp with urine, his face and fingers filthy; he pulled a primary-school speller from his sack and stared at pictures until the book became a pillow. On the bench in Union Station, eight-year-old Joseph Conlon curled as if to sleep, though he knew he wouldn't. "Annie," he whispered. "Please come back."

Sea

1882

*M*am died on the third day of the crossing. After that, Joseph stayed in the dark, not on the day-lit deck where Old Ciara took Colleen. Even when he tried to make sense of Mam's death, he knew his picture of events had shattered and he couldn't manage all the pieces.

Steerage was dank, and there Joseph found Gerry, who walked with a limp, drawing smoke from a cigarette that fit neatly through a gap beside a gold incisor. Gerry said each card's a force. The queen of diamonds was his lady, but the ace of hearts was worth more. Watch out for the ace of diamonds. Gerry's knack for winning at maw had paid for the steamer and several bodily repairs. Diamonds were the strongest of all earthly gems. "You can cut through glass with a diamond, boy — slice a mirror into pieces and see your face in every one." Gerry's face was a tapestry of scars that Joseph committed to memory. Other images and events he worked hard not to think about.

"Look at me," Gerry said. "We're the same, you and me. I lost my mam, so I did — as a lad, just like you." When Gerry smiled, his scars smiled too, revealing grey teeth. His gold tooth was a mark of distinction, obtained with a five of trumps. "Fear not, boy. Friends are friends. We help each other, do we not? The Lord God Himself speaks through a fresh-cut deck."

Gerry's hands and forearms were mottled by foundry acid burns, but his fingers shuffled cards in perfect arcs, and sprayed secrets around the table where Joseph sat, privy to the men's spreads. Gerry carried a stone with a hole in it that he let Joseph touch, "For luck." He wore a bracelet of hammered metal, and on it, a woman's name had been melted over. His boots were shiny. An oilcloth coat hung loosely across his shoulders.

From Gerry, Joseph learned hand signals for revealing the other men's cards. "No one'll know," Gerry said, "if you're careful. Why would a poor lad such as you, Joe, give a fig what they were dealt?" They'd all seen what had happened to Mam. Even though Joseph refused to remember the details exactly, other passengers' memories made him an object of pity, not suspicion. In exchange for Joseph mastering the signs, Gerry took him on, just as Old Ciara took on Colleen — only she did it for nothing. She had tried to hug Joseph, but he'd screamed at her touch and bitten her. Later, when no one was looking, he'd bitten his own arm very hard, to make things even. Both bites bled. Ciara kept hers wrapped with a strip of cloth and didn't touch Joseph again.

Gerry's presence was a comfort; as the men played cards, the boy's hands were active. Gerry won round after round until he took a break from winning. "We have to lose sometimes — or the real game's over."

Under Gerry's tutelage, Joseph also learned to smoke. The smoke burned its own language into Joseph's lungs before he let it loose in clouds that made the men's faces vague. The haze also obscured Joseph's memory of his father's face. The last time he had seen him, the man placed coins into Joseph's open hand, saying, "You're a strong lad, Joe." Joseph often called upon the smoke-haze to interfere with his gift for memorizing detail.

"What's that you've got in your hand, then, lad?" Gerry asked on the fourth day, long after the last game had finished and Joseph paused from practising his shuffles.

He stared at the card he'd forgotten he was holding. The ace of spades.

◊ ◊ ◊

On the night of Mam's death, Joseph must have slept because he had no memories. The next night, when the lights went off, Joseph wished that he could sleep again, like Colleen, but he lay awake with his arm around his tiny sister, relieved that she was quiet, but tormented by pictures that came, unbidden, to take over his mind. When grief and horror arrived to crush him, Joseph crept through a passage to find Gerry, sitting up with the card players. Gerry let him sip from a whiskey bottle so that sleep would come. Whiskey drinking was warm and liminal, a place between waking and darkness where Joseph could remember the things he wanted to, instead of the things he didn't.

He remembered Annie.

Joseph was grateful for her presence, even when she was merely a recollection in a crowded, groaning, fetid ship. Joseph recalled his mother's faraway words: "The baby's name will be Annie or George."

"She's Annie, Mam," Joseph had confidently declared. Mam had laughed and ruffled his hair. She'd held him close.

Now Joseph's gratitude for his first memory of Annie knotted his stomach, as he realized that he could not fully hear the way Mam had said those words to him. Still, he remembered the reedy smell of her dress when she squeezed him, and her black hair straying from the pins after her shift at Darkley Mill. Joseph's hair was dark and wavy like Mam's. "Like your Uncle Seamus'," she had told him many times, smiling. When she smiled, if Joseph was lucky, she would tell him a story — of the Red Branch Knights, the queens and kings of Ulster, enchanted animals, and sorceresses. He could almost feel the skin on Mam's fingers, rubbed smooth with salve, and how she'd stroked his cheek. "Annie or George." Closing his eyes more tightly helped Joseph to hear her voice clearly, as did another gulp of Gerry's whiskey.

Months ago, Joseph had already seen Annie spinning a secret beam of light, little bigger than a spider, in Mam's womb. Would Annie look like Colleen? After that, Annie's spirit had visited him at night when Mam was sleeping. "I am here," she'd whispered in the darkness.

⋄ ⋄ ⋄

Joseph could not organize Mam's death into a coherent story. A spell had killed Mam. That much he knew, because he had watched it happen. Her medicine should have helped, but —

Nothing.

His cries had brought a crowd of people, who stood gasping and whispering. Joseph hated his cries for bringing them. He hated the circle of onlookers.

"Close her eyes."

"Get the Captain. Something needs to be done with her."

And he hated Old Ciara, clutching Colleen to her hip.

"I knew her. The boy and this wee girl are hers."

Joseph stared at his useless hands. Mam's medicine bottles were tucked in his sack. They couldn't save her.

When the Captain came, Joseph shrank as the man placed a hand on his shoulder.

He wanted them to go away, to leave him alone with Mam, though he couldn't look at her face. Instead, he touched her soft, cold fingers.

2

*O*n Joseph's second night of whiskey, more wins led to mounting grumbles from the card players. He settled under Gerry's arm, swigged from the bottle, and let himself be lulled by the sound of the men's talk, even though their talk was agitated. As discussion gave way to bickering, Joseph turned his attention to the prayers in his speller, and to his own petitions written in the margins. "Dear God, Holy Mother, and Jesus, please save Mam. Dear God, Holy Mother, and Jesus, please save Colleen. Dear God, Holy Mother, and Jesus, please save me from the sin of my very being." He added with the stub-end of a pencil: "Save Gerry, too."

A gull had flown into steerage and someone had swung a suitcase at it rather than put up with the commotion. Joseph studied the dead bird on the floor beside the card players. He sketched the gull's head, its open eye, on the page across from his petitions. Then, with whiskey filling the place where uninvited memories might have haunted him, Joseph stopped thinking — about the gull, about the card players. Instead, Joseph thought about Granny Dolan, whose presence seemed to follow him across the sea, and about Annie.

Annie's spirit had visited Joseph many times in the months leading up to their departure from Ireland. He'd felt as though he'd been waiting for her his whole life. He could not tell Mam, but he drew Annie in the basic lines that a stick could make in the mud. He drew

Annie in the ashes, and on stone, with a potshard. He made Annie's shape in rushes and twigs, and he planted her in the winter garden.

Joseph had not felt or done such things before Colleen's birth. The arrival of his sister two years ago had seemed as straightforward as a dumpling spooned onto his plate. Colleen was bland and simple, and usually wet.

Joseph could not talk with Granny Dolan about Annie.

"Because she isn't born yet. And Granny Dolan is not your real granny," Mam said. Real Granny was nestled in the earth. "She's in heaven," Mam added.

"In the flowers," Annie whispered in the dark, when Mam couldn't hear.

Joseph knew the true reason: because Mam wasn't married. Granny Dolan, and indeed, all of Darkley, had been bothered enough when Colleen was born. Joseph wondered if Annie had seen the Dolans yet, and if Annie was one of the trouble-makers in their shared garden, where the pots were sometimes broken, and Aideen Dolan's baskets pulled to pieces. Prayers were said over such occurrences, and blackthorn branches hung over the door. Once, a whole supper was left in the back garden to appease the small ones.

"They live here too — keep the Virgin working overtime. It's all travail, if not sin, Nora Conlon," Granny Dolan had said more than once.

Joseph had often talked to Granny. He chatted on and on about the visions that he saw, just never about Annie. "A gift for pictures is what you have, boy," she would tell him when he showed her his drawings and spoke of his dreams. "Lord knows what you have is a gift, a strange one. As strange as those grey eyes of yours, too big for a child, too old. The pictures in your head — you mustn't speak of such things to others. They won't understand you. I say it for your own protection, Joe; you're different."

Yet Mam had always encouraged him to speak freely of his dreams, and he'd tell her anything to see the burdens lift from her.

Granny Dolan said the Virgin Mary loved all children, even the ones who were different. "And she's your mother too, Joseph, your Holy Mother." He didn't want another mother, but he couldn't say that to Granny. Instead Joseph had said: "Tell me the story of that English king," because it often produced a treacle scone or, if he was lucky, a wedge of pratie oaten. Granny Dolan shook her head. "Henry Eight tried to take Our Lady's power right out. She made him uneasy, you see."

And so began another history — one that Joseph could eat his way through and lick his fingers to.

Granny Dolan knew all the stories and she observed the feasts of every saint. Her house on Mill Row was often busy with visitors, looking for guidance. "Make no mistake, boy, I belong to the Catholic Church: the One True Church that is Mary's Church. In my house you will give thanks to Mary and pray for her son Jesus to take away your sins. Your very being is a sin, Joe."

"If He takes away the sin of my being, He takes me away. Where would I go then, Granny Dolan?"

Granny never explained.

Joseph remembered Granny Dolan particularly blessed with a shank of mutton as big as her arm. She had a gift for cutting, one passed down by her father, who could trim a pigeon to feed an army, and who had got them through the Great Hunger by following the tip of his knife. "He could cut meat from a rock, my father," she said. "Have a piece of this bounty, boy, and thank the Lord for it. Thank Saint Agnes too, because it is her faith that we praise today. And the Blessed Virgin Mary — to take away the sin of your being."

Granny Dolan made the sign of the cross and offered the boy a cleanly severed strip of flesh before offering further counsel. Then: "Adam and Eve did a bad thing, so bad that they were accursed. The very strangeness of it angered the Lord, who saw sin each time a child was made — and greater sin in those who come to this world without fathers. Bastard children are the true children of Eve, and Eve was marked by Lucifer, who lives in hell. And because hell touches us, we can never be fully free of it, but for the power."

"What power?"

"The power of light, boy." She took his hands in hers and looked into his eyes. "The Virgin and her child, Baby Jesus. Even the greatest sinner can be saved if he chooses the light."

"Even Henry Eight who killed his wives and made the Protestants?"

"Well, of course, I don't know."

"Why don't you know?"

"Because I'm not God."

"I have a father," Joseph said.

"Ay, boy. Another thing best kept a secret."

❖ ❖ ❖

Joseph sat alone where Mam had lain, creating a memory. In his invention, he sat beside Mam for a long time after she was still. He closed her green eyes gently and set his ear to the bump that was Annie. Then he quietly asked the Captain to have Mam buried at sea. Captain Lewis told him: "She'll go free, and very gentle. You don't have to watch." But in his mind's creation, Joseph did watch, and made sure that holy words were said for her. Joseph imagined Mam on the sandy bottom of the sea at a table set for company. "You're my love," she said. Yet each night, despite Gerry's whiskey, Joseph awoke in a salt sweat, realizing that he could not swim back. Despite his panic upon waking, Joseph preferred the sea burial story to thinking of Mam's body in a refrigerated box somewhere in the hold.

When terror came, Joseph whispered stories of Ulster to Annie. He told her about Queen Macha's race against King Conchobar's fastest horses, and how, before she died, she gave birth to twins who both blessed and cursed the Red Branch Knights. "Ulster's warriors would be very strong," Joseph told her, "but they'd also have a weakness.

Sometimes they'd be sick." He told about the fight for the Brown Bull of Cooley, and how the bull's hoof-prints were still visible in a rock in Armagh. Joseph told Annie many tales of the great warrior Cuchulainn, until a stranger's deep voice cut through steerage: "Enough, boy! I can't sleep with your prattle." Joseph did not tell Annie the story of the children who were turned into swans. Something in Mam's last version of that story had bothered him. In silence, he picked up his speller and wrote a new prayer: "Dear God, Holy Mother, and Jesus please bless Annie." Not once before the sea journey had Joseph thought to bless Annie, because he'd assumed that she was safe with the Holy Ghost.

But the Holy Ghost worried him now.

Joseph sketched in the margins and over the psalms until morning. He didn't dare sleep.

During the day, when he was not with the card players, Joseph kept his speller with him. The animal pictures soothed him: Rat, Rabbit, Badger, Dog, Kingfisher, Frog ...

Eventually he threw Mam's empty medicine bottles overboard: one for the Father, one for the Son. The third, still more than half full, Joseph placed in his sack with the Brigid's cross, his father's letter, a jackdaw feather, and Mam's gloves, wrapped tightly in a walnut shell.

He dropped the dead gull's body over the rail and watched it splash into the waves.

3

*O*n the way to the sixth day's card games, a postcard slipped from a man's coat. Stooping to gather it, Joseph saw handwriting and printed language that he couldn't read; but on the front was a photograph of a naked woman. He tucked the picture into his speller, well away from the prayers of petition. She slid smoothly between pages listing easy words of one syllable.

During a break between hands, Joseph opened his speller and secretly studied the lady's breasts, the hair between her legs, her beckoning smile. The lady distracted him, and he was clumsy with his hand gestures during the next game. One of the men caught him out. "Right then, Gerry, your boy's a cheat! Holding up nine fingers, he was, just as I sit here with the nine of spades!"

Gerry threw his cards on the table and stood. "Go on, now, boy!" he shouted. "We'll not have cheating at this table. These are respectable men."

"But Gerry — " Joseph felt his heart quicken and his face grow flushed and hot. He couldn't stop the tears.

"You heard me. Go!"

"Gerry," said one of the players, quietly. "Have some mercy, man. Remember the wee lad's just lost his mother."

But Gerry's gaze remained fixed and angry, and Joseph cringed before running from the table to his berth, the hot tears stinging. He tried to conceal the sound of his crying because he wasn't a baby, but wished he could hide himself entirely.

When he got to his bunk, he curled under Mam's Monaghan quilt until his body settled. Only then did he lift the cover. Hours later, Old Ciara arrived with Colleen. Joseph tried to take Colleen to his bed to tell her a story, the best one — about Cuchulainn killing the fiercest hound in Ireland and earning his name. But Colleen was tired, said Old Ciara, and curled with her on her berth until the two of them drifted off.

As the evening wore on into night, Joseph couldn't talk to Annie because someone would complain, even if he whispered. He wouldn't sleep without whiskey, but remembered Gerry's angry face. Joseph picked the scab over the bite marks on his arm until they bled. He took a metal jack and scraped lines into his other arm. When he felt the tears come again, Joseph opened his speller and, by lantern light, studied the naked lady. He placed the postcard close beside him, and sketched her body over the word lists.

Later he tucked the lady away and put out his lantern, rubbing his fingers along the stitches of Mam's quilt. Every patch was from the Monaghan house where she was born, cut and sewn by Real Granny and Mam's sisters, before the Hunger killed them, and Uncle Seamus buried each one in turn. The quilt felt like home, and under it Joseph allowed only chosen memories. Closing his eyes, he decided that the best place to send his mind was Keady — two miles away again. He wouldn't complain about the distance now. "I promise, Mam," Joseph whispered into the thin mattress so no one would hear. "No stomach ache or leg cramps. I can carry Colleen. I can." The mattress stank of damp duck feathers, and the air of human excrement. "Stay with me, Mam."

In his mind they walked. First along the old Black Pad, covered in cinders from the mill furnaces. Then, at the Slither, along the main road to Keady where the bells from two St. Patrick's churches rang: one for them, and one for the Protestants who, Granny Dolan said,

Saint Patrick's soul must pity. Little shops, the grist mill, and Joseph's father.

When Mam, Joseph and Colleen walked to Keady, they usually went to the dispensary which sold Mam ointments for her aches and pains. Sometimes Mam was sick. She had spells — like the Red Branch Knights, thought Joseph. Mam would never take a drop of liquor from the spirit grocer. "No remedy in spirits," she said. The medicine that made her better could be found only once a month on a Friday, when the Bottle Man rolled into Keady Market. No one knew where he came from. Some said that he walked from St. Mochua's Well, where the waters were curative if the stone was turned sun-wise. People whispered about the Bottle Man. And they whispered about Mam, who paid him a coin and thanked him for his trouble, and he nodded, as though to thank her for her own. On the label a lady with pink flowers smiled at Joseph, but Mam quickly buried her in her sack.

At Bridge Street, Mam often left him to wait for her. He and Colleen would run in the field behind the butcher's. To make the game worthwhile, he did somersaults in the grass and let Colleen fall on his back when he got dizzy. Each time she threw herself down he roared, and she giggled, until her laughter became exhausted and he chased her into a new spree of shrieks. When he stopped their game, she hit him on the legs and growled. Then she squeezed him with her little fingers and cried. "Don't cry. Being a baby won't help, Colleen. Stop crying!" scolded Joseph, as he'd been told many times. Sometimes he pushed her away. Sometimes he pinched her. Finally, he hoisted her onto his back, where Colleen's wails found a rhythm with his pace until she quieted. He set her down by the beech trees near the bridge and told her stories.

The tales that Mam taught Joseph were better than Granny Dolan's histories. They had come to her in childhood from her older brother Seamus, the best storyteller "perhaps in all of Monaghan," though Uncle Seamus had gone off to Canada years before Joseph was born.

"To have a better life," Mam told him.

"Now you're the best storyteller in Armagh, Mam," Joseph had whispered to his mother, earning a hug and the smell of her skin.

"Ah, you're my love."

Down by the Callan River where the old bridge waited, Colleen listened while Joseph told her Mam's stories of Ulster. Eventually, sucking her fingers and curling onto his lap, Colleen would fall asleep.

At winter's end, Annie had spoken to Joseph after Colleen settled. As he listened, Joseph pressed a piece of burnt wood lightly over a section of stone. An eye opened under his hand. "The Holy Ghost," Joseph whispered. When he glimpsed Mam on the bridge with his father, he did his best to wipe away the eye. Granny Dolan called Joseph's parents sinners. Joseph's father was a Protestant. And: "Being a Prot's not the worst of his sins," Granny said.

"When we get to Canada," Mam said, "we'll have a better life." When Mam placed Joseph's hand on her belly, Annie was not a whispering presence, but an actual baby, swimming inside her as he must have done. With his ear to the smooth drum of his mother's abdomen, Joseph heard surges and imagined pink legs kicking a message for him. Mam reached for the lady in pink flowers. "Just one swallow to keep away a spell," she said.

❖ ❖ ❖

Joseph awakened to the sound of his own scream. Colleen whimpered, Old Ciara stirred, and the other passengers grumbled.

"There now, boy. Friends are friends."

Gerry.

Joseph saw the orange lantern glow and a cigarette's burning tip; immediately the night's terror vanished. He smelled the oilcloth coat and the smoke. He clung to the man's sleeve as Gerry walked him away from the bunks, down a passage.

"I thought I ruined it for you, Gerry. I thought —"

"The game is the game. Now look at me."

In the dimness, Joseph saw that one of Gerry's eyes was blackened, and a fresh gash on his cheek had bled and dried. Gerry grinned his gold-tooth grin. "You don't let on. You never let on. That's why I spoke the way I did to you. Part of the game."

"But they beat you, Gerry."

"No! Indeed they did not." Gerry opened the breast pocket of his coat to reveal his lucky stone with the hole, and a wad of bills. "My ticket to Toronto bought and paid for. I'm grateful to you, boy, for the wins."

Joseph and Gerry stayed well away from the other card players, whose game had changed from maw to faro. "I don't like faro much, myself," Gerry said. "Time to practise shuffling." Boy and man sat together at a dim bench and table, where Gerry taught Joseph a patience game and two card tricks. He let Joseph sip from the whiskey bottle.

"No remedy in spirits," Joseph heard Mam say as he drifted back into a short-lived sleep.

"Part of the game," he repeated.

4

*T*he jaws of the land opened and they sailed down the St. Lawrence toward the gullet, Montreal. "Montreal is a second Ireland," Old Ciara said. "So many Irish, they say you'll think you haven't left Derry."

At Montreal, smoke stacks loomed and docks extended sullenly along the foamy shore. Captain Lewis found Joseph in steerage, gathering items into his sack. People stared and whispered as the large man walked among them there, in his crisp blue uniform with his gold watch and chain, in the stench and squalor, and the dampness. "Perhaps we should bring you and your sister to the Catholic church here. I could take you to St. Patrick's — just up the hill," the Captain said. "We'll tell the priest up there about your mother, Joe. She'll receive a proper Catholic burial."

But Colleen was a part of Old Ciara at the moment, and Joseph let her be.

"No, sir," Joseph replied, blinking away the Captain's words. For a moment, he saw Mam waving to him from the ocean floor, but he blinked that image away too. "We're bound for Toronto."

"Are you sure, laddie?"

"Uncle Seamus will meet us." Joseph's words held some power, because saying them made the Captain go away.

Seamus. Joseph imagined his uncle arriving like the warrior Cuchulainn himself, a shining hero and fearsome storyteller. In truth,

Seamus had come out so many years earlier that all Joseph knew of him were rows of spider writing on yellowed letters to Mam. Joseph could not read his uncle's hand any better than he could read his father's fancy script on the letter he had put away with Mam's gloves and the Brigid's cross. Joseph bit his nails and tasted dirt. People praised God when the ship finally landed. All the bunks were cleared; tin plates and cutlery were stuffed into sacks and mattresses were rolled and tied. Old Ciara paid close attention to the packing of Colleen's things, and Mam's, and took the Monaghan quilt.

Colleen whimpered to be lifted, but he said no; carrying three bags was enough. Old Ciara carried her and insisted they stay together getting off. When they stepped down, the Captain said: "I think it best that I take you to St. Patrick's, lad. I wouldn't want you getting lost with your sister. The nuns here can help you."

"No." Joseph stared down at the man's polished boots.

"The boy has his uncle to meet in Toronto," Old Ciara said. "And I'm headed there myself, so I don't mind taking them. Their mother wished for them to go to Toronto, to their kin. I'll watch over … both."

Two sailors carried a board tied with ropes bearing a blanketed form to the back of a carriage near the dock. People bowed their heads as Mam's body passed. "I'm all right," Joseph heard Mam say, "because I'm dead."

Joseph understood. He was learning how to be both alive and dead.

He let himself be led by Old Ciara up the hill to the train station.

❖ ❖ ❖

"Mam," Joseph had said. "Mam … listen now, and I'll tell you what I dreamed last night."

In this memory, spring stirred the fields beyond Mill Row where Joseph fancied he could hear Annie's voice.

"I saw people, shining people — whole crowds of them with light shining through them, like jewels!"

Mam had looked at him in a way that made Joseph believe Mam could shine too, if she wanted.

"You were there with me, Mam."

The memory of her made him ache with longing.

Mam had smoothed the dark curls back from Joseph's forehead, and studied him. Usually, she would smile and say: "What wonders you see in that head, wee gasson." Or: "Oh, ay, a fine dream, my chirpy bird." Mam even held Joseph's nightmares to be among his most spectacular visions. "A bard, you are," she would say to comfort him, "telling me such fine horrors."

But not this time.

"I must tell you what your father said."

Joseph had stared down at his buttered biscuit.

They needed four sets of tickets. "Say three if anyone asks. Your father says that we must only speak of three."

"Will he not come with us to Canada?"

"Oh, ay," Mam said, "but hush about that, now."

First they needed tickets for the Great Northern Railway of Ireland: a ten-mile ride from Armagh City to Portadown; then seventy-four more miles from Portadown to Derry where a steamer would be waiting in the River Foyle. The shipping agent would sell them tickets to Montreal. The final tickets would be most special, Mam said, "because your father will purchase them in Montreal. In Canada. Tickets for Toronto Union Station. So much money your father's given. For a better life."

Later, when Mam conveyed the news to Granny Dolan and the women at the mill, she didn't mention Joseph's father leaving Ireland with them, only that a brother would meet them in Toronto.

Before their journey, Granny Dolan surveyed their two rooms, empty but for the sacks of clothes, their quilt and mattress, Mam's oaten bread, salt pork and bottles of water. "It has been my Christian duty to help you, Nora Conlon. And help I hope I've given. May God forgive you and keep you." She touched Joseph's head, and her old lips trembled slightly. "May God forgive us all."

5

The train was more comfortable than the ship. Joseph and Colleen had their own seats and they watched as the land sped by. Colleen sang a song; Old Ciara watched with wet eyes. "My own daughter lost a daughter just last year," she said. "They wrote she went mad with grief. What can a mother do but grieve with her?"

Joseph twirled the jacks in his fingertips. He wished Gerry had sat in their carriage.

"All that would console her, they said, was her mother's company. So here I've come across the sea, by God, and at my age." The jacks kept twirling.

Joseph pressed the small points of a jack firmly into his right thigh, feeling the red letters forming beneath his pant leg. Soon "Toronto" was written in small abrasions.

Colleen fell asleep with her head in Joseph's lap. Her matted hair needed brushing, Old Ciara said, but the child needed sleep more. Soon Old Ciara snored. Joseph lifted Colleen and lay her down across the two seats. Then he crept away from the sleepers. As Joseph crossed to the next car, he inhaled the smoke from a dozen men.

"Gerry."

"By Jesus, boy." Each scar was a welcome sight. "Where have you come from, lad? Sit with us for a while then."

Joseph didn't need to speak, just to be there with the men's voices, the card decks, and the glimmering flasks as men tipped their heads back and swallowed. Occasionally Joseph was passed a flask and drank.

The conductor eventually came for him at Old Ciara's bidding. "I'll see you in Toronto, Gerry," Joseph called with a hiccup. Gerry's hand waved a mottled arm.

"Oh, you're back, then," Old Ciara said, staring out at the rolling land without turning. "I wondered what had become of you, boy." Joseph lifted his sister, who tensed, knocking her head on the arm rest. Her crying wearied Joseph, particularly as the whiskey had its effect. He wanted sleep badly, but feared it. He wanted to be back with the men and the flasks. "Colleen," he said quietly. "Don't be a baby." Joseph wanted to pinch her arm to show her that she needed to stop crying. He wanted to hit her.

"Mam," Colleen cried.

Then Joseph hugged his sister, breathing the smell of her hair and fixing her green ribbon to hide the tangles the best he could. He fumbled in his pocket for a jack, which he placed in one of her small, sticky palms. "Colleen," Joseph said. "Sing a song, Colleen."

"Mam," Colleen moaned.

"I'll tell you about Setanta — the day he fought the big hound and got the name Cuchulainn." Joseph had told that story to Colleen before, many times, and to Annie. Perhaps Annie was listening now. The jack hit the floor and rolled. Somehow he knew she wasn't.

❖ ❖ ❖

At Toronto Union Station, Gerry passed them by. "Not goodbye, boy," he called, "but good luck! And I'll see you." Gerry's hug smelled of ashes. When he waved, Joseph saw the lucky stone in Gerry's hand. He wished he had one.

Joseph hoped that Uncle Seamus would be like Gerry.

They sat on a bench in the waiting room under the station's

highest tower — the middle one of three, with the clock. Mam had told him his uncle would meet them there. Old Ciara waited too. She stared through the open front doors at the carriages and the lake, and as time passed, Joseph could see her impatience. All at once she turned to him, speaking carefully.

"Joseph, your sister, this wee girl here, won't be of any use to your Uncle Seamus. A burden is what he'll see — a burden. No use, a girl, only trouble for a single man. You don't understand that yet, but you will." He held Colleen on his knee, raised well above the chilly bench.

"I want you to let me take Colleen. Let me give her to my daughter."

At first the words didn't make sense to Joseph. Then, the old woman added: "She'll have a better life."

Mam's voice. Mam's words. "A better life," he repeated.

❖ ❖ ❖

Hours later, as he waited alone on the bench, Joseph remembered hugging Colleen and watching her disappear with the old woman. Seized by terror at what he'd done, he had run outside and seen a crowd of people on the street — but not Colleen. He'd run back inside the station, circling through a different crowd, shouting his sister's name, yet aware of the futility. Joseph found Colleen's green hair ribbon on the floor. It must have fallen as Old Ciara carried her out. He picked up the ribbon, and he held it to his nose to breathe whatever scent was left. "My name is Joseph Conlon and my sister Colleen's been taken," Joseph had tried to say to a man in a blue uniform, but the sounds didn't match the words in his head. What came from his lips was a kind of moan.

"She's gone. My sister's been taken." Each time that Joseph tried to say those words to a different pair of eyes, they looked away. Perhaps he was dead and people couldn't see him or smell his soiled clothes. If that were so, then limbo was Toronto Union Station.

But the station couldn't be limbo, because Annie wasn't in it.

6

All day and into the evening, Joseph waited on the bench beneath the station sign's gold letters. He hoped that, as Granny Dolan had once advised him, being quiet he'd make better sense, but Joseph doubted it.

Trying to calm himself, he opened his speller. The postcard slid, face-up, onto the floor; he quickly retrieved the naked woman and looked around to make sure no one had seen. For a few minutes, the sight of the lady brought relief. Joseph looked at the sketch he'd made of her, and adjusted it. With his finger on the card, he traced the outline of her breasts, her thighs; he touched the private place between her legs. He smelled the card, too, and put his tongue to her smiling mouth.

No. The card was bad luck. It must be. Despite the lady's enchanting smile and her body, the glimmer of pleasure she brought, he must have done the wrong thing in taking her in the first place.

Joseph walked to a waste bin, took a last look, and dropped her in. Maybe Seamus would come now.

An hour later, he pulled her out again.

❖ ❖ ❖

The conductor discovered Joseph once evening arrived, the man who had watched over Joseph, Colleen, and Old Ciara on their ride from

26

Montreal. Joseph stared down at his speller, his face expressionless. In his mind he implored: "Uncle Seamus — please find me! Find Colleen!" Then he flipped to the pages with the drawings of the animals. Rat, Rabbit, Badger, Dog ... Joseph smelled the urine drying on his trousers and he squirmed. He saw the dirt in crescent moons beneath his fingernails.

"There now, lad," the conductor said. "What happened to your grandmother and your sister, then?" The blood rose in Joseph's cheeks and caused a drumming in his chest, though his expression remained blank.

"She's not my grandmother," said a voice in Joseph's mind.

"What's happened then, boy?"

"Colleen's gone," said the voice that only Joseph could hear.

The man took Joseph's hand and led him to the big station office, and poured him a tumbler of water from a pitcher on the manager's desk. Joseph gulped it down, while the conductor had a word with the office manager.

"Something needs to be done with the lad, there. He's off a boat from Ireland, and arrived today on the Montreal run. I heard him speak on the train. Now the boy won't say a word."

"Defiant?"

"I don't know what's happened, sir. I saw him hours ago with a little girl and an old woman who I took to be his grandmother. I've done all my rounds and my paperwork, and the lad's still here. The woman and girl are gone."

Joseph closed his eyes tightly and concentrated. "Uncle Seamus," he urged silently. "You must have come when I ran looking for Colleen. I'm sorry I wasn't there, Uncle Seamus. Please come back. Come and find me. Find Colleen." Miserable, Joseph knew he would need to go back to the bench in the waiting room if his uncle was to find him. "It's my fault, I know," Joseph pleaded silently, "but please come back. Please."

The man put his large hand on Joseph's head, and Joseph shrank at the touch. "Mr. Nesbitt will help you when his shift's done." Mr. Nesbitt sighed, pulled a sheet down from a pile of paper, and wrote. Then he called over a young man in uniform and whispered something. The youth glanced Joseph's way and hurried out.

"I've sent for a police constable, boy," Mr. Nesbitt said.

Two young clerks stared at Joseph from their desks across the room. One approached, offering Joseph a plate of biscuits at arm's length. Joseph merely gripped his speller closer to his body and stared at the floor. The clerk returned to his desk.

"Wretched little mite. He needs a good scrub and a fire to take those clothes. He's a skull and bones, that one. He'll end the night at the House of Providence."

"Better to take him out and drown him," the second clerk said. "Spare the poorhouse another waif. Spare the city another bog trotter."

"Nesbitt'll have me drive him, to be sure — unless the copper takes the boy, which I doubt."

"Drop him at the corner and head on your way. Test his might. He'll only grow into another bloody papist if he's housed and fed."

"Have mercy, sir," the first clerk said. Joseph reread the list of animal names. He kept stopping at Dog.

"But I do, sir!" the second clerk said emphatically. "You're late at pints and face a double shift tomorrow: ugly business to lose the ale time. You can be sure all the Paddy Town taigs have been at their cups for hours — howling and brawling, and making miseries of themselves before they're on their knees tomorrow with the Hail Marys. You'd deliver the boy to that?"

Dog. Joseph pictured a wriggling pup in a biscuit-coloured sack. "Find a rock to weigh him down," Mr. Dolan had told Joseph. "He won't feel much."

Joseph had watched the sack as it sank. Maybe the clerks would tie him in a sack and toss him into the lake beyond the tracks.

He wove Colleen's green ribbon tightly through his fingers, and inhaled her fading smell. "You'll have a better life, Colleen," he said, aloud, as an elderly police constable entered.

"Where do you want to go, boy?"

Joseph gripped the ribbon tighter. "Darkley townland. In the parish of Keady. County Armagh."

As the clock sounded eight times, the constable's eyes looked sad, but his mouth smiled. "Come along for the night," he said quietly. He led Joseph outside into the cold Toronto air, lifted him onto a buggy hitched behind a chestnut mare and offered the boy a flask of water. Then he drove.

In the spring breeze, Joseph no longer smelled his dirty clothes. He smelled lake water and chimney fumes.

As they travelled, the city buildings grew smaller and the sky turned to ink. After a long time, Joseph asked: "What's the House of Providence?"

"The House of Providence," the constable replied, startled. "Why, a Catholic house of charity, boy. Did you want to go there?"

"No."

The constable relaxed, though his shadowy face still looked grim. "Providence is a good place," he said, "but I'll do you one better. Here, west of the city, I know a home the nuns run. Fresh air, no factory smoke."

They pulled up to the biggest, darkest house that Joseph had ever seen. "Sunnyside," the constable said. "Our Lady of Mercy." The old man stared at Joseph for a moment more. "Here you'll find people of your kind. You'll be taken care of, boy. I wish you well."

*T*he nun brought Joseph to a dim room with a hearth and a metal tub of tepid, cloudy water. She warmed the bath with a pot from the fire, and then left so that Joseph could undress and bathe. He kept his bag of possessions closely guarded. He didn't let her take it, and she didn't insist.

Alone in the semi-darkness, Joseph reached for a pitcher on the stand beside the tub and filled it with water. Crouching naked and shivering, he poured water again, and again over his head.

❖ ❖ ❖

When Joseph lay down, he gave in to the silence that replaced the ringing in his head. The nun sat on a chair beside his bed. She was a bird on the ship's rail and her eye was a perfect circle. She was a granite angel in St. Patrick's churchyard. She might have had wings. She was the moon's face drifting across the blanket of night, watching over him.

Occasionally, Joseph opened his eyes, reminding himself of where he was, though he preferred to imagine that his journey from Armagh was a dream.

As he'd done on the ship, he allowed memories of home, even sad ones, because they kept him safe from the nightmares of the ship and Union Station. Joseph accepted the memory of their walk to Armagh City. He thought about the engraved images in his speller of Rat, Rabbit, Badger, Dog, Kingfisher, Frog, Chamois, and Swan.

"What's a chamois, Mam?" Joseph had asked.

"Like you, a clever little goat good at hiding. Now off to bed with you." In his mind, Joseph could see Mam again and hear her voice clearly, even as the nun kept watch. Mam had laughed and run her fingers through his hair. He leaned into her, then. "My love," she'd said. Joseph whispered those words into the dormitory bed.

He knew his speller. Lesson ten, page twenty-seven: "The Lord is my light, and my health; whom then shall I fear? The Lord is the strength of my life; whom then shall I dread?" Joseph had listened to Mam repeat the psalm long after he was meant to be sleeping. When she prayed for mercy, he became afraid, for the prayers often came at the beginning of her spells. He'd learned that saying prayers aloud was dangerous. Maybe God didn't like to hear them from some people. Maybe that's why Mam died.

Mam's spells started soon after Colleen was born. Mam would return from the mill "filled with the weakness" and in need of her medicine. Later, when Annie's spirit visited, she whispered how to keep warm in the house while Mam was having a spell.

Annie told Joseph how to light the fire, and he almost did, imagining the warm flames.

More unsettling than Mam's spells were Granny Dolan's words afterwards. "The Lord only helps such ones as help themselves, Nora Conlon. No good can grow from a tree that's rot. Forgive me, Holy Mother." And she would make the sign of the cross to alert the Trinity.

❖ ❖ ❖

The morning they left Darkley forever, Mam said: "Nine miles we walk." Nine miles to Armagh and to Joseph's father. "Two miles more and we'll sleep, all four of us, under the stars at Navan Fort tonight."

"All five," Joseph said quietly to Annie.

"I am here," her spirit had whispered.

❖ ❖ ❖

Mam carried a large sack of their belongings, and Colleen, who carried her dolly. Joseph had two sacks. One contained clothes that Mam had folded and pressed flat, and tied with dried grasses from beside the Black Pad. "I wish I had yarrow," Mam said, but the season was too early for flowers. The sack held private things too. Joseph didn't see them at first, in a smaller bag within, though he knew her special gloves were there, and her medicine.

Joseph's other sack was his own and only he got to see its contents. Among his chosen pieces was Mam's Brigid's cross, which he had removed from the thatch of their roof in secret. "Bad luck to take down a Brigid's cross," Granny Dolan always said. He had watched Granny's daughter, Aideen, pull the rushes for cross-making at Brigid's Supper on the last night of January. Aideen wove quickly and soon transformed her rushes into diamond shapes and three-legged crosses. Mam worked more slowly, but her cross was more beautiful than all the others. Real Granny moved through Mam's fingers, plaiting a four-legged cross: a star.

As they walked along the very old road to Armagh City, Mam smiled. Joseph knew that she was thinking about his father.

A man gave them a ride part way in his cart, dropping them off just beyond the town's edge. There, two swans glided on the surface of the Callan River. "Will you tell me the story of the children turned to swans, Mam?" The story felt like home to him. On many nights, Mam had told him that story as he fell asleep, and he was sleepy now. "The swans flew far," Mam said, "but their wings were cursed by the sorceress Aoife. She was jealous because her husband Lir's children weren't her own." This part of the story always made Joseph picture the lady on the steps of the Protestant Church in Keady, standing beside Joseph's father. The lady had stared at Joseph, but Mam had pulled him quickly past.

On the road to Armagh City, Joseph thought about the story. Tied together with silver chains, the swans gleamed as they flew for nine hundred years before Saint Patrick came to Ireland and brought the word of God. The curse was broken by the tolling of a single church bell, and the swans changed back — only instead of being children, they were old, wizened people. Joseph loved that part the best because of the way Mam described them, just as Uncle Seamus must have described them to her. She made their old faces so clear in Joseph's mind that he could see relief etched in their wrinkles for a shining moment before they turned to dust.

As they approached Armagh City, Mam pulled from the waist of her skirt a small, handwritten map. They followed it to a house and knocked upon the door.

A man gave Mam a letter from Joseph's father.

"He said he's sorry," the man said and quickly closed the door.

Mam read the letter silently several times as Colleen slid from her hip to the ground. Then Mam, too, slid onto the muddy ground to catch her breath. "I'll just rest a moment," she told Joseph, but all three remained a long time before the door of the Armagh house.

❖ ❖ ❖

The road took them west from the city's edge, through fields that were not yet sown, in line with the old straight track of hedges. Joseph knew not to speak to Mam, even though she was silently crying. If only Annie would say something.

When they finally reached the hill that was Navan Fort, the sun gleamed orange and sank below the earth. Mam unpacked the bedding and made a place for them to sleep under one of the old trees in the ditch that encircled the mound, where they could watch the moon rise. For a few minutes she sat with them, but then she needed to go up to the top of the hill, she said. Her voice was breaking.

Joseph had tried to sleep under the Monaghan quilt, with Colleen curled in a warm ball beside him, but he couldn't. Mam's sobs guided his steps up the mound.

She was on her knees praying, rocking in the grass. The lady in pink flowers smiled at Joseph from Mam's medicine bottle.

❖ ❖ ❖

For a few minutes, as sunrise illuminated the windows of Our Lady of Mercy, Joseph slept dreamlessly. When he awoke, in full daylight, a girl was staring down at him. He blinked twice at her heart-shaped face.

"Deary's in the boys' wing!" someone hollered.

Before he could blink again, the girl darted down the long hall.

"Where's my sack?" Joseph asked, suddenly panicking, though he wasn't sure to whom he was speaking. His sack was on the floor beside him, tied with the green ribbon that had fallen from Colleen's hair. He opened it to return the medicine bottle and the speller, and stowed it under his mattress.

Joseph dressed in the white shirt and black trousers that had been folded and set out. Boys lined up to go out to the latrine before morning prayers. Each held a cup of drinking water. "There's one for you," a boy with an eye patch said. But an old nun led Joseph away.

At the end of a long hall, in a room with a large wooden table, sat the Sister who had received Joseph the night before. Beside her sat a priest. "This is Sister Patricia," the man told him. "I am Father Thomas — originally from Kilmurray."

"We're fortunate to have Father Thomas with us today," Sister Patricia said. "His work takes him many places. This morning he's come all the way from St. Paul's parish."

"But you've come much farther," the priest said. "From Ireland, Joe, like I did, long ago. Father Tom, you may call me."

Sister Patricia's spotless boots were laced tightly through tidy hooks. Joseph stared at her ankles, remembered the lady on the post-card and blushed.

Another scene unfolded in his head — one he couldn't stop from coming. He was on the wooden bench at Union Station with Old Ciara and Colleen. Joseph heard Old Ciara's voice above Father Tom's words. She said: "Your sister Colleen will be loved and cared for, boy. It's for the best." And Joseph knew it was true. To the priest, he said: "Our Uncle Seamus came, but I got up from the bench. It was my fault for missing him. I shouldn't have got up. I shouldn't have gone looking for Colleen — because she'll have a better life."

Father Tom placed his hand on Joseph's head.

He shook it off. "She will!" Joseph kicked the chair. "I shouldn't have left the bench! Uncle Seamus came! He came and I wasn't there!" Joseph bolted through the centre hall, past the patch-eyed boy, who stood watching. Joseph shoved the heavy front doors open and ran into the yard.

When he reached the wrought iron fence he found the gates chained shut. Beyond the property he glimpsed a dirt road, several houses, and stands of tall trees. Uncle Seamus wouldn't know where to find him now.

Looking over his shoulder, Joseph saw only the priest, the nun, and the girl he'd awakened to. She'd followed him out.

"Go away!" he screamed. Joseph fell to his knees and clutched the iron bars. "God, help us!" he remembered wailing over Mam's dying body. He saw the whites of her eyes. He wiped the vomit from her mouth. "God, please help us! Make it stop!"

"I can help you," the girl whispered.

Weeping, ashamed, he let her touch his shoulder.

"Deary Avery!" the nun called. "Deary Avery, come inside!"

Deary Avery led Joseph back, away from the iron gates.

String

1882–1886

8

*I*n the back pages of his speller Joseph made a sketch of Sister Patricia's slim, laced boots beside one of many old prayers: "Blessed Mary, forgive the sin of my very being. And Colleen's. Please forgive my mother." He sketched lightly in pencil, careful not to smudge the ankles, which were the best part. He also made a sketch of her face and imaginary body, one that he later had to erase; although afterward, looking carefully, Joseph still could see the faint lines of cartoon breasts and a triangle of hair.

He had torn out the word lists where the drawings had been copied from the bad-luck postcard, and buried them along with the card itself in a stumpy patch of earth beside the orphanage vegetable garden. Several times in the course of that rainy, humid summer, Joseph had dug up the card and studied it in various phases of decomposition, until the lady was safely beyond providing secret pleasure.

During morning prayers, he thought about Sister Patricia's body, well hidden by the black habit, but still accessible through his imagination.

During recreation time, Joseph made a ritual of squinting to see his rubbed-out naked Sister Patricia in his speller, until one day she saw him doing it. In a pique of shame and a display of feigned studiousness, Joseph wrote his signature twenty times over the erasures, adding "Darkley townland, parish of Keady" before erasing again.

Thereafter, he was mindful to watch Sister Patricia as she patrolled the boys' yard. Even at a distance, her ankles pleased him.

On Mondays and Thursdays, the boys and girls came together to sing for old Sister Martha, who coughed through much of the singing. Occasionally Mother Superior came down to listen, and Sister Martha coughed in another room until Mother returned to somewhere high up in the house. One Thursday, at the peak of summer's heat, the orphans and several Sisters travelled by street railway, all the way into the city, to sing at the House of Providence. Joseph stood in awe of the grand structure, remembering that the station clerk had called it the poorhouse.

Some of the old ones smiled and nodded when the children sang; others had only empty stares. "They're returning soon," Deary Avery whispered, mostly to herself.

Joseph hadn't found the courage to speak to Deary all summer. Her offer to help him that first morning had left him in awe. Unlike his attraction to Sister Patricia, which was physically exciting and secret, Joseph's attraction to Deary was reverential. She was three years older and mysterious in her devotions, which often got her into trouble. Deary seemed to possess magical knowledge. Joseph wanted to ask her where the old ones returned when they died. If she knew, then she might also know of Annie's whereabouts. Of any person he'd ever met, Deary was the most likely to understand limbo.

Deary wandered hallways where she wasn't supposed to go. She wandered the grounds, past the boundary of the girls' yard. More than occasionally, Deary wandered off the property — a source of consternation to whatever nun was supervising; somehow the Sisters never saw the girl's flight. Once Joseph helped hoist Deary over the fence, and they didn't see him either. His shoulder tingled after Deary had stood on it, and he took pleasure at watching her leap.

Deary always returned, accepting of her punishment. "I love the nuns," she said, and meant it. Deary wandered west to Grenadier Pond, because she needed to be with the willow trees. "So I can hear the spirits better." One day, Deary ran east all the way to the ferry docks. "I would have gone to the island," she told Sister Martha as she led Deary by the ear past Joseph and the other children, "but I didn't have five cents for the ferry. The island's a sacred place. May I borrow five cents for next time, Sister Martha?"

One-eyed Tim McCready, who often shadowed Joseph, but who kept away from Deary, told him about the days when she first broke into roaming. "They sent her to bed without supper," Tim said, "but Deary got too thin. Then Sister Martha caned her across the palms, but Deary didn't mind. Now when she's in trouble, they put her in a room under the cellar stairs. I'm glad, if you ask me, because she gives me the shivers." Joseph didn't ask for Tim's opinions, but he was grateful to learn the place of Deary's confinement. While she sat in the musty space on the other side of a locked door, Joseph found opportunities to sneak down to her. Eventually he found the courage to speak with Deary. She was the only one he could trust with the story of Annie.

When Deary answered from behind the door — "I met a spirit like your Annie once" — Joseph shed silent tears of grief, then relief. Finally someone knew of his secret sister, of the possibility that Annie's whispering presence had been — and perhaps still was — real. He curled on the dirt floor beside the crawlspace door, pressing his open hand to the wood.

❖ ❖ ❖

Deary collected strings and, under the stairs, tied them into knots, each with its own name. Often, she brought them upstairs to braid in the little girls' hair. String somehow found its way to Deary. She turned it into rings; she wound it into elaborate patterns — her language, she said — the language of her people, who studied things from the air in the silent places others couldn't reach. Deary's unseen people read spider webs and snowflakes and the way the ice dissolved on a roof. They read the paper caught in branches and birds' nests, pond ripples where stones were tossed and raindrops speckled. They read tracks in the mud made by wagons and shoes, and street lamps on an otherwise unruly ground.

At night, when Joseph didn't sleep and he'd exhausted the memories of Mam holding him close, telling him stories, he thought of Deary's unseen people. When Mam's dead face ripped him from his fleeting sleep, and Joseph sat upright, suppressing the cries that knotted his throat, rocking, and praying that Mam hadn't gone to hell, the thought of Deary's people gave him solace. He depended on them to fit somewhere that wasn't heaven, hell, or purgatory, to reinforce his belief that Annie was real, and that she might someday return to him.

Rat, Rabbit, Badger, Dog. Joseph copied the animals into circles he'd traced on the pages of an old seed catalogue, and cut carefully. After morning mass, when the boys and girls were briefly together before departing through separate halls to the refectory, Joseph gave Deary the cut-outs. "Thank you for your people," he whispered, "and for meeting a spirit like Annie."

She raised his drawings, one by one, above her head. "I think Annie came to me once," Deary said. "She told me you'd be here."

Joseph's heart skipped a beat. "I can make more drawings for you."

Alone in the cellar with Deary, despite the locked door between them, Joseph often felt the ache in his chest disappear. When they talked, the wings in Joseph's stomach stopped fluttering. She spoke of her people, and in return he told her Irish stories, but the pieces of his own story remained broken. When Joseph said: "I have something to tell you about me," it never meant: "I'll tell you."

❖ ❖ ❖

The evening before a trip to sing at the House of Providence, Sister Patricia announced in her kindest, gentlest voice: "Children, I have been reassigned. I will be staying on at Providence to help the old ones. I care about each one of you deeply. I shall miss you, and look forward to your visits. My work is God's will." All that night, Joseph could think only of how her pretty face and perfect ankles would be wasted.

After the concert, Sister Patricia hugged each of them goodbye. Joseph felt himself shrink at the shock of her touch. On the crowded horse-car, Joseph re-experienced Sister Patricia's embrace countless times, wishing he'd been different. In his mind she hugged him again and again, and he hugged her back, while the children chattered and the driver called the street names all the way to Sunnyside.

❖ ❖ ❖

When winter came, the snow swirled into drifts so high that Deary's wanderings were limited to hallways and off-limit rooms; but Joseph knew that her spirits were not diminished.

"I can put my feet behind my head," Deary told him at the Christmas social, where boys and girls were allowed to stand together, eating the bland, sweet dough balls prepared by Joseph's now-favourite nun, Sister Mary Margaret. When no one was looking, Deary led him to the pantry. She sat on a bench and lifted one leg, then the other, until she was done up like a parcel, perfectly balanced on her grey pantaloons. Terrified that something worse would happen, Joseph said only: "That's very good."

"Wait." Deary unpacked herself and hiked up her skirt again over the gull-coloured ruffles. Suddenly she bent over, crouching on her head and hands, and kicked up against the wall. Deary stared at him until her skirt, momentarily caught on a bootlace hook, broke loose and fell around her face.

"How did you learn that?"

"Easy," she said, flipping down again, and unburdening herself of the dress. In her underwear, Deary walked on her hands until the shelf of pickled beets became an obstacle. Joseph was desperately trying to think of something to say when Sister Martha opened the door. "Deary Avery! Put that dress back on and go downstairs this instant."

In the weeks that followed, Joseph watched Deary through the fence of the girls' yard. Practising how to stand upside-down against the wall, Joseph glimpsed Deary's ankles, and didn't fall.

Looking at Deary brought Joseph comfort and excitement, yet he didn't think of Deary the way he'd thought of Sister Patricia or the naked lady on the postcard. He thought of Deary the way he should have thought of Our Lady, but couldn't. He couldn't look the Holy Mother statue in the eye.

9

*D*espite the many prayers, psalms, and lessons at the orphans' home, each evening in the boys' dormitory was an opportunity for sin. The boys secretly waited for the nuns to go to their own quarters, and for the younger boys to fall asleep. Then Joseph and Tim gambled with Benny White. Tim considered the invitation to gamble another service to Joseph, one he added to explaining routines and personal histories, sitting with Joseph in the chapel, and following him in the yard — except when Deary was near. Joseph knew that Tim was uncomfortable around her, and he knew two more things besides. First, the only way Tim could reliably command attention was by exposing his empty eye socket. The younger girls always gasped and begged to see it again. Second, Joseph knew that Tim revered Benny. Benny liked to bet, but they had no money; so on days when Sisters Anne and Bernardine took the children on walks, the boys went scavenging.

"A world of riches is right at our fingertips," Tim told Joseph, who hid treasures in whatever pocket, sleeve, or pant leg wouldn't raise the nuns' suspicions. The beach was littered with bones. Bird skulls were nothing to scoff at. Dead fish, while not collectible, were satisfying to poke with sticks. Fragments of bottles smoothed by the waves lay waiting in sand. The collectors devised systems of equivalency. Three buttons were worth the sole of a shoe. Glass was valued by rarity of colour: red being high, brown from the brewery bottles most common, and blue — while attractive — in the middle. Colourless glass was almost worthless, but Joseph kept it anyway. Good nails rated higher than anything rusted — with the exception of one corroded spike from the rail yards, which Benny claimed had merit due to its usefulness as a weapon. He wouldn't bet with it. Tim wouldn't bet with the ribs of a decapitated groundhog, which he claimed had magic.

Joseph was willing to gamble with anything. One night he ran through all his leather and shards, a dog's bottom jaw, two forks, and a corset from Doctor Boylan's house. Tim won it happily, but he did not believe that it belonged to the doctor's wife. "Not enough bosom," Tim said. Just who had owned the corset and how it ended up in the doctor's refuse pile remained a mystery that made fingering the laces more pleasing.

Despite his losses, Joseph still did not fold. Of the objects under his mattress, the only thing of monetary value was Mam's half-full medicine bottle.

"What is it?" Tim asked.

"It's medicine."

"For what?" Benny asked.

Joseph tried not to hear the wheels of the Bottle Man's cart and the clinking cargo on the shelf marked "Goods for healing ailments of the Spirit."

Benny won Tim's last buttons and the bottle in a single round.

❖ ❖ ❖

The next morning, Deary turned a cartwheel, not looking at Joseph.

"Deary!" he shouted. "Where are you going?"

"I'm staying out of the way."

"Of what?"

"Of the commotion inside."

"What's happened?"

"An uproar. Sister Martha's in a lather. She called the doctor. The Mother Superior's come down, and Sister Mary Margaret shooed the lot of us out, but the little ones hid in the cellar to eavesdrop. I can't get any peace."

"Shall we go for a walk then?"

"All right. But we have to come back before Sister Martha finds out. More going awry just might kill her."

He hopped over the fence to the girls' yard. Surprisingly, the gate was unlocked.

"Let's go to the shore then."

Alone with Deary, Joseph felt a surge of excitement.

They crossed the wooden bridge over the rail ties to the hanging trees, so called, Deary said, because more than one man had tied a noose for himself there. "Sometimes at night I've heard screams in the dark."

"Whose?"

"I don't want to know. Once I found a torn shirt on the ground, not ten feet from a hanging tree. And a man was thrown from his cart when his horse got spooked. I heard Sister Bernardine tell it to Sister Mary Margaret."

She paused, tree by tree, running her fingers over the bark. "Here." She took Joseph's hand and lightly ran it over a spot where the bark was gone, revealing a smoother surface. "He hit here." They studied the trunk and the ground, looking for other clues.

"When did it happen?"

"In the winter."

"I never heard."

"I never told. His blood must have frozen in the snow."

Willows creaked in the breeze. "Let's climb one, Joe," she said, pulling up and straddling a bough. Joseph climbed above her. Deary rolled onto her back and stared off through the trees. Then she sat up, wriggled out of her blouse and skirt, and dropped her shoes and stockings to the grass. Naked, she lay back, still gazing through the trees. In shock and wonder, Joseph climbed higher, until her face was partly hidden by the branches; then he settled on a branch where he could study her small breasts, arms, and belly. Deary lay silently as the clouds shifted, and the first glimmers of sunlight burned through.

Eventually she jumped down. Her clothes on again, she bent over, lacing her shoes, as Joseph touched ground.

They returned up the beach wordlessly as the children of neighbouring Parkdale Village ran by with pails and shovels, their mothers following. He tried to ignore them, as he did all younger children. Then he heard someone call "Colleen." Joseph froze, his heart beating frantically. To calm himself, Joseph thought of her better life. His Colleen would have the shiniest red pail and shovel. Her castle would stand tallest.

He stole a glance, but his sister wasn't there.

Deary continued on ahead of him, across the bridge, as the black ribbon slipped from her hair. "Your ribbon," he called, but Deary didn't answer. He stuffed the ribbon in his pocket, running to catch up. They sneaked back into the house.

Inside, Mother Superior was livid. Sister Martha appeared to mix anger with gratitude as Doctor Boylan descended from the dormitory rooms, Sister Mary Margaret closely behind. All up and down the stairs hushed children crouched. Joseph and Deary joined them, unnoticed. Had someone found the corset? Joseph wondered. Tim would have hidden it well, but he and Benny were nowhere to be seen.

Doctor Boylan held an empty bottle out to Sister Martha. "Laudanum," he said. The lady in pink flowers had been ripped almost entirely from the glass; her waving hand was all that remained. "But the lad's pulse was steady, his breathing back to normal. He'll most likely awaken in time for tomorrow's supper."

❖ ❖ ❖

Sister Martha struck Joseph's palms ten times each with her bamboo cane in the cellar room beside a wall of crooked nail heads and knotted strings. Each strike was as painful as any he'd received at Darkley school, but each was a mercy for consuming his attention. After the Sister left him to consider his sins — about his possession of the bottle and his gambling, and about Benny who could have died from swallowing the poison, Joseph's real punishment began. He saw Mam on the mound at Navan Fort and wailed. He saw her head tipped back as she drank from the bottle he held to her lips on the ship. He saw her eyes, frightened, then staring. Now he understood that the Bottle Man had lied. Joseph wanted to stay on the cellar floor forever.

When Sister Martha came back to get him, he didn't speak. That evening, he went to her desk next to the statue of the Holy Mother. At first her cane was hard to grip because of his stinging palm, but he rolled his left pant leg and struck his shin until it bled. He wanted the Holy Mother to see how much it hurt. But when he looked into her eyes, they were blank.

10

*J*oseph didn't talk for two days after the canings. He didn't raise his hand in the school room. He didn't respond when the Sisters spoke to him, and he didn't reply to Father Tom when he questioned Joseph about the laudanum bottle.

"You had better search through his other things," Father Tom told Sister Martha. "I'm surprised that Sister Patricia let him keep them."

"She wasn't suited," Mother Superior said.

Joseph kicked the table leg hard after Father Tom and the nuns left the room. Then he kicked the wall. Sister Martha would read his father's letter. She would see his prayers, his most secret words in the margins of his speller. She would touch his mother's Brigid's cross, and the walnut shell that held her gloves. She would touch the ribbons.

Kicking the wall didn't allow tears to come.

Sister Martha removed only his old speller. "No need for two," she told him quietly. All his long-ago prayers went with it, and the animal pictures, the cartooned bodies not entirely erased, and Darkley townland, parish of Keady.

Neither the laudanum nor the canings stopped Joseph from gambling late at night with the dormitory boys. Since their scavenging walks were now forbidden, they bet imaginary money. One night he won a thousand make-believe dollars. He wished Gerry had seen. He wished for whiskey. Above all else, he wished for Deary.

After a week of being kept in during recreation time, and count-less Hail Marys in the boys' empty school room, Joseph finally was allowed to rejoin the others in the yard. The first place he went to was the fence to look for Deary. His palms were still too sore for a hand-stand, but she did one — their code for "Hello." Eventually she came to the fence when Sister Anne wasn't looking. "I have things to tell you," was all Deary said, before she cartwheeled away.

Deary didn't boast, but clearly she possessed unusual powers, including magic ones. After morning mass, or talking through the fence between the boys' and girls' yards, Joseph saw that Deary's spells were quantifiable. She offered proofs: a cloud dissolved above her gaze; an arrowhead appeared half-buried under the back steps; a hawk's sudden swoop caused shrieks in the yard and scattered the children. When Tim McCready flashed his eye socket at Deary, her cold stare cured him of the habit. The nuns finally allowed Joseph, Tim and Benny to join on supervised neighbourhood walks again. "I knew they would," Deary whispered. Tree spirits had spoken to her. "I hear them."

"How do they speak?" Joseph asked through the fence.

"Through my thoughts. Try it."

Joseph touched the smooth bark of an ash tree. He thought of Annie, though no words came. Just the thought of Annie's spirit — the tree's gift, Deary's — was a marvel. Joseph hadn't given up on Annie returning.

In the numbering of Deary's marvels, Joseph began his second year at the home. She taught him the language of new birds: belted kingfisher, cormorant, and great blue heron. In Sister Mary Mar-garet's kitchen, when boys and girls were called upon to help clean up, Deary taught Joseph herbs. "Sage for wisdom, rosemary for remem-brance, and thyme for courage. And healing. Though Sister Martha's beyond it," Deary added sadly.

Joseph lit votive candles and expanded his collections. He found more arrowheads. When Joseph glanced at the Holy Mother statue, and at her image in the paintings in the orphanage foyer, he didn't expect her to look kindly upon him. Not expecting brought relief. Joseph tried not to think about the Holy Ghost.

"My people move in all elements," Deary whispered in a pause on her rosary after "glory be."

Sister Martha made a routine of taking short walks with her each day after lunch, before afternoon prayers and classes. As far as Joseph could tell, their walks allayed her urges to wander.

Occasionally, when Sister Martha's cough kept her inside and the others weren't looking, Deary still shinnied the fence. Now, instead of being intrigued by Deary's wandering, Joseph fretted during her absences. One day Joseph missed her so much that he used the power of his worry to climb the iron bars without receiving a boost from anyone.

He found Deary on Indian Road and walked behind her, keeping a distance in case she wanted solitude. He saw the beads move through Deary's fingers. Her lips moved too, and he knew she was sincere in whatever words she whispered, even though the other orphans took her for a faker — or for crazy. Sisters Anne and Bernardine rolled their eyes at Deary's behaviour and her stories. But they couldn't see her now, as Joseph did. He saw Deary's devotion, even from where he knelt in the vast park, hidden in an old man's garden.

The nuns had spoken about the man who lived in the cottage by that garden. An old architect. And his wife lay buried beside the path. Watching Deary, Joseph also caught sight of a black fence and vaulted tombstone. When Deary moved, he followed, only this time he realized that he, too, was being watched. On a chair by the cottage sat the old man himself — white beard and glittering eyes, his paint brush in motion.

Thereafter, when Joseph followed Deary, he took care to be extra quiet. He did his best to avoid the painter's eye, though Joseph imagined that somehow the old man saw everything.

Mostly, when Joseph followed Deary, he felt elation. The feeling was compounded when Sister Martha announced that instead of attending choir practice, on Mondays and Thursdays, some of the boys and girls would gather to rehearse religious dramas; best of all, Deary had been chosen to lead them. Deary's spells were her prayers, she told Joseph privately, and the plays were her gifts. Under Sister Anne's supervision, plays became central to Joseph and Deary's world. Joseph painted scenes on white sheets that were then washed and re-used for the next production. Watching and painting, Joseph forgot his troubles.

Angel plays were presented through all four seasons. Sometimes Deary set her productions in the orphanage parlour; other times in the yard, or at the edge of the King Street bluff, or farther abroad in the neighbourhood for donations.

In spring, Joseph watched an angel visit Mary in a Parkdale Village garden. Another called to Zacharias from behind a clothes line, announcing the conception of John the Baptist in a woman "as old as Sister Martha!" the actor exclaimed, departing from the script in an extemporaneous moment of wonder that caused the other actor to gasp and leap from his overturned bucket. "Impossible!" shouted the four-foot Zacharias, shaking his fist, and, at a loss for his other lines, initiating a tag game through the drying sheets. From then on, Deary cast those boys in non-speaking parts.

In summer, as Jacob and the angel, the same two boys simply wrestled.

In fall, a special angel with six wings required wires, much sewing, and an actor who was promised a garter snake skin in return for not fidgeting through Isaiah.

In winter, an angel shut the lions' mouths as the cold winds roared over Humber Bay.

During Joseph's third Sunnyside spring, he watched an angel guard an empty tomb at dug-away hill above the lakeshore. During Deary's Passion Week production several free roaming cows were impounded at the tomb site after a tiny Mary Magdalene patted each of them, wishing them well as they plodded into the police wagon. Farther east, an angel spoke to shepherds on the clay bank at Dowling Avenue. In a parlour remount, before Joseph's painting of an empty tomb, Deary addressed the big girls, who kept their heads down, knitting in even rows. "See that you do not despise one of these little ones; for I tell you that in heaven their angels always behold the face of my Father." After the performances Deary joined the big girls. Her wool was blue and her stitches were neat. The big girls rarely spoke to her.

One warm day, at last, Deary invited Joseph to join her on a secret walk in the park. "You're older now," she told him. At ten-and-a-half, he felt almost grown up, though he didn't look it — especially beside thirteen-year-old Deary, who seemed more like a woman than a girl.

Joseph's thrill at accompanying her overpowered his foreboding that one of these days they'd be caught. He saw the architect's glittering eyes and brush. Off they went to the wilds of the park and pond.

Grenadier Pond contained the bodies of soldiers who'd put too much trust in the ice — or so the village children said. Joseph bristled at their laughter. "The pond is so deep they were never found!" cried one excited little girl to another. Deary rippled the water, first with a willow branch, then with the toe of her boot. "Maybe they swam down far enough to find a current. A passage to the lake," she said. "I can swim under water."

Joseph had promised to make a paper boat for her and he pulled it from his pocket where the walnut shell accidentally tumbled open, revealing two wispy white hands. Mam's gloves. "The boat will sink and the gloves will never go back in." He wasn't prepared for the sudden well of panic.

"Nonsense," Deary said. She put on the gloves and hummed as she gently pulled the boat along, making little ripples through the reflection of her sleeve on the water's surface. "These are a queen's gloves."

"Macha was a queen," Joseph said, staring at the mud as his diaphragm contracted. He turned the empty shell halves in his fingers.

Under Deary's power, the boat didn't need a sail.

"Queen Macha was beautiful ..." Joseph continued through the tale just exactly as Mam had told it to him. Crunniac's love for Macha, his joy, his boast to the King of Ulster, the race, the birth of Macha's children, Macha's curse and her death.

The little boat made its way at the end of the string and the willow branch.

"Do you think Annie will ever find this place?"

"I think she will," Deary said. "She has things to show you."

Deary twisted the gloves into a perfect ball and gently took the walnut shell from his hands. The two halves of the shell were whole again.

"Maybe she'll show me why I'm here."

"Look. I'll show you something!"

In what seemed like a single breath, she wriggled out of her dress, pulled her boots off, and flung the garments behind her as she tore towards the pond in her underwear. Before Joseph could find a voice to speak, Deary made a running leap into the water, sending the ducks into a frenzied flutter of honks. The pond surface rippled, until — nothing. She was gone. The birds settled as Joseph forgot the walnut shell in his pocket and ran back and forth along the bank, unable to call her name. Then he grasped a fallen branch and hacked at the water. Useless. Drawing air into his lungs at last, Joseph sank heavily to his knees in clay, as above the gulls cried, and he pictured the dead grenadiers below. He saw Mam's body at the bottom of the sea. "Help," Joseph called hoarsely, but for once, the Parkdale Village children and their mothers were nowhere in sight.

Suddenly he heard his name. Looking up, he saw nothing but water, land and sky. Looking down, he saw a white feather on the grass.

"Here!" the voice called. Deary's face appeared, a distant oval at the north end of the pond, grinning. She waved and disappeared under the surface again.

By the time she swam back he breathed normally, and his heart had stopped pounding, though he still felt weighted to the ground. "Don't do that, Deary."

"Why?" She shook herself off, laughing. "I told you I could swim." Then she reached for her dress, pulling it up over her soaked undergarments. "Water gives me life."

"Here," Joseph said, holding out the white feather, which she pondered for a moment, then stuck brightly into the wet and straggly nest of her semi-pinned hair.

"Thanks."

Sister Anne waited for them by the orphanage fence. Back inside, Deary was sent to the girls' school room, where she would serve a series of detentions, Joseph to the cellar. Sister Anne used the cane on both his hands. Left alone under the stairs, he retrieved the walnut shell of his mother's gloves and held it tightly in each palm, making the pain last.

"Annie," he whispered. "Where are you?"

11

*I*n his recurring dream, Joseph walked to Navan Fort with Mam. Grey streaks ran through her dark hair, making it look very soft. Joseph wanted to reach out and touch it, but he didn't. "Tell me the story of the children turned to swans."

Mam settled them in the ditch beneath the Monaghan quilt. "Their father missed those children very much," she said. He watched the blue hem of her skirt glide away across the grass. Then Joseph saw only blackness until the Armagh Railway Station gates swung open. The screech was just the train whistle, Mam said, but Joseph knew the sound of the Banshee.

❖ ❖ ❖

One morning after the children had eaten and gone with Sister Martha to the school room for prayers before the lesson, Joseph remained behind to take his turn at sweeping the kitchen for Sister Mary Margaret. The nun rarely spoke, though her large hands were almost always moving: as soon as one meal was done, Sister Mary Margaret prepared the next one. She sliced meat with a special knife that had belonged to her before she became a nun. Benny once said that on the day that Sister Mary Margaret joined the House of Providence she walked up Power Street carrying that bone-handled knife covered in blood. "She'd sheared her own head with it." Then he added: "I bet she stabbed someone," regal in his vision above the rummy game. "Her old man. I bet she killed him."

"Why?" Joseph had asked.

"Because he didn't like her soup." Then Benny belched, sending Tim into knee-slapping convulsions of laughter. In a day, Tim had perfected his own belch, which he practised frequently within earshot of Benny, who ignored him.

The knife had been her sign, Mary Margaret once said, before Sister Martha changed the subject. Each day Sister Mary Margaret put the knife away in a special case, like a relic. For all Joseph knew, Jesus had cut the loaves and fishes for the multitudes with it, and Abraham had raised it above Isaac before his own sign came.

"How long has Deary been here?" Joseph asked Sister Mary Margaret, as the sweeping came to an end.

"A few good years for certain. Deary were eight when she come to us."

"Why?"

Sister Mary Margaret cracked six eggs into a bowl and beat them. "You'd have to ask Sister Martha."

The best time to ask Sister Martha was in the evening after bedtime.

When he wandered through the house, Joseph worked hard to imagine the feel of turf under his feet and rush crosses under a roof. Wood was solid, but it burned. Houses were forever going up in flames here. That was why Sister Martha checked the hearths each night before settling onto her knees in prayer beside her bed. Sister Martha's door always remained open. When she turned to Joseph, her eyes looked sparkly in the lantern light, as though she might smile, though the same light cast serious shadows along the hollows of her face.

"Sister Martha, why did Deary come here?"

Sister Martha's attention was steady and her voice was firm, but soft, as she led him back to the boys' hall. "Each child of God has a story. Each story is private. What's gone before is only for God to know and care about. Goodnight, Joseph."

"Goodnight, Sister Martha."

Joseph dreamed that he was stuck in the earth, halfway up Navan Fort.

❖ ❖ ❖

On large outings with Sisters Anne and Bernardine, Tim McCready's scavenging turned into hunting. Tim stoned his prey, and prided himself on his efficiency.

"With baby birds," Tim explained to Joseph, "stoning puts them out of their misery. You know that when a newborn drops from the nest it doesn't stand a chance. Have a go at this one."

He put a rock in Joseph's hand. The bird's tiny chest heaved and its beak opened and shut; its eyes were glazed, knowing. "Go on," Tim said. "It'll only be food for a cat or a raccoon. They'll tear it to pieces."

"But what if we could fix it?"

"Are you willing to chew worms and spit them up? And even if you did, this bird's already bust."

"Come along, boys," Sister Anne called from far away.

The rock drove hard from the force of Joseph's arm and struck the bird. When Joseph opened his eyes, expecting to see a crushed corpse, the bird's contorted body flipped and fluttered in the grass. The second blow was final, but what stayed in Joseph's mind were the flutters.

After that, Joseph didn't watch Tim hunt. Occasionally, when the nuns let them roam a little, Joseph saw evidence of Tim's conquests. In the ditch behind the chemist's on Queen Street was "one less rat," Tim said. "That squirrel over there exploded. See?" Once, Tim killed a rabbit. So proud was he that he showed it to Sister Anne. She gasped, but let him bring it to Sister Mary Margaret for stew. In secret, he fashioned lucky paws for himself and Joseph. Tim dried the hunks of hastily cut fur with a pen knife and wrapped them with scrap metal from a tomato tin. Joseph kept the rabbit's foot in his pocket with a pair of dice.

"I want a gun," Tim told Joseph one late summer day as they threw rocks into the water. "I want a gun and a good knife. Then I could survive on my own."

Three nights later, when the boys were cleaning the kitchen, Tim told Joseph to come and stand watch. First, Tim picked up a vegetable knife. "It's not sharp enough for skinning." Then he drew Sister Mary Margaret's hallowed tool from its case and held it by its blackened bone handle.

"You can't take that. She'll notice."

"What's the difference? I'll be long gone. I leave tonight. Come with me."

Joseph felt a tightness in his chest, and the inability to match language to it beyond Deary's name.

"You don't have to," Tim said. "I just wanted you to know you're welcome. I know you won't snitch on me."

"What time are you leaving?"

"After a last round of cards."

They played rummy alone that night and didn't bet. The cards were comfortable and familiar like the stray cats that strolled about the yard and lazed under the thorn bush. The girls stroked them, but Deary paid them no mind, sitting alone in the back garden of the girls' yard. Deary's solitude had nothing to do with others. Joseph could call to her, and still she was alone. He could offer her marigolds from a sweaty palm, and she could take them through the bars and stare into his face, and he would know that he had brought her nothing, even when she thanked him. For a moment, watching her, Joseph's own solitude lifted. But the feeling didn't last.

Deary was growing up too far ahead of him, he realized, and didn't talk about her people anymore, or her spells. She stopped directing theatricals, though he caught her making character faces at her reflection in a window. Mostly she looked sad. What they did not say was still enough for Joseph to bind them; but he worried about Deary, even when he was playing cards.

Joseph also worried about Tim.

"Tim," Joseph said, laying down a pair of aces. "What'll you do when winter comes?"

"I'm going to travel. See the west. I'll bring you back a chief's feather headdress, and a rock from the mountains. Maybe gold, if I take to digging. Will you stay in the city?"

"I figure."

"Then I'll find you."

At midnight they blew out the candle. Tim took his pack and left.

All night Joseph heard a barred owl whistle, and he lay staring at the ceiling.

In the morning, Sister Anne pushed hard to emulate Sister Martha. "Tim McCready is missing from the dining room. Has anyone seen him today?" After a moment of silence the whispers started. "As well, Sister Mary Margaret has lost an important possession, one which affects us all directly. Should anyone know anything about either disappearance, know that God wants you to tell us."

Joseph carried the silence that followed into the school room and into his dreams of Keady Fair. The street was a sea of people moving among the carts with yarns and trinkets and the livestock shuffling and sounding in their makeshift paddocks. A fiddler played where the streets converged, and Mam said: "Take care of Deary, Joseph."

Two days later, Joseph watched from an open window as Tim was brought back on a coal cart. The driver pointed inside. Instead of bolting, Tim stood before the man and shouted something that drew the nuns outside. Joseph thought he heard one say: "Obey your father." For a few moments Tim's hollering turned to crying, which Joseph felt he shouldn't watch. The cart pulled away. Sister Martha tried to put her arm around Tim, but he waved her off, as the nuns quietly stripped him of his pack, including Sister Mary Margaret's knife, still wet with the blood of a groundhog. "Sweet," Tim said later, "but tough to chew."

"What was it like, Tim? Being out there."

They sat in the yard near the tom cat sprawled beneath the thorn bush, sleeping off a new rip in his shoulder.

"A wonder, Joe."

12

*D*uring the fourth winter, Benny moved to the Catholic boarding house for newsboys and apprentices — a rite of passage that some boys yearned for, but few experienced. Mother Superior and Father Tom preferred the Sunnyside orphans to stay and learn trades in the west end. Only the most wayward of the older boys went to board downtown, and then, only on condition that they would comply with the St. Nicholas Home rules. The Home was an upright place, said Father Tom. Most of the St. Nicholas boarders were in trades; the few who insisted on merely selling papers had more freedom, yes, but also faced more challenges.

"I want you to have this." Benny handed Joseph the spike.

"But this is your best weapon."

"There'll be plenty more where I'm going."

"I can't take it, Benny."

"I'll have it," Tim said.

"Very well then."

The tracks left by the cutter in the new snow were soon covered by the footprints of the orphans, who kicked white clouds into the air and rolled, making fortresses and angels.

❖ ❖ ❖

Deary made a snowman and studied it for a long time. She melted snow in a pot on the hearth to pour on her snow man so that he would turn to ice, digging with her bare fingers to shape a real face. "Frostbite!" Sister Martha said. "That's all we need."

The next morning, before breakfast, Deary was first out in the girls' yard to gather more snow for melting. The snowman had turned completely to ice. Joseph walked to the fence to study the statue, sensing that he must not say a word. Even though Deary no longer spoke of her magic, Joseph believed that when the time was right something great would be revealed. Sometimes, when she was looking, he stood on his hands and she nodded. Sometimes he wanted to cry because they didn't speak, but in secret, Joseph couldn't cry anymore.

Deary's breath touched the face of her frozen man. His eyes looked back at her, and at anyone who passed. His nose was straight and he had a full mouth, a torso and legs, and finally a robe. On the third day, after the schoolroom was tidied and the children had gone from the yard, Joseph watched Deary hacking at the neck of her snowman with a branch from the woodpile. She gouged at his face, sending the head rolling to the ground, where it broke in half. She stood for a moment with her head bowed, then returned the stick to the woodpile, brushed off her skirt, and came in for supper.

"Why did you do it, Deary? Why did you break your snowman?"

Deary's eyes shone. "I wanted to know what it was like for God to let John the Baptist die like that."

❖ ❖ ❖

Three days later, Sister Martha sat on a parlour chair before a man in a black woollen jacket and a lady in a feathered hat, and a cameo brooch clasped tightly to the brown piping at her throat.

Joseph crouched outside the partially open parlour door.

"She is an anxious girl. She needs to be kept busy. In truth, too much time has been a problem for her here of late. She is the first to finish her lessons and they are always correct. She is bright, and capable of hard work."

"Is she tidy?" the woman asked.

"Very."

"Well mannered?" the man asked. "My wife and I do a lot of entertaining. She needs to know how to behave properly as a domestic."

"She is exceptional," Sister Martha said.

"Has she been with you a long time? Who were her parents?"

"The girl's grandfather was a minister of the Anglican Church. The girl's father, we were told, was well-educated, and at one time a teacher. His wife pre-deceased him. The girl came to us at age eight, after her father was killed in a road accident. We do take Protestant children, of course. They worship with us and are welcome."

The man shifted in his chair. "Her breeding—"

"—must be no cause for concern," his wife finished. "We have our own children to consider."

Desperate—livid—Joseph fled to the yard. He ran at the ash tree and kicked it. Then he ran and kicked the shed, and the coop where the pigeons squawked and fluttered. Joseph kicked the brick wall below the refectory window. When he punched it, the wall stopped him. He sank down in the snow, holding his left hand and breathing hard. "She can't leave. I won't let her." He said it so many times that the cold numbed his lips and battered knuckles. Joseph glowered at the dull sky, not caring if the Holy Ghost watched him. He wanted to pray, but he didn't, because God wouldn't answer him; an unanswered prayer was worse than none at all.

Deary's belongings were quickly gathered into a carpet bag.

Deary was radiant. "I've been adopted."

Joseph stared at her, and she was gone.

Paper

1887
---

uring Joseph's last summer at the orphans' home, Sister Martha read Deary's letter to the children. They had gathered in the parlour as though one of Deary's plays were to be performed. Paper trembled in the old nun's hand and periodically she pressed it to her chest. Deary wrote of angels in the plaster of her new house — angels who reminded her of the Sisters. She wrote of her new "parents" and her rose-striped attic room which she shared with Cook. "A good daughter is kind," Deary wrote. Of the heat in the attic she had no complaint because the angels on the floor below cooled her with their wings. Myriad wonders awaited Deary each week in the Rosedale ravine where, in her few hours off, she communed with all that was holy there. Swaying trees and countless blooms whispered to her, reassuring her of every living thing's worth. The ravine was Deary's temple of gladness and she gathered its bounty in arms that eagerly bore wildflowers home.

Deary wrote of her "brother," a horseman, who was teaching her to ride. She could stand barefoot on the horse's back, she said — the horse showed her how. The horses spoke to her through her thoughts. At that point, Sister Mary Margaret smiled, though she seemed puzzled. She looked at Sister Bernardine, who rolled her eyes heavenward. With her smile fading, Sister Mary Margaret looked at Sister

Anne who muttered: "God save the poor girl's mind," too audibly to go unnoticed as she left the room.

Joseph understood that Deary communicated with the horses, and with the trees, the flowers and ravine animals. He didn't doubt her. If anyone could turn being hired as a domestic servant into an adoption, Deary could. Losing her only strengthened Joseph's yearning.

Sister Martha resumed reading. "Glory be," Deary said through the old nun's hacking cough. "I keep up my knitting. I keep up my beads." More spasms of coughing followed, then: "Tell Joseph a butterfly walked with me two miles and I heard the name Annie."

Sister Martha regarded Joseph for several watery seconds after her spasms ceased. He knew that she didn't doubt Deary either, though the other nuns thought Deary was touched. Despite her gruffness and rules, Sister Martha had a way of showing that she valued and quietly delighted in the girl's imagination, and Deary had softened the older nun in a way no one else could, least of all Joseph. Sister Martha had gasped at the sight of Joseph's broken hand on the day Deary left. She had seen through his lie about an accident and called the doctor. She prayed for Joseph, he knew, but she'd also seen his old speller and the laudanum bottle. She knew he was tainted. When Joseph thought of Sister Martha, he felt the weight of his sins; when he thought of Deary, he felt the excitement of longing and that miracles were possible.

Joseph urgently wanted the letter. Deary's hands had touched it. Her pen had written "Annie." But Joseph knew that Sister Martha, too, treasured it. She whispered a prayer, wiping a tear from her cheek and left the parlour in the other nuns' care. Joseph sneaked after her. In the front hall, she opened the desk with a key that she pulled down from behind a picture of the Madonna and Child. Joseph, hidden by the doorway, listened to Sister Martha recite a psalm that all the orphans learned by heart, and he mouthed the words as she spoke: "If I ascend into heaven, thou art there; if I descend into hell, thou art present. If I take my wings early in the morning ..." Sister Martha paused, shaking. Some of the words fell away. "There shall thy hand lead me: and thy right hand shall hold me." Sister Martha tucked Deary's letter in the desk and locked it.

In the weeks that followed, Joseph often went back to the Madonna for the key, avoiding the Virgin's tranquil gaze, and that of Jesus who held out his neatly severed, shining heart. Always, after reading Deary's letter, he folded the page carefully and slipped it back in the drawer. Sometimes Joseph paused to touch the cane that sat on the desk's shiny surface beside the Douay-Rheims Bible.

One day Joseph decided to write to Deary, and he stole a sheet of paper from the desk. More and more sheets went to his room, where Joseph whispered news and thoughts, imagining that Deary was listening.

Deary,
I saw three swans on the pond today. I thought one was you.
    And I was a swan too.
— *Joseph*

Deary,
I held the handstand for three minutes.
— *Joseph*

Deary,
Should I move to St. Nicholas Home? It would make Sister
Martha's life easier. I only cause her trouble, and she's very sick.
— *Joseph*

He planned one letter that he resolved to post to Deary — the story he had wanted to tell her, through their silences and even through their handstands. Father Tom might call Joseph's story a confession, but the story was too big for the confessional box: the box — and more — would break. But Deary would listen and understand — and not break, and he might not break either. If he could just put his story in words to her, the weight of it might lift. She would know how to answer.

One day, instead of finding Deary's letter in the drawer, Joseph found another one. "Dear Sisters," it read, "I write with regret to inform you of the disappearance of our serving girl, Miss Avery. The circumstances of her unannounced departure remain mysterious to us, though I am compelled to add that her time here was neither peaceful nor pleasant for our family. Under no circumstances is she to return here. While we bear the girl no ill will, please understand that we found her unsuited to our needs. You have done your Christian duty by her as we attempted to do, unsuccessfully. Sincerely yours ..."

As soon as he finished reading, Joseph knew that he had to move to St. Nicholas Home. In order to find Deary, he would have to be in the city. With the newsboys, Joseph could at least please God to some degree by remaining a lodger under the auspices of the Catholic Church. Sister Martha said: "Joseph, stay out here and learn a trade. You can grow up strong and skilled right here." Joseph saw the goodness in her watery old eyes, and that she wanted to help him, despite his many sins; he also saw that he was failing her again.

But Joseph had to find Deary.

14

*B*efore he became a newsboy, Joseph had not fully known the January cold. Waiting for the pre-dawn streetcar to get the papers, Joseph watched Tim's reddened fingers fumble with the match for their first shared cigarette of the day. At the *Toronto Mail* building, Tim reached for as many papers as his arms could hold: great twine-bound heaps. "Tomorrow I'll have money for even more," Tim said, grinning through chattering teeth. Joseph couldn't imagine surviving the winter.

Soon Tim earned enough to buy blacking and brushes for the two of them. "Take the money first," Tim said. "Never shine before you get the money."

At St. Nicholas Home, the day did not begin with mass, as the boarders had to get out to work. Most were apprenticing tradesmen —"upright boys," said Mr. Rory Murphy, the home's watchful superintendent, who lit the lamps at five in the morning, and dimmed them after the evening mass, a light supper, and night school for the boys. Joseph could see that Rory Murphy considered the home's few newsboys a dubious lot. Benny, for example, was long gone. Rory Murphy made sure that the Christian Brothers and four resident nuns maintained order. The Sisters provided the meals and lessons, and saw that each boy paid. But Rory Murphy walked the floors. He visited each room. The boys called him by his full name to his face, and by several others behind his back. Joseph and Tim gave up on playing cards.

Each morning Joseph ran north up Yonge Street to claim a corner. Men stepped down from the trams, reaching for coins, seeing only the words sprawled on mastheads, not the boy who sold them. For Joseph, saying "Thank you, sir" to deaf ears became like breathing. Adding "Good day," occasionally met with a grunt. When a corner dried, Joseph ran west past hotels and stables with signs on the doors: "Irish need not apply."

When the church bells rang at noon, Joseph gave up. He kept charcoal in his sock and drew on unsold newspapers. Joseph sketched women as they stepped out of church, doing his best to hide behind trees, or at least to divert his subjects' glances if they noticed him. One husband finished a sketch with his boot. At close range, Joseph's challenge was to memorize details of the scowls of the men whose shoes he shined. Each man's mouth ended exactly below the centre of each eye, even as the mouth opened to say: "Watch what you're doing," "Rude little street Arab," or, "What's wrong with you, boy? Get on, you dirty Irish!" Each man's eyes were central on the front of his skull. Every human face, regardless of its fury, followed rules.

In the late afternoon, Joseph found a tavern where the men playing euchre still occasionally took a morning paper. Joseph sold what he could, but the cards drew him. As Joseph watched the players set down trump cards and slough, he listened intently to their accounts of evenings at the music halls. Recitations of performers' names and gag lines became almost liturgical; yet the magic of the gaslit halls fell short of the images Joseph assembled in his mind. As he hurried to five o'clock mass, on his knees in the St. Nicholas chapel, Joseph made the sign of the cross and offered his prayers, works, happiness, and miseries of the day to God, but his visions of the theatre were his own. Perhaps God didn't want his visions anyway, he told himself. Like so much of Joseph's experience, perhaps his imaginings were incongruent with anything God would want.

Yet Joseph knew the real reason why he couldn't offer God his daydreams of the theatre: in his mind he placed Deary centre stage. Joseph said prayers for her, but he felt little comfort, because he prayed selfishly. He refused to make an offering of the joys and sufferings the thought of her brought him; he refused to give up anything about her, and God must have known. Maybe that was why He had taken her away.

Occasionally, instead of lingering with the euchre players or going to mass, Joseph took a meal alone at his favourite dining hall, Kit's Hashery on Queen Street, a dark, wood-panelled room where the victuals were cheap and the patrons kept to themselves. Newsboys were allowed to forego night school for sales, as long as they were back before evening prayers and the dimming of the lights.

At dusk, the doors of the Telegram Building blew open and a white-bearded man appeared. "All right, then, boys," was all he ever puffed at them as he counted their pennies. Joseph ran west, hugging the still-warm papers to his chest: "Appalling Tragedy! Whole Family Exterminated! Awful Crime at Battle Creek, Michigan! Get your *Telegram*!" Parked carriage horses whinnied and scuffed at the cobble. "Spring outbreak planned to avenge Riel's death. Read *The Evening Telegram*!"

A woman lit a lamp in a rooming house window and for a moment Joseph paused to watch her. Undressing her in his mind, he lost track of time.

Then, "Cold and storm in all parts — severe snows in England! Chicago! Galveston Texas! Zero degrees in Palestine! Get your *Telegram* here!"

❖ ❖ ❖

A girl on Leader Lane with a frayed white mantle and hair in tangles offered to show parts of her body for twenty-five cents. He followed.

"What do you want to see?" she asked.

"I'd like to draw you."

"Fifteen minutes," she said.

Her fingers gripped his wrist, pulling past law offices and a butcher shop, through a door that opened onto stairs leading up to a cracked sign: "Dressmaking. Millinery at reduced prices. We invite fine trade." Upstairs, the girl led Joseph past a door where a woman's voice whispered over the sound of a man groaning, to a storage room where dusty bolts of fabric lined the walls under a barred window. The girl's coat fell to the floor. Joseph settled onto a stack of folded cotton.

Joseph drew the girl on "Situations Vacant," "Help Wanted," and "Personal." Pencil marked the paper more precisely than charcoal, but never as darkly as he wished. He drew the naked front of her without looking at the page. When she turned around, she looked more like a boy. Focusing on the light and shadow was easier then, but at times his pencil tore the page.

When she pulled her dress on, he drew her face. She posed past their allotted time and told him that her name was Myrtle Wren and he could come again on Thursday. He did, bringing his charcoal sticks, paying her for an hour.

Tim could not understand why Joseph didn't have more money. "You're a fool not to go to Union Station," Tim said. "Why can't you move more *Empires*? If you won't work Union, you could at least try the Summerhill Station — or take the street railway to the west end, Joe. You could work Sunnyside, or go up Jarvis. Down here every block is crawling with street boys." Tim had taken to calling the others by that name. He had opened an account at the Home Savings and Loan and referred to himself and Joseph as salesmen.

But none of that mattered to Joseph, because the words "Union Station" stopped him cold. He almost punched Tim in the mouth. Instead, Joseph kicked an electrical pole and thrust the day's newspapers onto a fresh heap of horse dung. For once, Tim stopped talking.

On the days when Joseph visited Myrtle, he usually heard her humming as he rounded the corner at the top of her lane. When Myrtle hummed, Joseph knew that she was alone, unless a dog was by and she was patting it. Sometimes she was busy, ushering a man upstairs. One day in March, Myrtle sat snugly between the buildings, chatting to rags that had been cut and stitched into a miniature person: buttons for eyes and red piping for a smile. When Myrtle saw Joseph, she quickly tucked her doll away.

But Joseph had seen her doll, and his hands felt useless. He would not draw her naked again.

"Keep your things on today, Myrtle. I need to work on drapery. After a while, a body gets easier to draw. Your face is a challenge. Your hands are a challenge. And so are the folds of your skirt."

Myrtle did not watch the clock. When he had money, he paid her for their full time together. When he did not, he left her the pictures. While he drew her hands, day after day, she told him about her sister, Beatrice. Myrtle giggled. "At first I thought she was killing them."

"When was that?"

"Oh ..." She paused. "About two years ago. When our parents died of a fever, Beatrice said it would be better to live for ourselves than go to an orphanage where we'd be forced to become serving girls. Like prison, being a serving girl. You get old scrubbing clothes and stirring soup. And getting beat. Better to be together, making money for ourselves.

"When she gets enough money, Beatrice might learn a trade —like real sewing. Or work for a lady in a fancy house. Bea does real well. The men always come back. She'll get richer ones working in a proper house. But for now she's fine. What happened to your parents?"

Joseph's drawing made no sense. The fingers were misshapen, bent at the wrong angles. "I have to go," he said.

15

*B*y April Joseph had earned enough capital to sell three daily papers. "*Globe, Mail* and *World!*" was the morning call. People drifted into the streets more frequently, as the last of the slush trickled on the cobbles. Robins hopped through tiny puddles of melt-water and urine. The sun shone on Joseph's face. "I'd like a paper please." Because the woman was drunk, Joseph waited to see the coin before the *World* changed hands.

"The old sluts come here to die," Tim said as they walked through the Ward. "And don't let a fortune-teller stare you in the eye. If you're lucky, a teller's curse only brings the clap. Don't let one touch you. A thread from your shirt, one strand of hair is all they need. I hate it here."

"Loads of Irish live in the Ward."

"A sorry lot, Joe. No offense to present company."

By early May, Joseph's body was too big to slide comfortably between the dressmaker's building and the one beside. If Myrtle wasn't in sight, he had to wait for her in the open, listening for the sound of her humming.

Joseph drew Myrtle's feet and her ears. Each study required a number of sessions to the accompaniment of groans from the next room. He didn't tell her that he wanted a change of model.

"Myrtle," Joseph said, "what you said about orphanages — you

78

might be wrong, you know." She was curled on a dusty stack of oil-cloth, her head cocked like a magpie's. He was very close, drawing her left earlobe and speaking softly into the canal. "You would learn skills. The nuns would teach you real sewing. Even fancy needlework. I've seen it, Myrtle." Deary's fingers winding blue yarn.

The next day Myrtle wasn't waiting for him. Instead, a young woman stood with bare arms and a dress cinched tightly at the waist. Her brown hair was pulled back from a rouged and cherry-red-lipped face. "Your name must be Joseph. My sister says that you would like to draw me."

Beatrice's room was much bigger than the storage closet and every bit as dusty. "I'm a little more expensive. I understand that you like drapery." She lifted her skirt above one bare knee and removed the pin from her hair. Joseph fumbled for a stick of charcoal, hastily sketching a leg while the stiffening in his groin made it difficult for him to form the ankle. Her hair spilled onto the next page, and the next, as he worked to get past the distraction of his own body.

On the back of her bodice was a series of hooks that she invited him to undo as the charcoal tumbled from his fingers. The metal clasps were snug and warm. He wanted to press his fingers into the skin of her back, to make a picture with his hands there in smudges and smears that he could lick away, leaving her wet. She unhooked the waist of her skirt as he pulled the bodice from her full breasts. Her skirt slipped to the ground. She unbuttoned Joseph's trousers and yanked them down, and suddenly the two were on the bed. Beatrice's taste and her smell took him well beyond thought into the rhythm of his own body. Eventually Joseph heard the sound: a long moan from the core of his being as she mounted him, and he exploded into light.

Beatrice gathered up her skirt. "You can draw me if you pay," she said. "Just don't talk to my sister about orphanages."

⬦ ⬦ ⬦

At first Joseph didn't care about the persistent spring rains, as thoughts of Beatrice kept him occupied. He discovered that his penis offered a world of diversion. Recreating Beatrice in his mind each night ensured at least a momentary escape into bliss under the covers. If Joseph could have, he would have thanked God for the privacy of his bed; but he knew that would only compound his mortal sins.

With the rain, newspaper sales dropped. Only the boys at the rail stations managed to pull in decent revenues. Joseph thought about learning a trade, but he couldn't do it. Not only did he, a fallen lodger, feel unworthy of the upright apprentices at the home, but he also knew that as an apprentice he'd lose his daily access to the streets. He needed to draw. He needed to see the Wren sisters, and he imagined following other street girls. He needed to visit the card players — particularly as they now let him join. One or two even shared their whiskey. But more than anything, Joseph needed to find Deary.

One particularly wet morning, Joseph stood on the steps of the Manning Arcade with papers that were too damp to sell. He could have gone back to St. Nicholas early, but Father Tom was visiting that day, preparing a service before Pentecost, and since Joseph's encounter with Beatrice, he couldn't bring himself to celebrate the descent of the Holy Spirit. The pleasure that Joseph had experienced with Beatrice, and his repeated fantasy about the experience, was directly proportionate to his dread that God's airy minion might be watching him.

Thoughts of the Holy Spirit brought no comfort — and pleasure didn't last. If he could just stay in the middle of it, he'd be fine, but he couldn't. No matter how many drawings he made, women he imagined, euchre rounds he played, or cigarettes and whiskey swigs he mooched, pleasure always turned to despair. Seeing Father Tom usually made things worse. Father Tom counted on Joseph to be good and saw that he wasn't. The nuns told him when Joseph was behind on his weekly lodging payment. Rory Murphy told him when Joseph skipped evening prayers and lessons. Yet Joseph knew he'd end up at mass with Father Tom.

Joseph bit his nails until they bled onto the wet papers. His shoes had been wet for days. He wiggled his toes, watching the water around them bubble. At the St. Nicholas chapel, Joseph stood shivering before the statue of Mother Mary. It, too, had smooth, unfocused eyes. Suddenly ill, he wanted her to see him. Joseph set a stolen daffodil at her feet. He lit a votive candle, but the wind snuffed it out.

Shivering hot and cold, Joseph tried to listen to Father Tom's words. His head throbbed and his teeth chattered, and he envisioned John the Baptist shouting at the corner of King Street and Leader Lane.

As Father Tom spoke, so did someone else: Cuchulainn. "You're on the Plain of Ill Luck, Joe." Then Cuchulainn became a man at Keady Mill with a watch on a golden chain and three coins for Joseph's palm.

Burning up with influenza in the St. Nicholas Home infirmary, Joseph was both a wizened old man and a child, in a common grave. Then he was neither: Joseph was nothing. And being nothing, he was free.

During the first week, in his more lucid moments, he expected to hear the Banshee. During the second, he recognized Father Tom speaking Latin, making the sign of the cross above him. Mary Magdalene appeared. "You need to refine your skills, Joe." She opened the *Evening Telegram* to "Situations Vacant," where Myrtle's picture smiled back.

During the third week, a Sister helped him to sit up and drink broth. His ribs were visible ridges beneath the skin on his torso. His legs were like sticks and his feet were bony.

"You'll get new boots," Tim said, allowed to visit for ten minutes before the evening lesson.

Joseph wanted to tell Tim about Myrtle and Beatrice, but the words stuck.

"Lucky bastard," Tim said with a wink.

◊ ◊ ◊

Joseph dreamed of a blue skirt's hem drifting across a grassy hill. He heard: "I am here," and knew it was Annie. Then he awoke mouthing the words of an unsent letter.

> *Deary,*
> *What if something goes wrong and someone dies. Is there a*
> *spell to undo it? What if a fairy isn't a fairy at all, but an*
> *angel, a real one. The kind you see with six wings. Or any*
> *kind. The kind that speaks to you in your dreams. And*
> *something happens and the angel goes. And you spend your*
> *time waiting for a voice that doesn't speak to you anymore.*
> *Is there a spell to get her back?*
> *If an angel falls, can she rise again?*
> *—Joseph*

❖ ❖ ❖

Myrtle wasn't singing when Joseph rounded the corner. The air was warm and clear, and people had been buying newspapers. She wore a dress that Joseph had never seen — yellow and musty, stitched unevenly along the seams, and slightly wrinkled from her time on the stairs. She was weaving a chain of dandelions. "Fancy seeing you," Myrtle said, looking down at her fingernails: ten small crescents of earth.

"Sorry, Myrtle. I've been sick."

"Sick? I took you for dead." She looked squarely at him and took a step closer. "I *heard* you the day you were with Beatrice. And anyway, she told me." Myrtle had always seemed resilient in family matters. He certainly didn't think that she'd be bothered by him seeing Beatrice, as the sisters were, after all, business partners; but all at once, Joseph realized that Myrtle was jealous.

Her words bored into him, filling a place of shame. What could he say? His unmentionable act with Beatrice had been mentioned. He couldn't take it back.

At last Joseph's voice escaped like crumbling plaster. "Would you let me draw you today? I brought enough money for an hour."

"I've raised my fee," Myrtle said, "... but I'll make an exception since you're a longstanding customer."

In the storage room, Myrtle could not help but smile, which allowed Joseph to relax despite the bumps and mutterings on the other side of the wall.

When Joseph returned through a back door days later to draw Beatrice, she promised to keep their meetings a secret from Myrtle if he paid her more. So he did. His challenge was to complete a full figure or a study of an anatomical detail before quietly succumbing to her body. Joseph moved into ink, and, after a particularly auspicious week of sales, colour. With water and a brush he learned the two models all over again.

The paintings became souvenirs. They dried quickly, concealed and sometimes smudged amidst his evening newspapers. Although his voice had deepened, he was impatient to grow taller, to feel his limbs and torso thicken. At night, eventually Joseph drifted to sleep to glimpse a blue skirt move across the grass at Navan Fort. When he saw his own legs, climbing, he sat bolt upright, soaked in sweat, his teeth so tightly clenched that his jaw pounded. But when he painted, he was already a man: one who moved easily from the page into a woman's flesh, forgetting all that had brought him there.

16

*O*ne warm Sunday morning in June, as Joseph made his way to the newsboys' chapel, he paused briefly before the statue of the Virgin Mary, whose slightly averted gaze had become a relief. Joseph nodded, crossed himself, and joined Tim, who said, amidst the Latin, that he had a plan.

They were going to Hanlan's Point, Tim said. They needed enough money for the ferry and for ice cream. Twenty minutes after they set out along King Street, Joseph heard his name called. He recognized Myrtle's voice; he could see her from the corner of his eye. He walked faster, babbling to Tim, with no idea what he was saying. Myrtle shadowed him, calling his name until finally Tim stopped and stared at the girl on the opposite sidewalk.

"What do you want?" Tim shouted.

"Where are you going?"

"Hello," Joseph muttered, staring down at his boots.

"Do you know that girl?" Tim asked.

"I might have seen her before."

"I've seen her, too. She's one of those sluts in the lane by the gasworks. Sorry, darling," Tim called, "we're not buying today," and turned down Brock Street.

The wharf was freckled with people carrying picnic baskets and parasols. A lady walked a cat on a leash. Tim's eye gleamed as he paid his five pennies for the ride on Doty's steamer; but he was cautious stepping on. "Darned if I can swim," he said, winking at Joseph and chuckling, a little nervously, as the ferry pulled away.

Joseph and Tim moved to the bow and beheld a green horizon of amusements. Hotel flags snapped in the breeze. Windmills turned, fountains purled, and a wheel of painted horses twirled beside the Hall of Living Curiosities.

"I've been thinking," Tim said.

"Of what?" Joseph blinked to clear the image of Myrtle's waving hand.

"Of the future, Joe. We can't stay newsboys forever." The odds were against paper boys and they knew it. Many who didn't progress to trades or factories found their next lodging in the reformatory, the streets, or the Don Jail. "We need to move on to something better. In the meantime, we save money."

Joseph swallowed.

"We should save together," Tim said. "Already I've got an account at the Home Savings and Loan. I want you to help me build it. Alone we're next to nothing, but together we're worth something. If we make the right moves, in a few years we could get a house, get our own boarders. Think about it, Joe. By twenty we could sell and make enough to get our own places. What do you say?"

Joseph said: "All right, Tim." He had no idea what he was agreeing to.

Liquor was illegal on the island, but Tim pulled from his pack the best secret of the day: a bottle of sherry, "acquired in a fair exchange." When the bottle was empty, Joseph's head was finally free of pictures.

❖ ❖ ❖

Myrtle's smile was tenacious, though something about it had changed; when Joseph drew it again, he could not isolate the difference.

"I didn't recognize you on the street that day."

The lie stayed with her, as though folded in her lap beneath her clasped hands. She was learning the trick of accepting lies without flinching—an art form comparable to portraiture, though not as obvious. Myrtle sat wordlessly through Joseph's stories of the island. Her silence forced him to fill it.

"Today is my birthday, Joseph," she finally told him, as he gathered his bits of charcoal and chalk into the Mullins cigar box. The clasp made a small exclamation.

"Best wishes, then."

He did not hand her the picture, partly because he was dissatisfied with it—but also because the gesture seemed thin. "What would you like for your birthday?"

Suddenly, her smile widened. On her feet she twirled around: "I want something to look forward to ... I want you to take me to the Industrial Fair!"

Joseph's awkwardness in watching Myrtle's flurry of happiness and expectation was in some small way an antidote to his guilt, and one he was vaguely grateful for. That he agreed was a foregone conclusion and released both of them from their earlier discomfort.

❖ ❖ ❖

Deary,
If a person did something terrible, would the person go to hell
or would hell come to the person? I just want to know.
—Joseph

❖ ❖ ❖

"This Catholic business is holding us back, Joe," Tim said. "Nobody hires Catholics for the good jobs, only for the dead-end work they save for taigs and half-breeds. The way to go is Protestant. Now, the way I see it, the Anglicans would sniff us out. They're like that. And a pew at the back of a church would take years to afford. To be safe, I say we go with the Methodists. Hell, the Eatons did and they're tycoons. I don't take you for a Presbyterian, Joe."

Tim had grown whiskers above his lip that he trimmed fastidiously with a razor blade housed in an otherwise empty soup tin which, Tim boasted, was a perfect example of why factories were changing the world: each tin was exactly like all the others. Tim had amassed a sizeable collection beneath his bed. One tin housed his comb, another his rolling papers and a small packet of tobacco. A third held bank statements in the teller's spidery hand and folded into tiny squares. Others held soap, a tooth pick, and matches in their E.B. Eddy box —an assembly-line item that Tim could not bring himself to part with. Little match boxes lay flattened beneath his mattress where, occasionally, he retrieved them in order to study their perfect uniformity.

Joseph's sack of items remained stowed beneath his straw tick, not to be looked at: one green and one black ribbon, the Brigid's cross, the Sunnyside speller, a walnut shell of gloves, his father's letter. The unsent letters to Deary.

"Tim," Joseph asked while they studied the Help Wanteds, "when you ran away from Sunnyside, did you ever hope to be caught? What I mean is, were you disappointed to be brought back like that?"

Joseph's question was as preposterous as asking a newsboy to talk about his family: he had broken a taboo. Joseph's embarrassment grew as he tried to take back his words. "Forget I asked," he said, attempting to make the image of the man, the boy and the coal cart vanish. "Sheddon needs machinists," he added faintly.

"Better to be a dog in this town," Tim said, "than an Irish Catholic. We've got to turn, Joe. And no going back."

❖ ❖ ❖

Every swallow of the Host sank like a stone in Joseph's belly now.

He had made a stash of his sketches, all the smiles and limbs, the pubic hair shaded quickly, the difficult hands, soles, and ears. Each drawing represented a separate, unconfessed sin.

Father Tom called on Joseph to assist in both the Liturgy of the Word and the Liturgy of the Eucharist during the summer months. Joseph knew that he was beyond merely disappointing God; thoughts of wrath and indignation haunted him. Joseph strained to see every moment as Father Tom became Christ at His last supper, offering His body, bread raised above His head, and His cup of blood. "*In meam commemorationem*," said Christ in the voice of Father Tom. Joseph had lied to that man. In all those Saturday afternoon confessions, Joseph could not pronounce his many mortal sins. He hadn't known how or where to begin.

"Look at me," Joseph's mind implored, as if to do so might bring a saviour's intervention. "Please look at me. I beg you." For as much as Joseph felt ashamed before God, he felt greater shame and abject fear at the thought of leaving what was, in Granny Dolan's words, God's "One True Church."

Surely Christ would see His own betrayer at the table.

◊ ◊ ◊

The best way to walk to the Don River for bathing was northeast through the workers' cottages. People called it "going to Ireland." Joseph went through the lanes past plots of beets and cabbages and carrots. Penned goats bleated and dogs dug for bones. Women shook their brooms at squirrels. Cabbagetown was too crowded for Darkley, but the sound was right. All the banter at the back doors — the scrape of buckets and calming curses and calls across lanes — gave Joseph comfort. He stripped off his clothes like the other boys and waded to his thighs. Entering the Don was the closest thing to absolution now. He reached down, watching the charcoal stream from his hands.

Then he reasoned that Christ didn't need to see him. Better to stay where the willow branches hid him, listening to the laughter and splashing of the Irish boys. Let God look on them and be pleased.

❖ ❖ ❖

The city braced for the Toronto Industrial Fair of 1887. Posters appeared on lamp posts and telegraph poles. Out by the Crystal Palace, workmen climbed the iron tower to install electrical fixtures. Soon the lights would be visible even from the east end of the city, illuminating rooftops and factory chimneys. "More magic than the moon," Tim said.

Extra trains were brought in to deliver visitors by the thousands. Union Station was jammed. For Tim, the station became a horn of plenty. Fist over fist, he sold *Telegrams*, *Globes* and *Empires*, each paper offering its own information about the fair. The hotels were packed, but still took customers, who slept in billiard rooms and bars; even the proprietors' offices were fitted with cots.

Joseph's plan was to take Myrtle to the fair on Children's Day when lower admission meant more to put down on attractions. They would have ice cream if he could manage it, perhaps a ride and a small souvenir.

Their walk took the better part of an hour; the sun was still low, overtaken at times by rain clouds that Myrtle warded off with an incantation under her breath. Lines of children approached the Dufferin Gates. Girls with their hair in braided rings, farm boys from the concessions, school boys with shined shoes and pale skin. Street boys dodged the attendants collecting the entry-fee nickels. Joseph recognized some of them and turned his head away. Myrtle grinned in amazement at every detail, telling him about how pretty the girls were and what beautiful baskets their mothers carried. She moved in a near trance towards the Crystal Palace.

Tim should be here, thought Joseph. But not with Myrtle — or Beatrice, by now not the only woman Joseph had lain with. As Myrtle stood in awe of Rogers' Grand Display of Furniture, and then in even greater awe of the stages of silk production, Joseph allowed his thoughts to wander to two other street girls. He had not asked their names.

Tim would have approved of the uniformity of the cheeses and the distinctly British packaging of table salt. He would have been impressed by the pyramid of Moxie Nerve Tonic and towers of identical cans and boxes.

Beyond the Crystal Palace were a bagpipe contest, a dog and cat show, and prizes for the best pig, pie, and petunia plant. Foot races, horse races, and balloon rides abounded. An electric train took visitors around the grounds. By the Carnival of Venice, school ma'ams listened to the piano players; school girls collected business cards from corset makers. "I want a card for the sewing machines," Myrtle said.

"What will you do with it?" Joseph asked, as they watched two men tug on a rope and pulley, lifting a car holding eight screaming children into the air.

"I'll save it," she said.

"I can see King Street!" a child shrieked. "I can see the island!" bellowed another. Beads of sweat glistened on the bare chests of the rope pullers.

"When do you plan to make a go of it? Your sewing, I mean." He could never bring himself to imagine her whoring — if that was what she did. At the very least she was supported by a whore. Joseph was grateful that Beatrice's income supported the sisters; but he was also repelled. Myrtle recognized the real question, and let it fade behind another burst of laughter and screams from the children in the raised car.

"Colleen!"

For a moment, Joseph's world went silent. A child on the ride across from them waved her bonnet at a woman nearby. His sister might be here at the fair. His Colleen could be the girl in braids with a mother who watched her, waiting with a picnic basket — and a better life. He couldn't yet see the waving girl's face. Then he did. She was not his sister.

Joseph took Myrtle to see tight-rope dancing, fighting dogs, and the Eden Musée. At Harry Piper's downtown zoo, she laughed to see orangutans in ballet skirts. She gasped to see Myron the Mastiff Man gnaw on a sheep's raw femur and growl. But for a long time all Joseph could see was the waving girl on the ride who was not his sister.

Myrtle suggested they move on to Galatea's tent, where a statue turned into a living woman. Myrtle remained spellbound long after the transformation. Joseph wanted to be happy at bringing her such delight; instead, he felt empty. Then emptiness turned to anger that he tried to hide, every time, after hearing Colleen's name. The sadness beneath it was worse.

Myrtle's unfaltering smile became a burden; Joseph only wanted to leave. A boy crossed in front of them with his small sister on his back. Joseph shut his eyes. "How long do you want to stay?"

"As long as we can."

"Until sunset then," Joseph said, measuring the sky between the falling sun and the trees. "We can watch the fireworks from King Street."

He tried to feel glad for Myrtle, but merely compounded his misery by buying her a five-cent bracelet that she wore like diamonds beneath an unravelling cuff.

As the sun sank below the silhouettes on a lane beyond the fairground gates, they succumbed to one last attraction: for three cents a person could look through a tiny hole in the canvas to watch "Shizelda the Enchantress and Her Captor Raoul." After Myrtle's time was up, Joseph dropped three of his last pennies into the jar. Through the hole he looked into a world of potted palm plants and Oriental carpets. A gas lamp illuminated a woman who emerged from behind a panel of burgundy silk. She wore a veil over her face and a dress of gauzy white, and moved to the slow drum beat. A man entered. She turned her back to him, stepped barefoot into his cupped hands and straightened above him. In the air she bent backwards and placed her hands on the man's shoulders in a perfectly sustained arch, while he walked in circles to the music. The backs of their heads touched lightly as the woman's veil revealed her face before she stepped upside-down into the air, and down to the carpet.

Deary.

❖ ❖ ❖

By mid-September the city emptied out. The hotel taverns were quiet. Men struggled in grim sobriety to repair their pocketbooks after the Grand Exhibition. The factories were no less busy, but newspaper sales were down.

Joseph had returned to look for Deary three nights in a row, but behind each canvas was a different show.

His fleeting glimpse had produced a mix of elation and devastation. Joseph worked longer hours and travelled farther to sell the morning news. He gambled at cards, half-heartedly hoping to win, when all he really felt was loss.

Joseph took a break from seeking models, but he drew. He made fast sketches at intersections where fruit sellers discarded crates that he could sit on. Joseph sketched apples that had fallen into the road. Sometimes, after drawing them, he ate them. Eventually Joseph found his way back to Myrtle's lane, where she ushered a man in a brown overcoat up the stairs.

"Do you know what day it is?" Joseph asked when she returned to her post.

"What?" she answered, betraying no notice of his recent disappearance.

"It's my birthday."

For this, and on this day only, he could draw her for free, Myrtle told him. Joseph concentrated on the folds of her dress, which were slightly more challenging in their increased state of decay; but he was not in the room ten minutes when the screaming started. Suddenly Beatrice was in the hall, struggling with the man in the brown overcoat. He pushed her hard against the wall, with her blouse half open and her hair in tangles, and pinned her arms.

"He's a constable!" Beatrice hollered. "He's a bleeding, righteous cop!"

Myrtle shrank, or tried to, into the doorway of the long-departed dressmaker. A uniformed man mounted the stairs, produced handcuffs from the leather pouch at his side, and clamped them firmly onto Beatrice's wrists. As the first man approached Myrtle, Beatrice screeched: "Don't you lay a hand on her! Not a god-damned hand!"

"We've been watching you two long enough," the officer said calmly. The hand he held out to Myrtle was one that might offer sweetgrass to a pony before stroking its forehead. "How old are you, little girl?" Her only response was to chew the inside of her lower lip. "You know you would be happier in a place where people would care for you. You could have your own bed, and lessons, and warm meals."

The familiarity of the words took Joseph back to the orphanage parlour. Children given up by their parents were always hardest to convince. A child found living for days on a jar of beets would sooner have returned to the house of an absent, drunken father than been served a year of suppers in an orphans' home.

As Beatrice writhed, resisting each step down to the prison wagon, Joseph could feel a divine presence at work. An image of Father Tom raised the bread and then the chalice. He stared at Joseph in the transubstantial instant and a message became clear: "If you leave the church, you must find a replacement."

Joseph ran to catch up with the policeman who was holding Myrtle's hand. "Sir!" Joseph called. "When you're looking for a home for her, remember — she's Catholic!"

Dust

1888–1889

17

$\mathcal{A}$ year later, on their last Sunday as newsboys, Joseph and Tim agreed to attend mass at St. Michael's Cathedral. Joseph kept his head bowed during the Eucharist, except for the occasional glance at a nun whose presence was unexpected: Sister Patricia from the Sunnyside orphanage, Our Lady of Mercy. The years had made her more beautiful. The tiny lines on her face were delicate, like those in glaze on china cups. Joseph wondered if she would know him now, or remember his first Toronto night, when she had watched over him. He associated her with things that had been smoothed by time — white bones on the road, a perfect piece of beach glass. But only some memories were smoothed by time.

The boys made no goodbyes to anyone at the St. Nicholas Home.

During the day they sought work and at night they slept in the doorways of Protestant industries. Occasionally, when they found themselves on hotel steps, Tim pulled out his blacking kit and charged a nickel for a shine. "Commercial travellers," Tim said, "are the only ones who care properly for the condition of their shoes." Then he followed with his usual catechism:

"Where are we from?"

"Farms near Belleville."

"Why did we leave?"

"Too many hands and not enough land. Second sons of second sons."

"You're a third son."

"Right."

"What did we farm?"

"Whatever our employer knows least about. To be determined by code. A scratch on the forehead means cattle."

"Which kind?"

Joseph concentrated on making the agriculture columns appear in his mind's eye. "Jersey for dairy ..."

"Yes, yes. And for beef?" Tim yawned: a cipher.

"Angus."

"And your dog?"

"Bill."

"And my dog?"

"Big Ben."

"If we grow crops?"

"A single cough."

"For what?"

Worse than cattle. "Wheat?"

"Be specific."

"Red Fife."

"An armpit scratch?"

"Corn."

"Which *kind* of corn?"

"The kind on the cob."

Tim scowled, but only briefly. The litany established their corn as Golden Bantam, their mothers as sisters — Penelope of the rheumatism and Dot of the cherry pie — their mode of transportation as train, and their reason for coming to Toronto: "It's the Queen's City, sir. The best city in the world." Variations of their story were repeated through the Polson iron and Gurney stove companies, which did not hire minors, dashing Tim's first choice of bending metal. At

Heinzman Pianos, the pair was too scrawny; they were shown the door before they could speak of their bucolic Belleville beginnings. At Callum MacIvor's Flour Mill, when Tim and Joseph described their limited adventures in cattle, MacIvor hired them.

With the boys' new jobs came living quarters in the form of a boarding house recommended by MacIvor himself, though he had never seen it or its proprietress, one Mrs. Betty Roach. "A number of our boys have found reasonable accommodation there," MacIvor said, staring at Tim and Joseph as though to memorize them before they whitened in the mill. MacIvor prided himself on matching every employee's name with the correct face — one of the rituals for preventing a union — or so said one of their fellow workers, Slug Tully, a stubby youth who was a Knight of Labor and took the boys under his wing. "But he's a decent man," Slug said. "He'll say a word to you if he happens to cross your path, though MacIvor's mostly at the books."

The books were to be trusted and, as far as Tim was concerned, so was any man who toiled over them. "He's a Board of Trade man," Tim said. "The miller is a cornerstone of the community."

Mrs. Roach, while not a cornerstone, was certainly a sizeable brick. She gave a more rigorous interview, and she did not believe five seconds of their story. "I don't care what you done before, boys, as long as you pay on time and obey House Rules," she said, eyes darting from mug to blushing mug as if inspecting damage before it could happen. "We practise family reach at table. No fighting with fists, cups, or furniture. Any man who breaks a chair in here'll get his head broke by me and don't think I won't do it. It's five to a bed, no complaints and no cooties. Cooties gets the razor. You'll take your meals as they come and give thanks; I cook with grease. No man here goes hungry. Each night a pie of a different mash — seconds when the boys want it. Wipe your feet and address me as Mrs. Roach on workdays, Widow Roach on the Lord's. Smoke your pipe in here but chew outside. Any questions?"

None at all.

Joseph's first twelve-hour work day began with "Good morning," from Slug Tully, and ended with a message from Orland Pilch: "You're a scrawny little powder boy. I'll call you runt. Bet you can't hit a ball to save your life." The flour in the air made Joseph's eyes water. Orland's slit eyes, impervious to the dust, gleamed blackly. His crooked mouth, perpetually half open, issued insults, gases and profanities.

Orland's father, known as A. Pilch, had been the night miller for twenty years. The old man did not talk. He pointed, pounded, and squeezed. Orland was a packer, the stone dresser's assistant, and pitcher on the company baseball team. His twin brother, Orson — half as sensible and twice as large — drove. He had a disposition for horses and hauling, and a fondness for cats. "Because of his soft head," Jimmy Sykes, the cleaning-warehouse manager, said. Orson cooed to the creatures as they earned their keep, licking mouse guts from their paws.

Tim and Joseph worked the brooms and cobweb dusters — Tim in the cleaning house, and Joseph in the mill. Tim argued that sweeping was a skill to be mastered — even the lowest job was an opportunity. Look how Slug Tully, who was not much older than they were, had moved from brooms to packing. Slug even greased gears.

When not working or pitching, Orland was a bully. His fighting technique was to gouge his thumbnail between the eye and socket of his opponent until the adversary called mercy. Thus, he was known as Mercy Pilch. When, on his way to Mrs. Roach's house, Joseph heard Mercy's voice, he walked hopelessly faster. "Powder boy," the gouger said, "do you know what a baseball is? Or do you play with different balls, little powder boy."

Joseph figured that as Orland was a fixture of his new work place, he was best lost to — and quickly. Get it over with, thought Joseph, as he stopped under the gaslight of Virgil's Tool and Trade and waited for Orland, face to tightened face. But Tim interrupted their meeting. He had stayed late to sweep and to thank Mr. MacIvor again for the opportunity to learn in such a reputable, established, and worthy enterprise, featured regularly in *The Globe*'s "News to Grain Men." Tim lifted his eye patch. His empty eye socket had no effect on Joseph, but for Orland, it was a startling revelation. In its presence, the gouger had to reconsider his craft.

Tim leaned in close to Orland. Slowly, with the assurance of a shape-shifting *sidhe*, Tim stepped lightly around the gouger in a kind of dance, and hummed as Orland gaped at the oval of pink flesh, inadvertently turning a complete rotation, clicking his tongue in the back of his throat and blinking. Joseph prepared for the strange spectacle to end in his own bloodshed, but Orland merely clicked and gulped.

"Leave him alone," Tim said to Orland, "or you'll answer to me." Likely, somewhere on Tim's person was a pilfered vegetable knife, but the fight was over before it began. Orland simply leered at them, while the crooked channel of his mouth gave passage to the first day's parting words: "I know you lied about your ages, runts. Don't forget it."

◇ ◇ ◇

At Mrs. Roach's table sat an assemblage of labourers ranging widely in age, size, and occupation. Several were from MacIvor's, but most worked in wood or iron. Occasionally, a hand spearing a turnip lacked a finger or two. "More pie, boys?" earned assenting grunts and mumbles, though no conversation took place until the landlady's most senior boarder, Old Davie, arrived to hold court. His skin was magnificently leathered. He began with a proverb over the mashed potatoes, as Mrs. Roach delivered a wedge of pie that she'd kept warm during his routine stop at the local tavern, Phelan's House of Spirits. "It's the hand, boys," Davie said, "that educates the mind." The same hand doused his plate in gravy. "Expect no gift from life, but that won by your own toil."

The house was nonviolent for several key reasons. First was the quantity of starch, which had a leadening effect in the body. Each man's most fully automated feature was his fork arm. The landlady stood by her table, listening to the scrape of metal, grind of teeth, and semi-vocalized swallows, like a miller listening to the rhythm of the stones, rollers and bolters, satisfied the machinery was in running order.

The second deterrent to violence was Mrs. Roach's knife, twice the size of Sister Mary Margaret's, and more in evidence throughout meals. Mrs. Roach stated on a nightly basis that she would use it on any man who made a move against another. For that reason, Joseph soon discovered, her home was known as the Chop — a point that MacIvor had neglected to mention. Occasionally, when morning came, one less pig rolled in the yard.

The final factor in the pacification of tenants at the Chop was Davie's talk. Once begun, it had a soporific effect on all but Tim, whose supper helpings were smaller than the rest, but whose appetite for "improving speeches" was considerably larger. Tim was fed by stories of the rolling mills of Ohio — how Davie had worked across two countries, pausing only briefly to marry and lose his wife and child, which at first made Joseph wonder where they'd got to and if they might turn up. Old Davie was "Sojourner Davies" on workdays, and "Widower Davies" on the Lord's. "He is just passing through," Mrs. Roach regularly reminded them.

"Where a man's treasure is, there his heart is also." Davie's words, spoken over a schooner of beer, brought apples to the landlady's cheeks. Davie was allowed to chew tobacco in her house, but did as the rest of the men, and smoked a pipe. "The pipe is a tool of labourer and enlightened man alike," Tim said. Thus, the boys acquired theirs, and Davie offered his tobacco for their first good stuff. "A pipe is a man's own," Davie said, "but tobacco is common property." Fraternal smoke burned away the white cough of the mill. After the smoke, Davie exited into the night for his constitutional and a dram at Phelan's that set him singing.

18

*N*ick the stone dresser had a way of subduing Orland Pilch
with words. When the bully got out of hand, Nick called after him in
Hungarian. The words were indecipherable to all but the speaker;
but Orland thought they were a curse. Like Tim's exposed and pulsing
eye socket, Nick's language immobilized Orland in fascination and
horror.

And so, because Joseph liked Nick and feared Orland, his feel-
ings were mixed when he came to sweep the first floor of the mill,
where Orland was the stone dresser's boy. Yet Joseph felt protected by
the distracting whirl of line shafts, rumble of gears and rotating belts.
Often, Joseph could enter Orland's ground-floor territory unnoticed.
He could almost relax in the din of the gnashing rollers above him
and the cascades of particles shaken through the bolt machines and
sent back up for further grinding, or out into barrels, packed and hammered and pushed through a chute to the men who stacked them.

Joseph caught himself staring over at Nick as he re-carved the
surface of a French buhr stone with a power of concentration that
could only be described as holy. "The men of progress say the stones
will soon be things of the past," Tim said. MacIvor, who used to
chuckle at the "fad" of rollers, now ran six sets. Undeniably, mechanized rollers were more efficient than stones at grinding grain; rollers
needed re-grooving far less frequently. But Joseph didn't think about

progress when he watched Nick create a language of lines, precisely marked and radiating out from an empty centre.

Despite his vocal storms to reform Orland (often followed by a nudge and a wink), Nick was peaceful, which both drew Joseph to him and created distance. At the dinner break, Nick offered Joseph a piece of his wife's homemade sausage. The meat was more flavourful than any Joseph had ever tasted, heating his mouth and filling him with peppery satisfaction.

Tim rarely joined them on the bench, and when he did, he left early — not to avoid Nick and Joseph, but to continue work. Tim's sweeping was restricted to the vast cleaning warehouse, which Tim saw as a gateway to promotion, though Slug's progress had not included a spell in the cleaning house. Slug remained a source of interest and irritation to Tim; his quick rise at the mill, combined with his Knight of Labor status, was baffling. "With all their yapping about shorter work weeks and workers' rights, those Knights just stand for trouble," Tim told Joseph. He denounced the Knights' organized gatherings as "betrayals of the reputable men who lead."

While he didn't think much of Tim's fiercely independent views, Joseph said nothing. Listening and nodding were easier than arguing. Joseph also didn't say he'd heard MacIvor tell Sykes: "See that Tim works well back from the gears." Thus, when listening to Tim's plan to show MacIvor commitment and burgeoning skills, Joseph felt guilty, as he doubted Tim and his eye patch would get past the warehouse.

Tim quickly learned how to separate grit from grain, and lectured on the subject. "Dirty wheat meets the Champion, see — the separator, where the chaff, sticks, nails, and other junk gets blown or sieved right out." Tim beamed. "Then the smut balls get it in the Eureka. The brushing machine's next: a *beast* for dust! Then the magnets." He looked satisfied. "By the time the grain rolls up to the fourth floor and down into the bins, it's clean, tempered and conditioned. I tell you, Joe, the more I master, the more certain I am of promotion!"

Joseph just nodded.

"I can be patient, Joe. The best millers are."

Jimmy Sykes trained both boys in walking down the grain with their shovels when the two-storey bins were low, though Joseph was meant to help only occasionally.

"So I'm your main walker?" Tim asked.

"Sure," Jimmy said.

Tim blushed with pride at his first additional responsibility, and Joseph couldn't help smiling.

"Only go in when the grain's dropped a storey or so," Jimmy said. "If you see the level's low, like it is in this here bin, go down to the access door on the third floor." The "door" was really a small, square hatch that Jimmy dislodged and propped against the wooden bin wall. They slid inside, where Sykes explained how a chute below the four-inch central discharge hole at the very bottom, on the second floor, emptied the grain to a lower-level elevator. There, buckets were filled and hoisted by an endlessly rolling system of belts to the adjoining building to be milled.

"Keep the grain moving, boys. Walk it down," Jimmy said, as the three waded around the edges of the dim, room-sized bin with their shovels. "Push the grain towards the centre so gravity can do its job. When it's low like this, it needs coaxing. You gotta break up the crusts, get the clumps out, and knock it down from the sides where it's stuck. You gotta mind the grain don't settle and turn musty, and that it don't breach."

"Breach?"

"Ghost stories," a miller called from the beyond the bin.

Jimmy explained. "On top a grain hill forms a crust, see? But below's a hollow. Once the hill caves in, it pulls a leg in, too."

Keith Bigly, the foreman, stuck his head through the opening. "I come from a family of grain men, boys, and I've never witnessed breaching. But I have heard tell of it. If a person's leg sinks in the grain, the thing to do is lie flat, spread out on top."

"Like floating," Jimmy said. "But you gotta do it fast. There's the trick. If you panic and try to keep walking, the grain's like quicksand."

Keith said: "More like a sea. A man can drown in it."

Joseph flinched. Tim chuckled.

The older men smiled, assuring the boys that such occurrences were rare. "Just remember," Jimmy said, "like Keith said — lie flat. And leave the door open when you're in a bin so folks'll know where you are." Tim's eye twinkled. Somehow the danger elevated their rock-bottom jobs.

❖ ❖ ❖

Joseph could see that Old Davie's talk of labour and its virtues fed and sustained Tim. While Joseph didn't feel quite as nourished, he quickly agreed to accompany the two to Phelan's tavern. Within the dim-lit House of Spirits, Joseph was most receptive to Old Davie's proverbs and his stories. The taste of whiskey made the details vivid — the iron puddler's furnace with its molten sea of flame. "In those days," Davie said, "I looked on hell and stirred it, every fibre in me flexing to boil out dross and brimstone. Remember that, boys. Strong metal doesn't come easy. Pig-iron men are brittle. Only the man with a wrought-iron will can wrestle good iron from the earth." The more Old Davie swallowed, the more he pined for the hell that he described, and the more clear that picture of hell became in Joseph's mind. In Toronto, where the brief age of iron rolling mills had passed, Old Davie worked at a foundry merely making stoves; but the *Globe*'s Hamilton news columns never went unnoticed by the Sojourner, ever seeking a return to iron. He bought a newspaper each evening from a shivering newsboy.

Joseph's hand also ached — not for any instrument of Davie's description, and certainly not for his broom, but for his pencil and his pen, which remained buried in his sack. When he opened that sack and saw the two ribbons — one green and one black — something else in him ached. His aches disappeared when Davie handed him the whiskey tumbler.

One night Tim declared that, instead of joining them at Phelan's, he was off to the Mechanics Institute library. "I have taken a membership to improve my mind."

"Well, you can't keep a good man down," Old Davie said.

Joseph said nothing, but reached in his sack, without looking, to pull out his drawing kit. "Would you mind if I brought it along?" he asked Davie.

The relief of moving the pencil in concert with the furrows in Davie's leathered brow was almost enough to make Joseph forget his glass. His whiskey sat undisturbed for whole minutes as a wizened face emerged on the page.

"You've got a knack, boy," Phelan, the proprietor, said. "Would you do one for me?"

And so, at night, Joseph sketched quietly while Davie talked, moving from face to shadowy face. People offered Joseph drinks, or occasionally coins, in exchange for sketching them. "Here you are free," the voice in his mind said, but whose voice it was, he could not be certain. "Annie?" he whispered.

"We're closing," Phelan said. Old Davie began to sing.

❖ ❖ ❖

Reluctantly, Joseph accompanied Tim to a Methodist church service. "We can join this place," Tim said, preferring the back of a large, affluent congregation to the middle of a poor one. "In church, as in life, we must use strategy." Grinning, Tim tipped his hat at a young lady in a fox fur cape. She caught herself smiling before briskly turning away.

"I'm not coming back," Joseph said.

"Come at Christmas. And at Easter. Then you can say you're a Protestant."

For Joseph, Sunday meant the rinks. He could not afford the dime to skate on commercial ice, but watched from the boards, unless a sketch or a royal flush financed his entry. Stunts by touring performers drew crowds — especially the contortionists. Joseph trained his eyes to seek out Deary, whatever wig or dress she might be wearing, whatever alias she might bear. In a city of wheels and blades, surely Deary had learned to skate.

Sometimes, having searched Moss Park Arena with an empty pocket, Joseph walked down to the frozen Don River, where the working-class boys skated with the working-class girls in their thin woollen coats. No paid entertainments existed here, just the Irish. Joseph skated on a pair of dull blades he got free at a Salvation Army revival. He told Tim he'd paid a nickel for them, so Tim wouldn't lecture him that their days of accepting charity were over.

Like the rinks, the city's theatricals also drew him, and they were worth saving up for. Joseph kept those outings to himself. Dramatic productions supplied knights and heroes, though Cuchulainn never made an appearance; but at least, watching the protagonists on their quests inspired Joseph to obtain a decent suit. Someday, when he found her, he would show Deary that he'd grown up.

When Joseph took a young man's glass-buttoned grey serge suit free from the St. Vincent de Paul, he exclaimed to Tim: "A tremendous sale at the Golden Lion!" Tim responded: "Fair enough," although he cocked his head suspiciously as it happened to be bank day and Joseph was short of coin. Tim added: "You know I'm saving for my eye. I'm a little low on cash myself."

Their house purchase could wait another week.

Joseph's suit went nowhere near the mill, but appeared at the rinks or a melodrama in a rented warehouse. "All fancy are you, boy," Mrs. Roach said, without smiling. He took her words as a compliment.

In his suit, Joseph felt ready to face Deary, should she cartwheel into view. His recent spurt of growing was a source of comfort, though Tim was almost a full year older and a full head shorter. Tim ate too little and too fast, claimed Old Davie, as the boy bolted to the library. Books, Davie opined, did not bring muscle. But he conceded: "You can't keep a good man down."

For Joseph, defying Tim generally required lying, particularly the evening Joseph planned to attend a meeting of the Knights of Labor. Appropriately suited, he travelled with Slug Tully to his local chapter in a place called Claretown. There Joseph found a mixed assembly of chattering men and women, young and old, trades and "tribes" (as Tim would call them), including the Irish Catholic tribe, which compounded Joseph's guilt upon entry. A laundress, lately scalped by a rotating steam shaft, smiled through a gate of missing pickets. "Vincent, you've brought a friend." She took his hand and led him.

"Yes," Slug said. "This is Joseph, Polly."

"Welcome, Joseph."

Joseph nodded, smiled and looked around, working hard not to tally the absent appendages. Polly moved about the room, questioning every newcomer: "Do you believe in God?" Some nodded. Others, like Joseph, cleared their throats and reddened, which was construed as an affirmation. One man clearly stated his faith and was told that his denomination, while certainly worthy, was of no significance here. No sectarianism must exist amongst the working-class Knights — no ranking based on religion, trade, or gender. "If you believe in God," Polly stated quite simply, "you're in. Unless you're a lawyer."

A dance was being organized to buy her a wig, and a leg for an absent brother who had stepped on an unguarded gear. Signs around the room proclaimed: "We are not cogs!" "One day for God, five for labour, and one for humanity!" Joseph found "Succeed at home first!" difficult to picture in practice.

When the meeting began, only one word — "strike" — caused the assembly to erupt in heated arguments. The leader pounded on a table with his mallet. "Order, Knights! Tonight, we'll not speak of strikes. Let the Trade Unions do what they will." The grumbles faded.

"We need to apply our efforts to local legislation, my friends — laws for private business owners. Let us speak of minimum wage!" Cheers. "Let us help to bring about the eight-hour day!" At that, people rose to their feet and applauded.

As the meeting continued more quietly, with plans laid and stories shared, Joseph saw that in their conviction not to be trampled by machine or capitalist, members had found peace. People smiled, whispered, and applauded where they could. This solidarity unsettled Joseph — not for its messages, but because he didn't feel he belonged, like a prosthetic appendage that didn't quite fit, and felt ashamed.

After the meeting, tea and biscuits were provided. Issues of *Palladium* circulated to those who could read. Slug negotiated his way through the hall, shaking hands and patting backs in a way that made him radiate a warmth and charm that Joseph had barely glimpsed at the mill. Slug's graciousness was palpable. His air of trust in himself and in pure goodness, combined with an unflagging intention to serve, distinguished him. Joseph could see it — he might even be able to draw it — but he doubted he could live it.

Joseph was disappointed that the Knights of Labor had no uniforms. "Is there a badge at least?" Joseph asked quietly as he and Slug were leaving.

"I suppose there is," Slug said. Joseph's heart quickened a little. If he at least had a badge for being a Knight he could show it to Deary as proof that he was grown and, in some way, gallant. Not that he had expected shining armour or a sword — visions of Cuchulainn and the Red Branch Knights quickly faded, and not a chariot in sight. Just a streetcar.

"I was wondering, Slug — if I can call you that again — or Vincent. I was wondering if sometime you'd like to join us at Phelan's after hours. For some fellowship, I mean to say."

"Is it a tavern?" Slug asked.

"Oh yes."

"We're temperance, Joe," Slug said, delivering the final blow. "All the Knights are temperance. But thank you for the invitation."

"Don't mention it."

"I won't. And please, Joseph, don't you mention it either."

So much for the Knights of Labor.

19

*I*n spring, reputation at the mill was gained by demonstrating prowess on the baseball field. Training occurred every Monday, Wednesday, and Thursday, after the day shift ended. Neither the long hours of labour nor his persistent cough deterred Slug. Outfielders missed his hits every time. "But a batter alone doesn't make a successful team," Orland said. "It's the battery."

"Trouble is," Jimmy Sykes said, "our catcher, Roddy Newel, up and moved to Timmins last October. We need a catcher for the Victoria Day game against Sproll Flour. Someone to practise with Orland here." The men looked down and scratched at the dirt with their boots.

As he studied the ground, Joseph felt himself being stared at. He dug his right boot deeper into the earth, as if his whole being might follow.

"Someone whose hand does a good job of following his eye," Keith Bigly said, his spectacles guaranteeing his position as practice umpire and team steward. It went without saying that Tim need not apply — though his new glass eye turned heads.

"Does it help you see better?" Orson asked.

"Let's just say I'll be practising my batting," Tim said. Each morning at dawn Tim nudged Joseph awake and they went down to the street with a stick and a ball. Tim swung and swung, and sometimes he connected. His improvement, undoubtedly, was worth the investment, though Joseph's head ached most mornings, and by noon his limbs seemed to creak on the way to the bench beside Nick and his brief respite of paprika sausage.

In the draw for catcher, unsurprisingly, Joseph's straw was shortest. And so, his day included "leisure," as Slug would put it. Practices with Orland were comprised of avoided assaults. Joseph was handed former catcher Roddy Newel's legacy, an ordinary leather glove with the fingers cut off. It managed to stop a curve short of breaking Joseph's teeth. An interrupted speedball saved a rib or two.

The game against Sproll Flour was played on the rivals' turf, the site of a former business block, burned out so long ago that the grass had covered all trace except for the occasional stump of post to be avoided in right field, or beside third base. "Ankle twisters," Jimmy warned, having seen more than one man go down.

The MacIvor Mavericks lost ten to four to the Sproll Sprockets. Down York Street at the Walker House, the losers bought the winners beer. Slug Tully only shook hands with their victors, wished them well, and disappeared into the mists of abstention.

Their second game, against Duke's Commercial Flour, took place on the Mavericks' home turf in June when the light favoured all nine innings. The boys from Duke's had a pitcher who threw by the book, below the belt, but like Orland he wore his belt across his nipples. Slug, undeterred, hit a run of line drives into left field that ended in a manure pile behind the barn. Tim hit fouls, but he hit. Joseph stole third base, and in so doing slid into a familiar infielder, Benny White from Sunnyside — a foot taller and considerably more burly than their last encounter.

"Benny!" Joseph said, laughing. "What are you doing here?"

"Waiting to soak you if I can," Benny returned in kind. And soak him he did. Whatever allegiance the two shared in having emerged from the same house of charity was abandoned in Joseph's tear for home and Benny's tag on him.

"He could tell everything about us," Tim whispered, desperate to flee but bound by duty to stay with his squad.

"I don't think he will," said Joseph, whose need to fend off Orland's throws put things sharply into perspective. Greater dangers were at hand. Having survived Orland and another loss, Joseph joined the MacIvor boys at the Walker, where the Dukes awaited free beer. This time, like Tully, Tim bid goodnight and congratulations, and went home.

"How's Tim?" Benny asked, when he and Joseph found themselves in a dark back corner of the tavern.

"He's all right."

"I like his new eye. A little paler than the other maybe, but good and round. You both look very fine, Joe Conlon."

"So do you, Benny White."

The beer loosened their tongues and brought welcome relief. Joseph stretched the reddened fingers of the hand newly loosed from the team glove.

"Strange he didn't say hello," Benny said.

"He was tired," Joseph said, lying. "I'm not sure he recognized you."

"Tim would know me anywhere. I'm the first chum who stood by him the day he came to Our Lady of Mercy. A person always remembers that, wouldn't you say?"

In his mind, Joseph saw Deary. "I would."

"I held onto him, see, when he tried to run back to his old man." Then, as though it had happened only yesterday and not years ago, Joseph saw Tim returning to the orphans' home after his failed attempt to run away. Tim had struggled with the man who brought him back on the coal cart. Eventually Tim had stood down, red-faced, arms folded across his heaving chest. Joseph remembered the nun's words: "Obey your father."

"Tim's father," Joseph said. "Did he drive a coal cart?"

"Well ... yes. I suppose he did. It's strange the things you remember."

Joseph remembered Benny clearly, the lady in pink flowers waving from an ever-tilted laudanum bottle. "Very strange."

❖ ❖ ❖

Dominion Day was the biggest game day of summer. On the lawns of Government House and University College, and on those that sprawled behind the Jarvis Street mansions, men played cricket. Clubs accommodated paying players; gates closed quietly behind lawn bowlers, and not so quietly behind lacrosse teams. Everywhere else was baseball. Vacant lots were staked out for games organized by trades. Forgers played forgers; smiths played smiths. MacIvor Flour hosted Sproll — their first game on the Mavericks' home turf — and had an audience. Nick and his wife Nina brought a basket of bread and fruit for the team. Nina's beer, consumed before the second inning, so affected Tim's swing that he hit the ball to centre field. The assembly included Old Davie and Mrs. Roach, who maintained a respectable distance from each other. The Widow watched both the game and the Sojourner, dabbing her forehead with a cloth mainly used for binding cheese. MacIvor himself came out to take part in the festivities. Slug successfully landed three drives in the dung pile. Once the beer flowed, even Orland's twister mellowed.

MacIvor's was victorious and reeling in the mid-day sun. Men staggered into the Esplanade, avoiding carriages. MacIvor left two bottles of rye in Slug Tully's hands, knowing that his temperance star hitter would distribute the contents judiciously, and trusting that workers who played together tended to stay peaceful and productive.

❖ ❖ ❖

The season wound down in late August. Joseph welcomed the earlier darkness and a return to Phelan's. Tim returned as well, once more in the thrall of Old Davie's talk.

One October night, Tim presented Joseph with a proposition before the two set out for the tavern. "Old Davie's going to move soon," Tim said. "He's had it with foundry work. He's over-skilled, here, Joe. In Hamilton, Davie has a chance to have a furnace again. Without iron and steel, we stay wooden men, Joseph. And wood burns, it decays. All the great cities want metal for their bones. Think of it — to be a metal man — that's something. Imagine where it could lead."

All Joseph could imagine was not finding Deary in Hamilton.

"Davie's pretty old."

"I wasn't thinking for Davie. I was thinking for us. We could work with him. Look, every iron puddler needs a boy. He could vouch for us, Joe — get us jobs that are higher up than at the mill. MacIvor won't let me near the rollers, or anywhere there are more than two or three belts. He thinks I'm blind, Joe. I tell you, Hamilton could be the start we've been waiting for. New town, new jobs and Davie's blessing."

"An iron puddler only needs one boy," Joseph said. "It might as well be you."

"But he could get you work, too."

"No, Tim. I won't leave town."

❖ ❖ ❖

Two weeks before Tim and Davie's planned departure for Hamilton, Tim asked Joseph to draw his picture. "I'd like to see me there, on your page."

When the sketch was done, Tim smiled. "Not bad. You got the eyes right for sure." They were eyes that stared straight ahead. "I want you to keep it."

20

*T*wo weeks turned into three. As Tim waited for Davie to decide their moving date, he continued working shifts in the cleaning warehouse. Joseph continued to visit his friend during his own short breaks, letting the flour dust, and his cough, settle. Compared to the mill house, with its endless grinding, rolling, and bolting, the warehouse was relatively quiet. Sometimes, Joseph helped Tim shovel grain when a bin was low. The sound of the shovel, despite the shoveller's private discontent at the mill, was still a happy sound. But on this particular November day, Joseph didn't hear the shovel.

He looked for Tim sweeping, but didn't see him. He walked up around the cleaning machines, but Tim wasn't dusting, either. He knew that Tim occasionally assisted the men outside, unloading dirty grain. Joseph called down to Jimmy Sykes, but he hadn't seen Tim. "He's not in the privy. When you find him, tell him to get to work, eh?" Sykes winked.

On the third floor, the long corridor of wooden bins was eerily quiet. The only motion Joseph sensed, besides the constant, distant rumblings of the mill, was his own anxiety rising. The hatch to bin six was open. Except for slightly more than a half-storey of grain, the bin was empty. Joseph backed away from the access door, near panic. It wasn't like Tim to leave a hatch open, and he didn't take breaks. Joseph recalled Jimmy's long-ago words about how a hollow could form beneath the surface of the grain. "When a person sinks upright, the grain becomes quicksand."

"Almost unheard of," Joseph said aloud to steady his nerves. "Almost." But something in the shadowy bin drew him back. He'd seen it the first time, but hadn't allowed the image to register. There, floating on the surface by the far wall: a wooden shovel.

The Banshee was late, yet she came.

Joseph's scream brought the men running. Joseph watched Jimmy and Slug slip inside through the narrow opening. When Callum MacIvor and Keith Bigly appeared, MacIvor told Bigly to shut down the mill. After a long minute, the rumbling ceased. All Joseph could hear was the sound of men digging. Gripped by terror, he retreated down the passage and sank against the brick wall, hugging his knees.

"Dig there!"

"Pitch the grain to the corners! That's quickest!"

Then Jimmy Sykes said: "Oh Jesus. I've got him."

❖ ❖ ❖

It took a half hour to dig Tim out. Joseph didn't look as the men lifted Tim's body and manoeuvred it through the hatch, gently setting the dead boy on the floor. Scarcely aware of his surroundings, Joseph saw a ship's hull. When Keith Bigly said: "Someone cover him," Joseph heard: "Cover her eyes." Head tucked and body tight, quietly moaning, he rocked against the bricks until his back bled. Her open mouth, her cold, clammy skin, the dirty blue hem — fading.

MacIvor paced, Jimmy wept, and a visibly distraught Slug Tully said: "He never should have been alone on this job. We need laws."

"I trained him," Jimmy said. "I said lay flat if you sink. I said it more than once. Poor young fella must've panicked. A damn shame."

Joseph couldn't look, as he couldn't look at his mother's face after his scream had brought the passengers to their berth. People had said she was dead. He'd touched her hand; then she was gone. He should have done more. He should have stayed in Montreal with Colleen and heard a priest say holy words for Mam. He should have watched her coffin lowered into Catholic ground. If he had stayed, if—

His thoughts were too sharp. He couldn't think anymore — only move. He pushed his way through the men to the body someone had covered with a coat.

Joseph knelt down, allowing the smell of death to fill him. "Father Tom. I need Father Tom — in St. Paul's parish. Tim needs a priest's blessing."

The men looked away as Joseph lifted the coat and stared at his friend's blue face. Only Slug looked on with him. "I'll take you to your priest."

◊ ◊ ◊

Joseph pounded on the rectory door, beyond dreading the priest now. The moment was another sinkhole, and all he could do was flail. "Tim's dead," Joseph blurted to the priest, who blinked for several seconds before registering. "Tim's dead and you have to bury him. He needs a proper Catholic burial."

Father reached out to put his hand on Joseph's shoulder, but Joseph stepped back, every muscle tense, refusing to give in to the remorse that would choke him if he let it. He couldn't think of Tim's drowning moments, or of the boys' betrayal.

"We ran away. We worked at a mill. Tim died this afternoon. You have to say mass for him. You have to see he's buried Catholic. *Please.* He needs your blessing."

Then the story of the boys' flight came out. Yes, the mill they worked for was Protestant run. No, they didn't tell their employer they were Catholic. Joseph didn't tell Father Tom about Tim going to the Methodists; he couldn't risk him being denied a place in St. Michael's ground. The chances of saving his own soul were next to nil, but he could do his best for Tim.

Two days later, Father Tom met Joseph at the doors of the very large and almost empty church. The priest placed a new rosary in Joseph's hand as he entered. After the mass, the hearse travelled three miles up Yonge Street to the Catholic cemetery. Tim's father stood, hat in hands, his coal cart on the street outside the gate. Old Davie shed a few tears. Callum MacIvor, Jimmy Sykes and Slug Tully represented the mill. Only Slug shook the priest's hand and thanked him, after all was said and done. Joseph stayed by the edge of Tim's grave after the mill men left. The boys' Home Savings and Loan money was enough to pay for a decent burial. "It's a fine plot, Tim," Joseph whispered. "Sunny." What he meant was respectable. Joseph knew Tim would appreciate a central place, away from the paupers in the southwest corner. It was all Joseph could do for him now.

Tim's father stood silently for a few moments, and then said: "You knew my boy?"

"Yes."

"He was a good boy?"

"Yes."

The old man fidgeted with his hat. "I couldn't raise him after his ma died, see. Too many of them. Too much. The Sisters took him, eh? But I loved him. I loved my Tim."

The lump in Joseph's throat grew harder. He couldn't talk. He remembered hearing Tim cry the day his father brought him back to the home — all the shouting and the man driving off. Joseph recalled his own father handing him money, and Mam later weeping, holding the letter that Joseph still kept. The weight was enough to bury Joseph, too. Only anger kept him standing.

"That miller killed my son, eh?"

"No, sir, you did."

"I beg'r pardon?"

"It was an accident."

Tim's father nodded.

When Joseph finally crossed through dead leaves on the November cemetery ground, Father Tom was waiting.

"Only God can judge," the priest said. "Tim had no time to do penance for his sins. We can only pray for his soul in purgatory. But Joseph, you have the opportunity to confess your sins and do penance — to return to God."

After nodding silently, Joseph declined the offer of a carriage ride back downtown with the priest. He didn't join Davie in the St. Clair tavern, either. Instead, he walked. Down the long hill back to the city. He kicked tree trunks and trash bins. He pulled the rosary from his pocket, broke the chain, and watched the beads roll in the gutter.

❖ ❖ ❖

The day Old Davie left town, Joseph walked him as far as Wellington and York, but he refused to go near Union Station. Somewhere on the railway lands the old iron puddler would hop a freight train. "The way of a sojourner," Mrs. Roach said later, dabbing at her nose with a cheese cloth.

If Tim had been with Old Davie, the two would have talked incessantly. They would have been excited. Joseph saw Tim beside the iron puddler, looking back over his shoulder with a wave that said: "I'll see you, Joe."

❖ ❖ ❖

At the mill, no one challenged Joseph for having lied about his past when he and Tim were hired; however, most of the men avoided his eye when they could. Nick, Slug and Jimmy were exceptions. Nick arranged for Joseph to become his pick sharpener, releasing Orland to Packing full time. Nick's kindness was as dependable as bread — dull when excitements were at hand, but sustaining when they were not.

The Chop House table was quiet.

Weeks later, Joseph took his suit to a laundress on Duchess Street, who steamed and pressed it, and held his coin as though it were a fragile animal. He imagined her spread out on red velvet in a gaslit studio. Walking west, he passed a familiar lane. In his mind, Beatrice opened her body to him; but he didn't try to see her face. Instead, he saw Myrtle's face.

Then a young woman in an alley off of Lombard Street sent the sisters out of his head completely. Her dress pulled up easily. She was good at her work and he paid her. Afterward, the woman's smell lingered on him. Joseph paid her again. "You can't get it up that fast," the hooker said with a laugh, reluctant to interrupt the cigarette she'd just rolled. She was right, but he touched her skin and lay his head in her lap.

All at once, Joseph realized how close they were to the newsboys' home. The last person he wanted to see now was Rory Murphy — or worse, a priest. Suddenly repulsed, he left the woman without a goodbye. By the back stairs of a nearby commercial building, Joseph changed into his suit and rolled his other clothes into a trash bin. Then he turned south and washed his face and hands at a public fountain. At Jack's Jug on King, thoughts of the previous half hour dissolved in the first whiskey of the night. The next two kept them gone.

Suddenly a familiar voice jarred him.

"Here you are, then, runt," Orland Pilch said, as foam dribbled down his chin. "Haven't seen you here before. So this is where you made your plans to steal my job, is it?"

"I didn't steal your job, Orland."

"You're in your cups, I reckon, now that your little cyclops friend is gone — papist bastard. Filthy lying taig."

Sometimes three whiskeys spoke for themselves, and in a flash, Joseph and Orland were out on King Street. When Orland charged with his thumb, Joseph pulled up in time to bite it, tasting salt, and watching his oppressor recoil before he punched Joseph's face with the other hand. Joseph's mouth bled onto his suit jacket. Men from the tavern formed a circle around them.

"Take it back, Orland!" hollered the whiskey.

"You little runt. No cyclops to protect you now." Joseph lunged at the bully, sending them both to the ground where their breath, saliva, grunts and gasps intermingled. For a moment, Joseph's sweating body kept Orland down, flushed and writhing. Then a series of scratches, claws and swipes had them rolling to the sounds of tearing cloth and groans — a cracked skull, pummelled ribs, and oozing teeth marks. Anything but mercy. A choke hold unexpectedly bloomed under Joseph's weight when he happened to be on top. Watching Orland's face turn purple offered several seconds of fascination, before a man stepped in. "That's enough."

The next part was a blank. Joseph walked a little unevenly towards the Chop. Every bit of him hurt. He couldn't even answer the man with Ulster in his voice who said: "Good for you, Joe. He had it coming."

Joseph touched his bruised and bloodied jaw and felt strangely exuberant. He began humming the tune to "Slide, Kelly, Slide" because his mouth was too sore to form the words. One foot in front of the other carried him closer to the Chop, but nowhere near to home.

Twenty feet ahead of him, Deary Avery stepped into the street and crossed through a pool of lamplight. Joseph's heart leapt inside his battered ribs. He couldn't call her name — or run to the shadowy laneway where she vanished.

Glass

1893

21

*A*t nineteen, when a gear caught his right sleeve and nearly caught his arm, Joseph quit the mill, heeded Tim's long-ago advice, and bought a home. Free of attachment to any employer, he pitched a tent by the Don River. Joseph's savings paid for the tarpaulin, poles, and groundsheet, a daily meal or two at Kit's Hashery, blankets and prostitutes.

Joseph pulled pictures from his pack and lit a fire in a circle of dead wood by the river's edge. Of all the sketches, he selected only twelve to keep. A pair of eyes, the fold of a dress, a hand. The tavern-goers' discarded faces curled and blackened. Street scenes turned to ash. Tim continued staring straight ahead, but Joseph could no longer visualize Deary's face.

The next day, he walked to the shell of a burnt-out church, where workmen were attempting to extract an undestroyed window. Somehow the ruined structure was a comfort to Joseph. Here, where someone else was responsible for the damage, he wasn't burdened by his long absence from the church and countless sins. He didn't worry about God's love and God's wrath, Father Tom's disappointment, or the Holy Spirit. At the base of the church, Joseph found a shady place to draw the entire block of businesses across the street, each door a mouth, the windows eyes. Above him, in the remaining church window that the workmen were trying to save, a glass Jesus appeared to

Mary in the garden; Jesus had been entirely blackened, though Mary's face remained visible.

Then Mary's face fell onto the grass and gazed up at Joseph. When searing pain quickly followed, he thought she was the Banshee.

❖ ❖ ❖

"You're at the General Hospital," someone said.

❖ ❖ ❖

Somewhere out of time Joseph perceived a screen, and behind it a place he yearned for, of ticking grass and high red clover. Golden flowers bowed in the breeze and Mam's voice said: "Yarrow." A woman held his hand. Joseph didn't want to see her, because he knew that if he looked he would risk losing her. A needle was drawing a thread through the skin on his face. Then he slept.

Later, the world behind the screen had gone. In the corner of a room stood a man with cropped black hair and a pressed white shirt. His eyes were two smooth strokes of ink, wet and shining. He bowed.

"Mr. James Ramsey sent me," the man said. "You were hurt when the church wall fell. Mr. Ramsey, the window maker, pays for your care here. Drink this — you become strong."

The man appeared each time the screen fell away. Joseph would have stayed behind the screen where the breeze was cool and sweet, and the familiar female presence watched over him. Each time he sensed her with him, Joseph felt no desire. Wanting faded on the green hill behind the screen. When the room reappeared, Joseph's wanting returned. What Joseph wanted was whiskey, not the bitter liquid in the man's tumbler.

One day, Joseph could no longer make the room disappear.

"You're healing nicely," a nurse said.

Healing was submission, Joseph reckoned. The visiting man's

drink was medicinal, and added to the defeat of waking up. Joseph could do nothing more than say: "Thank you."

The man introduced himself as William, a workman at the church when the corner of the building collapsed. "I brought you here," William, the first Chinese man Joseph had ever met, said.

Day after day blood and pus trickled from a wrung cloth into a bowl beside Joseph's bed.

"When you were hurt, I sent word to Mr. Jimmy. I am his glazier."

When William talked to Joseph he looked directly into his eyes, but when the doctor spoke, he looked at the stitches laced through Joseph's right cheek, and at Joseph's leg that had been cracked in three places. "We are going to re-bind him," the doctor said to Joseph's knee. "Then, with a brace and crutches he may begin to get around again."

One day William arrived with a folded piece of leather. Inside was Mary's face, barely visible through a crust of blood, the edges newly smoothed with lead. "This very lucky for you," William said. "White man's goddess of mercy. Do not wash."

◆ ◆ ◆

Outside, the hospital walls were barely visible through the ivy. Occasionally cattle wandered to the high picket fence, turning their eyes placidly upon the towers, and ambled on. Joseph limped on sticks that window-maker James Ramsey had purchased for him, circling the building each day as instructed.

"You were a regular sleeping beauty when you arrived," chirped the nurse who spent the bulk of her time with the groaning men in Joseph's ward. Each spoon into a mouth stopped a strand of the noise. The cattle were better company.

William's visits, while brief, were predictable. He walked with Joseph under a darkening sky each evening. While Joseph did not wish William to stay, neither did he wish him to leave. "Mr. Jimmy will send for you soon," William said. "You will come to his house when the doctor says you are strong. Mr. Joseph, you are a lucky man."

William placed Mary's leather-wrapped face in Joseph's sack. Weeks ago its other items had been examined for clues to their owner's identity: twelve drawings; a handful of beach glass; a boy's unsent letters; a man's letter delivered long ago, opened many times, and heated to reseal the wax; a cross made of rushes; white gloves in a walnut shell; and two ribbons.

"Mr. Jimmy likes your drawings. He likes your charms."

In the ward, Joseph heard a fiddler playing. The music was thin through the closed window and air that stank of sewage. A pipe joined, and a distant drum. Joseph imagined banners and marching: the twelfth of July. Every Orangeman in the city would be out. To Joseph, who cared little whether a banner was orange or green, the music was simply Irish. His blood was red; that much he knew.

When the time came for Joseph to become acquainted with his new face, he asked William to be with him, as if the man's presence could change what Joseph was warned he would see in the mirror. A lace from a child's shoe was his first thought. The stitches created a sort of order to the forehead lacerations, and to the gash beneath the left eye that ran down the cheek. The doctor seemed pleased by the particular shade of the scarlet welt he talked to, as he coaxed it to give up its thread.

Joseph drank William's medicine before the mirror, watching the muscles expand and contract beneath the scars and stubble. "Your face is special," William said, "like everyone's."

"Thank you," Joseph said, turning from the monster in the mirror and, for the first time, smiling at the man across from him. The night before his accident, Joseph had saved a self-portrait from the flames. The time had come to burn it.

22

*M*r. James Ramsey met Joseph in his Richmond Street parlour like an old king poised to worship at a sacred mound. This mound, however, was made of paper and untouchable. Even by Maud, "Mrs. Jimmy Number Two," who held dominion over the rest of the family home. Her portrait, a little larger than that of Mrs. Jimmy Number One, also hung a little higher on the parlour wall, yet neither was a rival to James Ramsey's mound of files, sketches, invoices, and letters. Nanny Polk, who was nearly as ancient as Mr. Jimmy, and whose last charge of the thirteen Ramsey children was Little Cora — "not sound of mind but God's creation just turned twenty" — learned long ago to avoid the white-haired Ulsterman when he was in his parlour. Even Kenneth Ramsey, first-born son of Mrs. Jimmy Number Two, sent abroad to study and retrieved to inherit the drumlin of the Ecclesiastics Department, would not approach his father's hill of paper. "That he meets you there — " William said. "Very lucky."

Shifting on his crutch, all Joseph could think was that, with his glittering eyes and full beard, the old man looked like the long-ago architect who'd watched Joseph follow Deary through his vast park towards the pond. The resemblance was unsettling. Then Joseph recognized three of his drawings on top of the pile that Mr. Jimmy prodded lightly with a slim cherry cane.

"So an artist's been lying up in that bed then," the old man said to the mound. "Do you fancy yourself an artist? Or do you just like to draw."

"I like to draw, sir. I've had no training."

The stick moved to an outlying area of exposed floorboards; Mr. Jimmy paused to inspect Joseph's face as he would a newly leaded mosaic. "Your injured hand is not your drawing hand."

"No, sir."

"And you've got a bust leg."

"Yes."

"So you'll take some time with us then, Joe Conlon. Seeing as you've no relations here to wonder."

"No, sir. No relations."

"And no job, I presume."

"No job."

"Good then. William will take you to the women who'll find you a wee room for a while. What part of Ireland are you from?"

Joseph could barely swallow. "I ..." he said, then stopped. "Darkley, sir."

The old man grinned. "Darkley of County Armagh?"

"Yes, sir."

"*Ay*, Joseph." Mr. Jimmy beamed. "I'm your neighbour — from Tyrone, near Dungannon, not far from Armagh city."

The black gates of the railway station swung open in Joseph's mind. He found it difficult to breathe.

"We're countrymen then. I suspected as much going through your pack." From his waistcoat pocket, Mr. Jimmy pulled a folded handkerchief. "And do forgive us that, Joe. A necessity of identification, the copper told us." The handkerchief opened to reveal a decaying, three-legged cross of rushes like those Joseph remembered from the underside of a thatched roof. Of Mam's four-legged diamond cross, Annie had whispered: "A point for each of us."

"My own mother wove this before my brothers and I left, fifty-one years ago. Five crosses for five brothers." Mr. Jimmy bowed his head, re-wrapped the object, and stared again at the mound. "We won't call you an artist till Kenneth has a go with you. But you've got a job if you like, Joe Conlon. In drawing." The old man smiled. "If you wish."

The next morning Joseph's drawings were returned to him with a note: "We assume you're Protestant." No reply was required. Joseph was beyond counting sins of omission.

❖ ❖ ❖

Joseph's curiosity inevitably led him to Nanny Polk, "Pokey" to the Ramsey children, and keeper of the family stories. "So it's William you want to know about." Nanny lit her pipe. "Smoke?" Sheer gladness. The crone handed Joseph the pipe and lit another. "William was houseboy to Rip Ramsey, the oldest of Mr. Jimmy's brothers — and the loudest and the proudest." Pokey cackled. "A regular California legend was Rip Ramsey, The Man who Discovered Gold. Our Mr. Ramsey had the church supply business. Not many churches, then, and fewer hands.

"Mrs. Henrietta Ramsey, my first mistress, died in the child bed with her sixth infant, Dermott, he of the Plaques and Banners Department. He also does brass chandeliers. Maud, the second Mrs. Jimmy, had seven. You've seen the last of them, Little Cora ..."

Joseph nodded.

"Now, not long after word came that Rip had died, came a knock at the door. There stood a Chinese boy. In a stage coach were candle sticks, a boa skin, Mexican pots, a silver spittoon, a squeezebox accordion with ivory inlay, Confederate Army whiskey — all sorts of bric-a-brac."

"And the boy was William?"

"Ay. Kenneth's age, I figured. Barely spoke a word of English and not a tribe for miles to claim him. He insisted on helping me with the cleaning, pushing that broom for days. He'd answer the door and even bow to the milkman, or fuss in the garden, snipping at the weeds to make you wonder.

"Mr. Ramsey made a room for William at the shop and he's lived there ever since. And been paid I might add, tending the kilns, preparing the lead cames.

"Little Cora was born soon after with an odd, screechy cry. I knew she wasn't right in the head, God love her. Maud Ramsey dotes on that bellowing girl, sits for hours while Cora leans on Rip Ramsey's squeezebox. Such a noise you're best to stay clear of. Your name again?"

"Joseph."

"Ay, then. Welcome to the Ramseys, Joseph."

❖ ❖ ❖

Stained-glass faces hung from lines across every window: men with white beards; chubby angels; praying saints. Surfaces held scrolls and lime dust, cut glass in half-assembled crosses, and vellum figures waxed on board. Heads bowed. Hands moved pencils, paints, blades, and cement. Stories took form in cusps, kites, and lancets bounded by lead. The ascension was a puzzle on a table: a disciple's arm, a white-petalled flower, a head and halo. A rose window, pure colour, beside Christ knocking — the same Christ who could not be pulled from a semi-ruined wall without collapsing it. Long ago, Joseph had stared at a stained-glass Christ while Deary recited the rosary. The knocking had been Joseph's own heartbeat.

"Jesus, this is awful," Kenneth Ramsey said. "Who did this?" He knocked the Good Samaritan's head out with his cane. "This face needs to be repainted."

According to Pokey, Kenneth had returned from design school with eyes gleaming like his father's, but fierce for having to return at all. Destined to carry the family business into the new century, Kenneth still dreamed of London in his suit from Savile Row. He happily would have expired in a thick London fog serving the great cause of Art.

"Kenneth is unquestionably brilliant," Maud Ramsey said the first time she met Joseph. "All my children are endowed with a fine intellect. Even Cora has gifts." Maud Ramsey limped to a chair. Her right foot stepped at a right angle to her body, and the ankle swelled and sagged beneath the dusty hem of her dress. "Kenneth will teach you what you need to learn."

In Kenneth's office, designs were drawn in pencil, then worked in watercolour on thick paper. Christs and Davids, Saint Johns, Saint Georges, Marys, and patrons lined the walls along with armorial bearings and words in various styles: "memory"; "sacred memory"; "all manner of sickness"; "family"; "even unto the end of the world". "Lo I am with you" lay crumpled in the bin.

"I should start you at the bottom," Kenneth said, "regardless of my father's notions. Do you know what a cementer does? Or a glazier?"

"No, sir."

"Where have you worked before?"

For a moment Joseph was on the steps of the Manning Arcade as the rain seeped into his bundle of newspapers. "I've worked in a flour mill."

"So you have no related experience."

"Only my drawing, sir."

"Yes, your drawing." The red blotches above Kenneth's starched white collar continued up into a receding, ginger hairline. His left temple pulsed. "I understand that you draw well, which is why I have decided *not* to start you as a cementer or a glazier. I must make it clear that this is *my* decision. What is your interest in windows?" he asked suddenly, as if suspecting that Joseph might have stolen some.

All that Joseph could think to say was that one had fallen on his head. "They're beautiful," is what he did say.

"Do you know," Kenneth said, "that it takes years to cut glass properly? You could apprentice as a glass cutter — a respectable position, second to painting. Design, of course, is the highest, but I'm not counting that. Have you ever seen anything so perfect that it made you weep? Weep — because you could never achieve that. Ever. Have you?"

"No."

"Good!" Kenneth said. "I shall start you in the painting department. Weep with inspiration, weep with awe, but never, *never* weep with defeat." He paused, staring up at some invisible ally. "You will begin each day at seven o'clock, waxing glass to the painters' easels. My sister Bette will teach you to mix paint properly. She will also show you how to trace backgrounds and teach you fundamentals of painting. Tracing will be your job for one year. Simon Fields, the head glass painter, will watch you. Then I will assess your work, after which, I will decide if you are to be a painter with this firm."

❖ ❖ ❖

At evening meals, the Ramseys sat around a long dining table. After serving, Nanny Polk took her place at the foot, where she could easily fill a pipe or save a child from choking. She watched everyone chew — in particular, the grandchildren, who occasionally accompanied their parents to the family home and, after eating too fast, ran in circles around the table before being shooed to the garden, where they dug battlefields for armies of carrots.

Maud Ramsey called William's boiled greens tonics. She and her husband consumed them after supper on the screened porch where Cora laughed as William brought her dandelion bouquets, saving leaves for tea that counteracted the effects of Mr. Jimmy's whiskey. Joseph took spirits whenever offered, and also received cups of the bitter potion, which he carefully disposed of after William had returned to the shop. Sometimes, while sipping his whiskey, Joseph winked at Cora, causing her to rock and laugh.

At the dinner table, subjects ranged from politics to petunias, tackled with equal intensity by any variety of visiting siblings; only Cora and Bette were present consistently. Bette, Maud Ramsey's oldest child, had achieved the distinction of being unmarried at forty, gaining her a steady, satisfying position in the glass-painting department.

Each evening, Joseph longed for dinner to be over; then his time was his own. He discovered a production of *The Count of Monte Cristo* at the Grand Opera House and spent a dime for standing room. At the Grand, little candles in sconces cast flickering haloes on the burgundy wallpaper; their glow remained soothing after the gaslights were dimmed. The Chateau d'If was a spectacle of painted drops, and Edmond Dantes, dining on rats and digging, elicited a feeling of calm in Joseph. He wished for his sketch book—that he could draw in fast gestures the way the man's body scrambled at first sight of the old priest. "There is no talk of God in here," Edmond Dantes said.

The theatre became Joseph's church and he attended regularly.

Back at the shop, Kenneth sighed as he scrutinized the background of another Good Samaritan. Unmistakable were Joseph's slight alterations; but the walls of the Chateau d'If passed inspection. At the two men's feet: flowers. "The thing must swirl with colour," Bette instructed.

When *Monte Cristo* folded, Joseph felt empty. The temple in which Joseph had worshipped for many nights—sometimes leaning on a crutch, sometimes sitting in a frayed velvet chair with his sketch book—had fallen. Joseph switched to *Twelfth Night* at Jacob's and Sparrow's, no conversion required.

As the plays came and went, so too did the subtle changes to a window background. A sea drawn calm might eventually turn stormy. A distant figure—the only kind Joseph was allowed to draw—might become as one tossed in time through a hurricane. Enoch Arden crept into the top right quadrant of the Garden of Gethsemane.

The voices of the audience, their commentary on the periphery of the action, lulled Joseph into a state of rest unattainable at the

Ramseys' table. He should have felt gratitude towards the people who had fed and housed him and given him work. He should have felt blessed in the house of a family where he was to stay "until you've got yourself back on both feet," Mr. Jimmy said, motioning to the crutch as though it was also a guest. But Joseph did not feel anything at all.

Only in the theatre could Joseph experience emotion. When Viola discovered her long-lost brother, Sebastian, Joseph's throat tightened. When Enoch softly called: "Annie ..." as he turned from her window, Joseph felt his heart beat faster. Listening to that name, in a chair in the fourteenth row, he let sadness come for a moment.

In an alehouse each night after the play as Joseph contemplated the amber of his beer glass, a flower-seller appeared offering rosemary and pansies; but when she saw Joseph's mangled brow and beard she hurried past. If only he could paint his face in lead oxide-based enamel, gum, and arabic powder, a single shade like that of a saint or a roadside sinner.

One night, after *Hamlet*, Joseph contemplated the ghost of his father — the letter in his sack, reheated and stuck back countless times in the orphans' home, newspaper boys' lodging, boarding house and by the river. Long ago, that honest ghost had written: "Dear Nora, The time is out of joint ..." and something about a sea of troubles.

Joseph wished that he could feel rage, even hatred, for his father, but he merely felt nothing, which was a greater curse.

Walking back to the Ramseys, slightly drunk, he fancied he saw a figure shaped by breath. "Have you forgot me?" he said. Or did she say it to him?

❖ ❖ ❖

Bette's hands were large and steady. She drew the boy's face in conté several times as it appeared in the sepia photograph, asleep on a high-backed chair. Bette liked the hard lines. Often Joseph simply watched as she worked. He learned to see the face as a dependable grid of mathematical relationships. The rules for this child and Jesus were the same. "Measure from nose-tip to mouth," Bette said, "multiply six times vertically and four times across, and there you have it. Notice how the relationship between the cheek, the ear and the skull base stays fixed."

What Joseph noticed, after confirming all the ways in which her face followed the rules, were the ways in which it didn't. Bette's face should not have been attractive, but it was. Narrow eyes, a broad grin, plump chin, and a hastily knotted mane of grey-brown hair created a charm that had nothing to do with geometry.

"People's faces are more than just fractions and sums," Joseph muttered, frustrated at struggling to draw the boy precisely, but creating Myrtle Wren's image instead.

"Of course, of course," Bette said. "You're an artist. Now draw this boy again in three-quarter profile." She winked. "And draw him smiling."

Quickly Joseph fell back on Bette's mathematics, crumpling Myrtle's face into the waste bin. As he continued sketching the boy in various poses, he asked: "Why did your mother leave supper on the table last night when I got in? She knew that I'd eaten." His words were aimed at the boy's mouth, which now extended past the centre of his eyes but not quite to the edges.

"Not my mother," Bette said. "Nanny. Didn't you notice that it was All Hallow's Eve?"

"I did. And so?"

"And so, each year on All Hallow's Eve our dear Nanny leaves a plate out for my father's first beloved. We don't call her that, of course; we don't say anything at all. Neither does Nanny. When we were children, Nanny taught us many of the old-country ways."

"What?" Joseph asked, leaving the white dot of light on the child's left iris.

"Once she saw our souls escape as butterflies while we slept."

Bette smiled. "They always fluttered back, she said, just before we awakened, so she knew that she could stay our nanny. And she taught us to spit. It's good luck."

Nanny's lore continued as the cartoon shifted into profile and a pensive gaze—the wind-man, and Jack of the Lantern who beat the devil at cards and was forced to roam the earth. Crows are best staying, not leaving, and some babies are fairy changelings. Beware a great mist where fairies are about.

"Does Pokey believe that fairies live here?"

"Of course."

On the page, the boy looked up; the boy gazed down. The expression on his face remained content, though slightly puzzled, as if a thought was not quite complete.

Bette stared at all angles of the boy's head. "Good work, Joe," she said softly.

"What is this window?"

"A dedication. Matthew 19."

"Are we drawing it?"

"I'm doing the lettering. You're tracing backgrounds."

"And the faces?"

"I'm drawing the boy. I imagine Kenneth will paint Christ, as usual. And Simon will take the rest."

The boy had drowned at Pointe au Baril when the wind-man capsized his rowboat. The inscription: "For of such is the Kingdom of Heaven." Three days later, Simon Fields, the head glass painter, set the last piece in place: the face of the man who had drowned trying to save the boy. "The boy's family insisted," Kenneth said, "even though the man was a stranger."

That night in an alley off Adelaide Street, Joseph finally experienced the rage he'd wished for—only it came as a torment, not relief. He sank onto the frozen ground, clutching at his face until it bled. Joseph collapsed on his side, the hard earth against his cheek. How could one man give his life for a stranger's child, while another turned away his own? Where, inside the cracked and ruined pieces of Joseph's memory, could he set his own father's face? He couldn't even visualize it; yet the face kept surfacing. Now it cut him like broken glass.

A few blocks south, he found a woman who took his money and didn't care how ravaged he was.

"Piss off," she told him after he'd come. "You're a fucking, bleeding mess. Don't come back."

On his way back up to Adelaide, he brushed the dirt from his clothes and straightened his collar.

Joseph burned his father's letter.

"*D*o not look at the moon sideways. Face it directly," Nanny often warned.

Tonight, from his seat in the nineteenth row, Joseph stared at a painted moon. The play was Tennyson's *The Cup*. Having consumed three tumblers of Rossin House whiskey unusually early in the evening, Joseph longed for coffee.

In the second act, Phoebe entered, a maiden faithful to both the goddess, Artemis, and Camma, the protagonist. From the moment the actress set foot on the stage, everything changed. In her pool of light, Phoebe called out to Artemis, and Joseph held his breath at the sound of her voice. From that moment, the play was lost on him. He had eyes only for Phoebe.

Joseph returned over and over to see Phoebe brought to life by a bit player, Miss Cyrena Ayre. Fair-haired and radiant in a gown of the palest, spectral blue, she moved from window to priestess and back again, almost dancing.

In the same company's *Othello*, Cyrena Ayre played Bianca a different way each night. Sometimes she sidled barefoot to Cassio; sometimes she cartwheeled, producing a flurry of murmurs in the house.

By the time *A Midsummer Night's Dream* opened, Joseph's knee had noticeably improved. "You're not limping as much," Bette said, surveying with some apprehension a portico that had appeared above the head of Saint George.

"I can move it over to Saint Paul if you like," Joseph said. When he shaved his beard, Bette broke the stunned silence with a giggle. "You have a face, my dear Joseph. And a nice one at that."

Joseph's face was not nice, though some scars had begun to fade.

In the *Dream*, moving to the notes of a hidden flute, Moth danced alone. Joseph watched the winged creature, enthralled, as she turned circles in a beam of light.

An hour later, at the backstage exit, Joseph waited in the falling snow. Moth stepped into the alley on the arm of a player struggling to open a tobacco tin. She laughed, stealing the roll-up cigarette from his cold-stiffened fingers.

"Deary Avery," Joseph said.

The couple stared. "Do you know this man?" the actor asked.

"You're Deary — Deary Avery."

"I'm afraid that you've mistaken me." She patted her companion's arm, loosening its hold. "I knew a Dora Avery. Or was it Doran? We did some shows together. You're not the first to confuse us."

He couldn't speak; she was so near.

"Did you like the performance?"

He nodded.

"Would you like an autograph for your book?" She gestured to his sketch book, which was open to a picture of Phoebe standing at the window of Artemis' temple. "Your name?" She held his book now, flipping through the many pages of Cyrena Ayre.

"Joseph Conlon," he said at last.

"I like this one." Hippolyta: silent, regal, and somehow still ethereal after her transformation from Moth. "Where did you know Miss Avery?"

"Here," Joseph said. "When we were children."

She reached into her bag for a pen. "Michael, go on without me."

"But, Cyrena—"

"This man knows Miss Avery, my old friend. I want to talk with him about her. A few minutes."

"Are you sure? I can wait."

"Dora Avery really was like a sister to me. I'll be along, after I've talked with Mr. Conlon."

"If you insist." He kissed her on the cheek and she grinned, blowing smoke in his face that he bit at.

"So, you knew her where?"

This time she was not smiling.

"In Sunnyside. Our Lady of Mercy Orphan Asylum."

She looked hard at him, closing his unsigned book. "And who were you at this 'orphan asylum'?"

"I don't know what you mean. I was me—Joseph Conlon."

"What did you do?"

"I—" He was at a loss for words. His cane dropped. "I did this." His upper body remembered the way to be upside-down and travel. His arms were strong and for a moment his knees floated before the handstand crashed.

"Let's walk to the lake," she said.

❖ ❖ ❖

"Did you ever notice," she said, "that birds disappear at night? You can't even see them in the trees." She bent, picking up pebbles. "I used to hate this place. But lakes are magic. How could a city on a lake be truly bad? There must be a spirit here to feed." Each toss rippled. "Or a dragon. What would happen if we dove for treasure?"

"We would die."

She traced the scars on his face with her fingers. "And how did you come to draw Cyrena Ayre so many times?"

Rhetorical, said those fingers, unbuttoning each boot. The stockings slid down easily. "I am going to alert the dragon to our presence.

Lend me your cane, gallant sir. I may need it to defend myself." He limped behind her, to the end of the pier where she sat, dangling one foot, then the other in December water, prodding the lake with the stick. "Here we are, you spirits of the deep! Reveal yourselves! Cast up your treasures so that we dreamers may wake and find our true inheritance!" She splashed him lightly. "Because it's too damn cold to dive!" He sat beside her, impervious to the icy drops.

"If my feet fall off, I'll be the footless maiden. Not a pretty picture; though it might sell tickets. I think it would annoy Agnes."

"Agnes?"

"Mrs. Tripp, our leading lady and company directress — who recognizes in me 'a gymnastic element that serves as an enhancer.' She's my mother, really."

He straightened.

"Just kidding. She might be someone's mother, though. Someone being raised as we speak by the gentle nuns. Thank goodness for the nuns." She crossed herself. "Or by the wolves of Chatham. One never knows. Least of all Mr. Tripp. He's the money. Did you notice him tonight?"

"Oberon?"

"God no, that's Randy."

"Theseus?"

"Bernard. Tripp was poor, ancient Egeus. If you want your own company you need an Egeus."

"You're a very good actress."

"He doubles as Mustardseed, that rotund fairy with the beard. The whole production is his gift to her. You can't tour this thing with a troupe of ten. We have fifteen — the mechanicals are five brothers from Hepworth who owe Tripp money. Tripp's not an actor. He buys islands in Georgian Bay. Who knows where he makes his cash, but Agnes gets it — and every role she wants. In the bright lights from here to Woodstock — no, all the way to Sarnia."

All her jesting did nothing to diminish Joseph's elation. He yearned to take her in his arms, to lay his head in her lap. Anything — just to feel her fully with him.

"And what about you, Joseph Conlon? What have you done with yourself since the days of bagging bones with one-eyed Bill."

"Tim." Saying the name brought its image carved in limestone, half-buried in snow.

For a moment, Joseph felt guilty to be so happy. Then the guilt passed. With Deary, he was overjoyed.

"I trace backgrounds for stained glass windows."

"You're like glass."

"I beg your pardon?"

"You collected it. In that old sack."

One black ribbon, one green. "Yes."

"We put it in our mouths to make it shine." She pointed to his book. "You're an artist. These are not backgrounds."

"I would like to draw your face," he said, now that he could see it in the half-light.

"Come to the theatre again. Now, my shoes." He passed her stockings first — their smooth nothingness before the leather. "You'll have to come to the potboiler: *The Midnight Express*, or, *She Could not Marry Three*. We always end with a melodrama. The worst show sells the most tickets."

"May I see you then?" Suddenly he measured possibility in curtain calls. Five more were left at best.

"Give a note to the box office when you come. On Friday." The second-to-last show. "I can see you then. Someday, you can make me a portrait for my parlour."

He walked her through the empty streets, trying to imagine such a parlour.

He made a statue of her in his mind: something still and holy, that he could kneel before and touch — not like the women he paid, though he found himself imagining her naked. Joseph concentrated on her communions and her beads. Then he remembered the asylum

Madonna, her blank eyes. Joseph had to look repeatedly at Deary's eyes, to make sure that they saw him. They did. Later, only the most important words stayed with him: "On Friday. I'll come to the show on Friday."

❖ ❖ ❖

Joseph didn't drink for the first two days after meeting Deary. In the mornings he arrived at the shop early, before Kenneth, stirring paints and fixing vellum on easels. In the winter sunlight, dust motes settled on palm trees, a saint's face, the folds of an angel's dress. Dust was indiscriminate. Lead oxide and lime made wings.

Joseph painted a storm of sparrows. "Too busy," Kenneth said. "Just trace."

Each night Joseph slept deeply, conserving energy like a starving animal. Once, Joseph dreamed of Deary's blue-veined feet. Then his mind's eye caught the hem of a skirt ascending Navan Fort. Joseph's panic upon waking gave way to the whiskey bottle he kept close at hand. As he drifted off again, Joseph saw his long-ago shipmate and card-sharp Gerry's gold-tooth grin and his metal bracelet where a woman's name had been melted over. Joseph consoled himself with thoughts of Friday. The whiskey almost took him there.

Kenneth's wife gave birth again. Mr. Jimmy awoke unable to move the left side of his face. A small stroke, said the doctor. By noon James and Kenneth were fighting. Joseph traced camels.

"Your work is getting better," Bette said. "What are you seeing tonight?"

"Just a melodrama."

❖ ❖ ❖

"Welcome, ladies and gentleman, to our production of *The Midnight Express*. Due to unforeseen circumstances," the boy called, "Mrs. Tripp is unavailable to play Bessie Brandon tonight. Instead we present Miss Cyrena Ayre in the leading role." The young announcer lingered during the applause that followed. "At least clapping will keep us warm," a man to Joseph's left said, grinning. "Someone turn up the heat!" Joseph unbuttoned his coat and removed his scarf. He was sweating.

As soon as he saw Cyrena Ayre, Joseph gave up on following the story; he simply watched and listened. She was funny, and she was sad — at one point, inconsolable. The audience loved her.

He wanted to be alone with her, to gaze at her up close, to touch her.

At the play's happy ending, the audience clapped and cheered for the heroine. The final bow was a kiss.

Joseph waited at the back door in the freezing rain while she dressed and the crowd spilled thinly over the icy streets. Then the back door opened and she was there. A tall man held her arm, and another man followed. They were laughing.

"Cyrena." The actors paused. "This was the night you said to meet you." Joseph realized his words were ridiculous. He had offered no congratulations on her performance. She would rush past him and his bones would crumble from the pounding of his heart.

"Joseph, come join us."

◆ ◆ ◆

In a Melinda Street tenement lived Skinny Michael's stout Cousin Albert and a pair of ferrets. The smell of opium partially masked the oily weasels' stench. Cousin Albert's pipe was a mercy.

"Did you like my dance tonight, Albert?"

"You were a sight, my darling. I wanted to eat you then and there."

While he enjoyed the red wine and opium, Joseph wanted the others to disappear.

"To Cyrena," Tall Michael said, raising his glass. "You carried it tonight."

"It's a terrible play," she answered.

Outside someone knocked on the glass and Skinny Michael gasped. "Oh God, it's Agnes."

Agnes Tripp entered stiffly. Cousin Albert quickly handed her a drink.

Agnes must have said something clever that Joseph missed, because people were laughing.

On the stage in Joseph's mind, Cyrena Ayre stood silently in her light. She began to undress: stockings first, until only a corset and thin slip remained. Tall Michael stepped forward in the fantasy, undoing the hooks with a practised hand and retreated. Shadows played on Cyrena's breasts and on her hips. Joseph gave in to excitement, though his breathing was slow, and he felt wonderfully at ease. Then the theatre faded from his mind, but not Cyrena. He watched her transform into a girl on a bough who saw only sky. Applause: wind through the hanging trees.

Startled, Joseph opened his eyes. Agnes was delivering a postmortem of the show. After addressing the male actors, finally, she directed her words to Cyrena Ayre. "My love," Agnes said in a voice that curled like fingers around a shiny apple. "I watched you tonight. Rarely have I been able to observe you closely, free of my own obligations to perform."

"What did you see?" Cyrena asked.

"I saw a girl." Agnes reached and lightly stroked that girl's hair. "My girl, and such a pretty one. I've made you well, Cyrena Ayre."

Joseph sensed Cyrena stiffen, though she remained poised, peering at Agnes' slightly blotchy face. "How was my work?"

"Your imitation of *my* work? Why, excellent, my love. For a moment I thought I was in two places at once. Remarkable. And just three autumns ago I plucked you from that Chatham peep show."

He couldn't stand Agnes' power.

Cyrena was good — not just a good actress, but wholly good. She was holy. Joseph had felt her grace the first moment she'd touched his

149

shoulder in the asylum yard. He longed for her even now, when she stood right in front of him. He wanted to fall to his knees or to stand upside down. He wanted anything but the scene they were in.

Cyrena knew how to make her own escape. "Thank you, Agnes," she said in a voice like honey. "I've saved this for you." She pulled a sachet from her skirt pocket. "*Artemisia vulgaris*. The herb of Artemis, protector of women. Like you, Agnes. Keep it with you for luck." Cyrena kissed the matron's lips.

Skinny Michael passed the pipe to Joseph, but he declined, unable to take the party any longer. While he craved the smoke, he craved an end to the scene more. He walked toward Cyrena, touching her shoulder, and she turned.

"Joseph," Deary Avery said, looking into his eyes with an expression he couldn't read.

"Let's go outside now," he said.

On the fire escape, they sat in silence. Joseph felt relief, as he had years ago, sitting quietly with Deary in the cellar and in the orphanage yard — the same feeling came from an even earlier time in his life, but he struggled to keep the older memories from rising. Eventually Deary stood and gazed down at the street as the players departed. She lit a cigarette.

"Did you think I would stay on in that stupid house? Do you think I'll stay in this one?"

He brushed a tear from her cheek.

"Agnes Tripp, my 'mother,'" she said, chuckling. "Ever caring, ever nurturing — cultivating one cliché after another. 'Culture,' she says, when she means mediocrity. It sells so beautifully. And so do I."

For a moment he saw Deary smashing her near-perfect snowman.

Instinctively, Joseph reached into his coat for a flask of rum he'd brought to the theatre. She took the bottle and swallowed.

"Everything for a price," Deary said. "Fill the house." She wiped her eyes on her sleeve and laughed. "Morpheus! envelop my faculties fast." She tipped her head and swallowed again; with a vague sense of horror, Joseph reached and took the bottle back, tucking it away. Deary pulled a book from under her shawl. The pages had been well worn. "I have a waking dream."

"What do you mean?"

"This play." She held the text out to him. "Agnes Tripp doesn't know about it. How could she? The old stories, the old jokes, hapless beauties, victims, 'Artemis' — ha! This play is different. When I've toured enough and saved enough money I will mount a production of *A Doll's House*. I'll be Nora."

Joseph started at the sound of that name.

"What did you do to your face?" Deary asked softly. "You were hurt." When he didn't answer, she continued. "The other night, I was being playful ... I try not to think of the orphan asylum days."

"Why?"

Deary turned her head in the direction of a passing train. Then she brightened a little. "You told me Irish stories."

"And you told me of your people."

She stared in silence.

"Don't you remember your marvels, Deary?" he said. "All the magic — the pond, the birds? All your plays?"

She lit another cigarette and inhaled, leaning back against the icy railing. "I remember you were looking for someone called Annie. Did you find her?" The orange tip glowed as she drew more smoke into her lungs. She held out the cigarette to Joseph, who set it down and took her hand instead. Her skin was cold, her hair too far fallen across her face for him not to move it gently to one side. Her lips were too wet, too vivid not to kiss, wanting it never to end.

The long kiss felt like mercy.

"Tomorrow," Joseph whispered. "After the matinee."

Deary smiled faintly, touching the lines on his face, allowing them a language of their own.

Flesh

1894–1899

23

"Tripp's company closed early," a box office clerk announced when Joseph arrived to see Deary in the final show. People grumbled in the line-up.

"Where did they go?" Joseph asked, forgetting to breathe.

"Not a clue," the clerk said shrugging. "Somewhere in the States, I think."

"Will they be back this spring?"

"No."

"In the summer or fall?"

"Not any time soon, not after cancelling. We're giving refunds, or you can apply your ticket to something else. Would you like comedy, tragedy, animal tricks, a concert? German or Italian? Maybe magic? We have a mind-reader in March who levitates people, saws ladies in half, throws burning darts."

"Cyrena Ayre," Joseph said. "I was supposed to meet her today. Did she leave a note?"

"Excuse me," a woman from the line said with a sigh. "We're all cold and some of us need to hurry."

"No note. Please move along."

That night, like other details lost between the tavern and his bed, the sketchbook, too, disappeared — Cyrena's final exit.

❖ ❖ ❖

"We are so very busy," Bette said. "You can do this."

Joseph began his first full-scale enlargement for a window on a February morning, half-way through his apprenticeship. In the painting of the Lost Sheep, the animal did not exactly seem relieved to be found; if anything, it appeared uncomfortable. The sheep's body sagged in the crook of the saviour's elbow. Another sheep grazed indifferently beside two sandaled feet. Another looked up at Christ's halo — quite a distraction, thought Joseph. After a night of hard drinking, Joseph's stomach churned. Bette knew not to pass the biscuit tray just yet.

"The dove isn't meant to be diving — it's soaring," James Ramsey said. The old man's criticism was not of the enlargement, but of Kenneth's watercolour original. James Ramsey didn't often voice admonishments directly to his son, and Kenneth was livid.

"This is design, Father. Design," he said, raging. "Everything in the picture is balanced — except for the bird that's deliberately inverted to command attention. It got yours. Clearly the positioning works. And I don't appreciate being challenged on what I do in my own shop!"

"Your own shop, is it?" James Ramsey said, reddening.

"Yes, whether I like it or not."

"Has the patron seen these paintings?"

"The patron!" Kenneth scowled, looking up to the ceiling as though the plaster might commiserate. "Of course the patron has seen the paintings."

"And did he get to have his say?"

Kenneth Ramsey stared hard at his father. "Yes, he got to have his say," he replied, quietly at first, then building: "He *said* he liked the paintings!"

"As long as you're listening to the people who pay you, Kenneth. I built this business on tradition and straightforward depictions.

People expect clarity. You have to be willing to tolerate criticism and adapt when necessary, even if it means compromising your new design principles for good, old-fashioned pictures that people understand."

"Have I tolerated enough now? I have four meetings today, and six paintings to complete this week. I would like to get back to my good, old-fashioned job!"

From then on, Mr. Jimmy kept his criticisms to grumbles that could not be overheard.

One rainy day, the old man sat beside Joseph, who had graduated to painting figures on glass. Mr. Jimmy stank of wet wool; water dripped from his coat into rivulets around the two men's boots.

"You've done well for yourself here, Joe. And you've done well for us. I wonder if you'll be staying on a while, now that Bette tells me your apprenticeship has ended early. I trust you like the work here?"

"Yes."

"You'll stay, then?"

Joseph nodded. "Thank you."

James Ramsey smiled, but his brow was furrowed. "Do you ever miss the old country, Joe? I do." One side of his face stared beseechingly, while the other remained frozen by his unresponsive muscle.

"No." Joseph's face was fully motionless beneath the scars.

Three more years passed under the Ramseys' roof.

❖ ❖ ❖

William planned to marry, his intended a Temperance Street laundress from his native region in China. "Our flesh will be our homeland," William announced at dinner one evening, causing Mrs. Jimmy to choke on a dry salt cracker and Nanny to strike Maud Ramsey between the shoulder blades until the offending wafer was airborne.

"Mr. Joseph," William said when they were alone. "I would be grateful for your help to make my marriage proposal. May I send you on a special errand?"

Joseph nodded.

"Thank you, Mr. Joseph. Tomorrow I will show you what to do."

The next morning William lowered a large, freshly slaughtered chicken into a sack. The bird was worth three days' wages. With it William handed Joseph a scroll, intricate brush strokes that were both a proposal and an apology. "I must apologize to the family because I have no birth paper. Without it, they cannot know who I am. I send you to represent me, for you are lucky."

After receiving William's instructions, Joseph found himself walking east on Richmond Street to Bay Street, turning right, then left past veterinarians and Methodists to a sign that said "hand wash" in small red letters. Beside it, on a tenement wall, the painted "k" in "Chinks" was still visible, although the brick had been scrubbed almost completely of "Go home."

"You take the work of a Christian mother with six mouths to feed!" called a woman in the direction of a Chinese girl scrubbing the wall.

Inside the shop a man ironed behind a long counter. His face pearled with steam and sweat, as his arm drove a heavy pan across a white shirt sleeve. In the back, more workers steamily pressed. An old woman squatted by a washing trough, scrubbing. A younger man stoked the stove fire, heating half a dozen ironing pans. Wordlessly, Joseph handed the sack over to the man at the front who set down his iron, assessing the blood on the fabric before he realized the bag's contents. Then Joseph handed over the scroll. For a long time the launderer stared at it, carefully reading the symbols. Then he stared at the bird, and finally at Joseph.

"You no family."

"No," Joseph said.

"Come back one week."

After several expensive ales at the Rossin House and a spell of listening to a street-corner cellist, Joseph returned to the shop.

"This ... is good," William said, bowing to his slightly wobbly ambassador.

The next week William sent Joseph with sugar in red paper. The paint on "Go home Chinks!" had been freshly reapplied, in size and boldness rivalling the sign on the Pei family establishment. When Joseph entered, the voice of the man at the front cut sharp syllables into the air, halting the other men's irons. A young woman stepped forward out of the rising clouds of vapour. A very old woman pushed ahead of her, to stand eye-to-eye with Joseph. The old woman stared at Joseph for a long time before he remembered to remove the second scroll from his pocket. William's second message, tied in seed beads, was a question: "If not now, when?" William's real name, Tan Zhou, was signed at the bottom of the curled page.

William had painted the sugar paper in cadmium gouache and dried it on his shelf beside a candle and a small stone figure that seemed to sit in calm reflection. The next day William had folded the paper and bowed to the stone man. When he'd placed the package into Joseph's hands William had bowed again.

"Go!" the old woman said. "Take," the crone added, pulling a warm and slightly damp letter from the folds of her smock.

"The man is Jing's uncle, not her father," William said later, reading the markings on the creased page. "He says he is afraid to give her into the hands of an unlucky man. Jing's father and mother are dead. Chen Pei, Jing's uncle, says he must honour their spirits by waiting for a sign to see if Tan Zhou is the right husband." He folded the paper and placed it beside the burning candle. "Chen Pei has answered my question."

◊ ◊ ◊

The next gift was a canister of tobacco in a hand-sewn bag with red brush strokes. William translated the third scroll for Joseph. "My message tells Chen Pei: 'A respectful son, I will wait for this sign.' I am not his son, but I must prove to the family that I am worthy. I will wait as long as I must for the sign. For Jing to be my wife."

"And what if the sign doesn't come?"

For a moment a look of sadness washed over William's face, but then he smiled at Joseph. "I must be content."

When Joseph placed the gift into the hands of Jing's uncle, Chen Pei studied William's short message and handed the bag to the old woman. The young woman looked up from her ironing only briefly. A bolt of silk, two brass candlesticks, and a year's worth of black tea did not convince the Pei family that they should accept William's offer. Joseph wished that he could draw the scene so William would see futility. But the glazier remained hopeful, despite knowing that signs, like luck, could not be bought — and even if they could, he was temporarily out of funds. He did not speak of Jing, but he smiled as he went about his work and continued to offer cups of boiled greens that he had dried from the summer garden. "Tonic for the spirit," Mr. Jimmy said, drinking the teas in moderation with his whiskey. "I want to see William in his own house."

And so, against what Kenneth called better judgement, the company purchased a small residential building behind a carriage factory. "For storage purposes," Mr. Jimmy said, beaming with half his face and handing William the key. "You will pay rent, of course. With a raise to ensure it."

William's smile faded. "To live in such a house alone ..."

From his waistcoat Mr. Jimmy pulled a second key, tied with a red ribbon. "Don't think an old man doesn't see."

Joseph delivered the key in a paper box that bore Jing's name. The old woman handed the box back. "No use," Chen Pei said.

Reluctantly, Joseph returned both box and key to his coat pocket, where they joined a packet of cards, a small pencil, and a ticket for a matinée that had never played.

When Joseph left the laundry, a woman's voice stopped him. "Wait! My uncle and grandmother cannot speak for me," Jing said in fluent English. "Only my brother. My brother is the one you must address. And he does not want to let me go."

She led Joseph to a lane behind the business block. Here amongst the sagging privies and the refuse bins, discarded chair legs, rusted springs and animal bones, a small boy sat playing with a set of brightly painted toy figures.

"You see," Jing said. "Cho."

When the child, Cho, looked up, he rose to his full height — at Jing's waist.

"You! Scar Man!" he bellowed, gnashing his teeth and curling his lips in a face that he had practised many nights since tasting William's gift of sugar. "I fight you!" The boy growled again: "I'm a tiger! I beat you, Scar Man!"

Then, for the first time in his life, Joseph bowed. He stared at the ground a long time before leaving. The bow was an act of submission, he realized — to the boy, yes, but also to memory. For a moment, Joseph wandered Union Station, crying out his sister's name.

The moment became unbearable.

When William heard of Jing's brother, William and Joseph walked to the lot behind the Temperance Street laundry. William told the boy that he could live with his sister in their house if he wished. William gave the boy a key, newly cut and tied with wire. The very sign that Cho Pei needed, and William had waited for.

❖ ❖ ❖

On the morning of William and Jing's wedding, Cho Pei walked behind his sister, his toy figures wrapped carefully in a cigar box.

In William's new house on Nelson Street a candle burned beside fresh flowers and the stone man. A chef, seconded from the Stanley Street Ale and Beanery, who had trained as a priest in Old China, presided in the parlour of the unnaturally quiet Ramsey and Pei families. Joseph studied the intricate loops of Jing's hair, and the draping of her scarlet robe. The Pei family chanted their blessings; the boy fidgeted. Then William and Jing served clear tea that, when consumed by a couple's parents, made the couple husband and wife. William carried cups to Chen Pei, Cho, and Jing's Grandmother Pei; Jing carried cups to James and Maud Ramsey. When all the cups had been filled, the company sat for long minutes of wordlessness and the sound of swallowing. When Cho found his way to the marriage bed —one with real springs and a Simpson's mattress, he jumped up and down for ten minutes.

After the ceremony, Cho's voice chased Joseph as he was leaving for the tavern. "Where you go, Scar Man? Wait! You live with us, Scar Man?"

"No," Joseph said, softly. Then he handed the boy a small scroll tied with a bootlace. Joseph had sketched a tiger from the best photograph he could find in the Mechanics Institute library. Unfurled, the tiger's face made a magical impression upon Cho Pei, like that of Joseph's scars. When the boy asked for more gifts, Joseph produced playing cards and a lesson in maw, the only game for two players that he recalled.

In the frozen lot behind the Nelson Street house, the boy's nose ran as he played. Keeping his cards hidden was a feat of small motor muscles for Cho, who marshalled his stubby fingers like beleaguered soldiers, attempting to conceal the high trump. Cho sucked back several streams of mucus before using a hand to wipe one, inadvertently flashing his cards. Cho's royal cards pleased him more for their faces than for their ability to win tricks. The ace of hearts caused mild spasms of delight that the boy couldn't hide since Joseph had told him it was lucky. In maw, the ace of diamonds was foe. Occasionally that card elicited Cho's growl during the deal. Cho unfurled Joseph's drawing of the tiger each time the bad-luck card presented itself.

"When I grow up," Cho said, "I'm going to have scars like you." He wrinkled his nose and bared his gums. New teeth had begun to advance, and the old ones waved at angles, somehow whimsical in defeat. Cho paused to wriggle one, dropping a jack of clubs in the snow and a five he could have won with earlier but had kept, because he liked fives.

◆ ◆ ◆

After Joseph made his goodbyes, he stopped for a drink, then went on to a Pembroke Street house where the ladies of the evening welcomed him back.

"Someone new," he said.

Always someone new. Susan, Nancy, May.

"How do you want it?"

He took May from behind and watched her ringlets shake each time he thrust, until he didn't see — only clutched at her hips and pulsed, glorious — the surge inside him finally crashing.

Four shebeen whiskeys dulled the memories of May's paint-smeared lips, her gasps. Yet the Irish voices haunted him, and he recalled Mam's story of the children turned to swans.

Deary was flying farther and farther beyond him.

24

*B*ette often cried in the mornings, when she and Joseph were alone, at opposite ends of the shop. By the time Kenneth arrived, her face was dry and the blotches on her cheekbones had faded. The distant sound of Bette's weeping unsettled Joseph to a degree that was beyond his understanding.

"Bette."

"Joseph."

Joseph could not avoid looking up. "You're crying." Her usually self-assured, peaceful countenance was ravaged. Joseph's heart pounded. Sweat seeped through his shirt. "What's wrong?"

"Joseph." She stepped so near that he had no choice but to remain fixed on her fervent, wet stare. Bette's face had turned to scarlet blotches. Her hair fell loose and damp across her brow. "I keep moving back, straining to see. The page gets farther and farther away. I can't work my eyes," Bette said quite simply now, taking a deep breath, and another. "I cannot tell Kenneth. I cannot tell my father. I cannot draw, Joseph."

The next day, Joseph walked with Bette to the storefront of Daniel Abrahms, Jeweller and Purveyor of Optometry Supplies. The proprietor stared into Bette's eyes for several seconds before putting on his magnifiers. "Very good, very healthy eyes. Very blue, I might add."

The jeweller held glass circles in his hands, lifted them to Bette's eyes, and shone light. She smiled as they forgot the chart altogether through long stretches of conversation. The two went together into a back room, the sound of their chatter and laughter making its way to Joseph. Apparently, time for the jeweller and his client passed differently than the time that Joseph measured on his watch, thirsty for his afternoon whiskey. Joseph heard Abrahms tell Bette: "No need for a doctor. I'll make your spectacles right now."

"Now" turned out to be another hour that passed as the jeweller and his client shared stories of their lives. Abrahms was a widower with grown children and a penchant for reading.

"Me, too," Bette said.

"And now you'll be able to read again, my dear. You'll paint masterpieces." He added: "I hope that you didn't mind me calling you 'dear' just now."

"Not at all, Mr. Abrahms."

"Call me Danny, please, if you'd like to."

"Danny. I thank you from my heart. I'd like you to call me Bette."

Joseph found himself agitated by his response to a scene that should have made him happy. He wanted to believe that he cared deeply for Bette, and indeed, for all his friends at the Ramseys', but he felt jealous of the joy that she and Abrahms had suddenly discovered. The realization disturbed him. Joseph couldn't imagine thanking someone from his heart, as Bette had done. Joseph couldn't feel his heart — not now, at Bette's happy discovery, or at William's wedding — only at the wrong times. Sitting alone with Deary on a balcony and kissing her, he thought he'd felt his heart then, but with Deary, his heart only tortured him; yet he so wanted to be tortured again. His wanting both angered and wearied him. Joseph's jealousy — unacceptable and repulsive — exhausted him. For once, he readily fell asleep. He dreamed of the sea.

When Bette tapped his shoulder and he awoke, her bespectacled face was resplendent.

Thus, at forty-three, Bette came to marry.

The widower Daniel Abrahms and his bride signed papers at the Front Street City Hall, because neither church nor synagogue would bless their union.

"They're too old to care about a difference in religion," Nanny Polk said. "What does it matter, as long as she keeps her faith?"

Bette did keep her faith.

With her spectacles in place, each week, Bette returned steadfastly to the drawing board that was her church. Danny Abrahms met her every evening in the long shadows, held her hand and walked her home.

Joseph kept his faith, too, in his misery at Deary's absence.

❖ ❖ ❖

One Sunday Joseph found himself on King Street where the land cut away to water. Continuing west, he turned down across the tracks to the shore, studying the ground where glass washed up — Joseph's treasures once. He pocketed a stone with a hole through it.

Up the hill, near a strip of newly sawn houses, was the orphan asylum. He felt compelled to revisit the place; but a form caught his eye and he headed back towards the cold, March water. A dark grey mound undulated, half-submerged. As Joseph drew closer, he recognized the wet weave of a man's woollen overcoat, then the corpse itself. It was almost faceless now, the skin swollen and white. The man's tongue was frayed, the lips gone, and a jaw of yellow teeth stuck open on stiffened hinges.

For several seconds, Joseph smelled the sick, sweet smell of rot. He let repulsion and fear travel through him. He let Mam's sightless eyes appear in his mind. He didn't fight the sight of Tim's blue face either, after he was pulled from the grain bin.

Joseph pulled a scrap of paper and a pencil from his coat pocket, crouched, and drew. He sketched a ruined hand, partially open, as though something had slipped from it unnoticed. The sketching kept

Joseph steady, and the intensity of the discovery dissolved into the calm that drawing brought him. As Joseph followed the edges of the disintegrating coat, trousered legs, and laced shoes, four geese glided past. One raised its head and flapped its wide wings, and reminded Joseph of the children turned to swans. They talked and sang with human voices. They wandered across the waters for nine hundred years, and though the children's father was god of the sea, he could not undo the spell placed on them.

"God of the sea," Joseph whispered, "what happened?" His hand began to shake and he stopped drawing. "God, where are you?"

Joseph's tears surprised him.

He placed the holed stone in the decaying palm. "For luck." He saw Gerry, the card player, oilcloth and ashes. He saw him waving good-bye in Union Station.

Children's shrieking roused him, and he realized that they were shrieking as much at him as they were at the dead body. A nun, following them at a distance: Sister Anne. All at once, he was glad to see her. Joseph folded the sketch into his pocket and rose. Sister Anne made the sign of the cross.

"I should notify the police," Joseph said, gesturing to the corpse.

"Was he murdered?" one of the boys asked excitedly.

"Did you know him?" another asked.

"You were drawing him," the first boy said. He stared at Joseph's face. Then he stared at the dead man and poked the cadaver with a stick.

"I was."

"Sean!" Sister Anne said. "Come back here. Immediately!"

"Why were you drawing him?" the boy asked, standing his ground, staring at Joseph, then at the corpse, and back at Joseph again.

"I don't know," Joseph asked. "Why did you poke him?"

"Why not?" the boy said, grinning. Then he prodded the body lightly with the toe of his boot, eying the bloated, half-eaten face. "He can't feel any more."

"No, he can't."

"And he can't hurt me. Old maggots can't hurt me."

"No."

Joseph walked the boy quietly back to Sister Anne. "God sees what you do, Sean," she said, but she was looking at Joseph.

"Sister Anne," Joseph said. "I'm Joseph Conlon. I used to live at the home." Abruptly, Joseph no longer felt glad in the nun's presence, but nervous. He'd failed the church. He didn't want to think of the sins on his head.

But Sister Anne's expression softened. "Joseph Conlon, of course! You'll come back up with us then. Sister Mary Margaret is about to serve supper. May God preserve and have mercy on this poor man's soul. I'll notify a constable when we're safely home."

Her recognition did little to assuage his discomfort; she may have been happy to see him, but Joseph recalled her rolling her eyes at Deary's stories and her letters. Now, Joseph couldn't look at her. Instead, he imagined the sound of Deary's boots and sought out the spot where he'd retrieved her fallen ribbon.

Sean led Joseph through the door of the orphans' home as though no time had passed since Joseph's last back-alley wander. The dining room seemed smaller to him now, though the number of children was greater. So many orphans. "Set another place," Sister Anne said. "Sister Mary Margaret, Joseph Conlon is back for a visit."

The kitchen door opened and Sister Mary Margaret appeared, wiping large hands on her apron and fixing her eyes upon Joseph. "God bless us!" the old nun said, stepping forward, embracing Joseph, and enveloping him in her familiar blend of chopped shallots, turnip, and sweat. Joseph felt relieved.

"Are you hungry?"

"Very," he answered truthfully. He ate heartily, as the children stared at him and Sister Mary Margaret patted his hand.

"Is Sister Martha here?"

"Sister Martha is with God in His Kingdom these many years,"

Sister Anne said. "She didn't live long past your time here. Now she's well at peace; God rest her soul." Both women made the sign of the cross. Sister Mary Margaret chewed, nodded, earnestly suppressed a belch, and crossed herself again.

After the meal, the Sisters invited Joseph into the parlour to hear about his life since leaving St. Nicholas Home. "Of course we heard the news about Tim." More crosses. Joseph adapted his story for their hearing: the taverns and the street girls disappeared, Joseph's scars were made by Protestant glass (a single point of emphasized accuracy), the stained-glass window-painting business was entirely ecumenical, and he prayed every day.

"Have another biscuit, Joe," Sister Anne said. The crunching sufficed to counter the nun's scepticism. Sister Anne patted Joseph's shoulder, excusing herself to supervise evening chores, prayers, and recreation time.

Then Joseph raised the subject that was foremost on his mind. "Sister Mary Margaret, many years ago I tried to learn from you about Deary Avery."

As the old nun nodded, a wash of joy and sadness coloured her face. "Ah, Deary," she said. "A marvellous strange girl."

"Yes, she was. And is. I met her again."

"You know her then? What's become of her?"

"She's working in theatricals, Sister Mary Margaret."

The nun sighed, shaking her head and smiling faintly again, though the look of trouble never left her eyes. "Marvellous strange."

"You know where she came from. You once told me to ask Sister Martha, but you know Deary's story."

The old nun stared at her empty hands. "Sister Martha said a story like that could hurt the child. Me, I talked only to the priest, because I felt he should know what we knew. And now, here you are, come along after all these years."

Joseph leaned closer. "Could you tell me? If I should see her again I might then know how to be her friend. How to stay her friend."

Sister Mary Margaret closed her eyes. "Forgive me, Heavenly Father, if my telling's a sin, and forgive me please, dear Sister Martha." Then she began. "The man who brung Deary to us were such a God-fearing man. He and his wife were neighbours to the girl and her father, you see. He knew that Deary needed a firm hand and God's house — so missing was the church from her life."

"But Sister Martha said her family was religious."

"The grandfather were a minister, and high up in his day, though long dead by the time Deary come into this world. She were scarce six years old when her mother died in the childbed with her infant son. The father's heart was broken. An educated man, he were." She sighed and stared off into nothing for a moment. "Well-schooled, university taught, though not one for church lessons. He worked as a teacher, but he roamed — moved from job to job. The man could never settle. After the wife died, his restless streak took a turn into darkness.

"He gave up teaching, claimed nothing good ever come of it. He burned his books, let his home go to shambles. But always he schooled Deary, even once he took heavy to the drink. 'Tis a rare strange thing to find a small child so skilled in her letters. In mathematics, too.

"He took on all manner of work so long as he stayed dry enough to do it. Print shop work. Tram driver. Delivery cart driver. The man who brung Deary to us said they'd even spent time with a circus — the father driving the wagons, putting up the shows, but nothing ever lasted, except his taste for whiskey 'til it killed him. The devil in the bottle drove him into a ditch.

"They found her in the snow, nestled snug asleep beside him with her arm around his broken back. God rest the poor man's soul. They brought her here. I wish she could have stayed." Then Sister Mary Margaret smiled up at Joseph through her glassy old eyes. "I wish you all could have."

Joseph managed a faint smile in return. Soon it faded, and he found himself staring at the floor. Eventually, Sister Mary Margaret said: "Come with me."

She led him to the kitchen. In the drawer, exactly where he knew it would be, was her great knife. She took a heavy block of cheese and cut a thick wedge. Then she handed him bread from the cupboard. "Take these, now, for your journey back to wherever you come from."

"Thank you, Sister Mary Margaret." Joseph let himself be squeezed in the warm, turnipy folds of Sister Mary Margaret's habit.

"I never did know the girl's Christian name," the nun said. "The man who brung her didn't know either. 'I'm called Deary,' were all she said. 'Deary.'"

The name in his ear caused him to linger a moment more; then they stepped apart.

"Goodbye, Joseph Conlon. Perhaps you'll come back," Sister Mary Margaret said, though her smile meant they both knew he wouldn't.

As Joseph walked through the yard, he caught sight of young Sean kicking a ball into the wall. "Sister Anne notified the coppers. That body'll be gone now," Sean said, frowning.

"I would think so."

"I wanted to see it again."

"Here." Joseph pulled the sketch from his coat and handed the drawing to Sean.

"Thanks." Sean stared at the picture for a moment or two. "Can I rip it up?"

"Please."

The boy tore the drawing to pieces and threw them in the air. "You're all right."

Joseph stood for a moment more and smiled. "Glad I met you, Sean. Be a good lad."

"How many years?" the boy called, as Joseph walked towards the gate. "How many years did you have to stay here before you went free?"

"Hmmm. Enough. But not too many."

At the gate, Sister Anne stood peacefully watching, though balls sailed past, and ropes were skipped, twirled, and jumped, marbles rolled, and children ran in circles. "Did you have a good visit with Sister Mary Margaret?"

"I did."

"And did she answer all your questions?"

"All the questions I asked. I have one more question."

The nun nodded.

"Did you ever have a girl called Myrtle here? Myrtle Wren."

Sister Anne smiled. "We did indeed. She was a fine seamstress. And a beautiful singer. *Dominus tecum*, Joseph."

"*Et cum spirito tuo*, Sister Anne."

25

*B*ette's husband copied poetry on pages torn from his ledger. She spread them open when only Joseph was near. "I spent so many years not being looked at twice, if at all, because I wasn't pretty, or because I wasn't young, or because I wasn't willing to live as a wife and give up my work. And now, I've married a Jewish man. Before, they didn't see me; now they see me, but avoid me. I hear the whispering."

"What do you do?"

Bette smiled. "What I've always done. I keep walking. And think how lucky I am that Daniel's walking beside me."

"What does he say when you speak of this?"

"He usually says something to make me laugh. Or he recites a poem — I don't know how he remembers so many. Yet his children still won't visit us. And my parents act strangely. Kenneth and Pamela, too — the whole lot — though of course, they try not to. What does it mean?"

"Your parents care about you, Bette. They care about you — both." As Joseph said those true words, the image of Old Ciara surfaced, haunting him after so many years. He saw her arms around his sister, Colleen. He heard the awkward "both" — spoken as a gesture to civility under the gaze of a ship's captain. She'd promised to stay by him. But Joseph was not chosen. The "both" had been a lie.

He remembered Colleen waving and wished that he'd been

chosen, too — for the first time, he acknowledged that he wished it — even though, had the old woman followed through, her acceptance of him would have been a lie. He would have taken her lie over a station where no one came for him.

"You chose each other, Bette — you and Danny. That's important."

Who, and what, had Joseph chosen after all these years?

Visiting Cho on the back steps of William and Jing's house, Joseph forgot about Bette's blessings and her troubles. He forgot about the mysteries of choosing.

With the boy, Joseph thought only of stories. They poured from him as though a great stone had been lifted. Each time he visited, he felt like he was rolling on the grass in Keady, staring up at a vast, indivisible sky.

❖ ❖ ❖

A last snowfall came after the branches had begun their swell of blossoms.

"A celestial calling card," Bette said.

"In April — bloody hell," Kenneth Ramsey said, leaning on his cane to lever off each rubber overshoe by the open back door.

All at once, Joseph saw Myrtle Wren emerge from a red-brick building. Despite the cold, Myrtle wore a tidy, cream-coloured spring dress fastened down the front by a strip of gold buttons. She did not wear a coat, but a brilliant orange scarf wrapped loosely around her neck. The sign on the building behind her said J. Crutchfield: Milliner and Haberdasher.

Joseph retreated to his drafting table. The corner of his eye twitched involuntarily as he attempted to settle into establishing a standard rendering of a doorframe and lantern. He had wanted to call out to Myrtle, but couldn't bring himself to do it. Now, instead of feeling relieved, he was agitated.

On the first warm day, the blossoms arrived, and with them,

Myrtle, who stopped Joseph in the alley beside the Ramseys' shop. His heart jumped as he stood speechless, and relieved. "I'm so glad to see you," Myrtle said again, because he had missed his cue to respond in kind. "You were my good shepherd."

"Don't say that," he quickly replied, blushing with guilt that he realized must have looked like modesty.

"Truly, you were. The things you used to say to me, what you said to the inspector — you changed my life." Myrtle told him about the skills that the nuns had taught her, and how they'd sent her out for higher learning when the time was right. Already she'd worked at several places, and just last week had taken a job at Crutchfield's making hats. Soon she'd have enough money to buy her own machine and, one day, her own dress shop. She lived with two old spinster sisters in a row house on Widmer Street, and walked each Sunday over to Bond Street to worship. On Wednesday evenings she had choir practice, and on Thursdays she served in a soup kitchen. Every day she thanked Mother Mary, Lord Jesus, and Joseph Conlon, who saved her life years ago, when she was hauled into the light.

She did not ask about the lines on his face or the lime dust on his hands, only: "How are you?"

"Well enough. But I must get to work." He didn't mean to be rude; he simply couldn't think of anything else to tell her. His mind was perplexingly blank. She looked into his eyes for several seconds before telling him about the strawberry social at St. Michael's and asking if he'd like to join her.

"Yes," Joseph said. The buttons on her neck looked like pearls. Her auburn hair was swept up loosely, perfectly smooth. He found it difficult to stop staring at her.

Joseph wasn't sure if he agreed out of an old habit, obligation, or something else. He settled on something else. Yes, he wanted to see her again.

✧ ✧ ✧

On Saturday he paid a boy two pennies to shine his shoes. The boy's face was smudged with blacking.

Myrtle wore a raw sienna dress with ivory piping and shiny acorn buttons. Joseph tried not to stare at the buttons.

"We won't actually be eating strawberries," Myrtle explained, taking his arm and leading him to the parish hall where people sat at small tables with white cloths and pastries and meats, and Christ was risen and the banner on the wall proclaimed "Good News."

Myrtle's hand, with the bitten nails Joseph had drawn so often, was warm. Under the hooks and laces of Myrtle's boots were feet he had made studies of. Joseph remembered how Myrtle's back could have been a boy's, the smooth narrowness of it in the dusty light of the dressmaker's abandoned storage room. He remembered her double-jointed elbows, and the bruises on her skin, all now snugly sewn into the smooth dress.

"I'm not a church-goer," Joseph said.

Something in her expression changed. Perhaps she was crest-fallen. "It doesn't matter," she said, swallowing beneath the smoothly fastened collar. "I'm glad you're here."

An elderly man at their table told them about Christ sightings in Milwaukee during Pentecost. The old woman across from him said such sightings weren't necessary. "The point of faith is to *not* need to see!"

Joseph sketched Myrtle in his mind, or tried to. Her childhood face he could almost draw from memory, but now her face was a woman's. He needed to re-learn her. He wanted to, he realized, and the realization compelled him; studying Myrtle had nothing to do with drawing.

"You be a nice friend to our Myrtle now," the old woman said. "She sings like an angel."

"I saw an angel once," the man said. "I think it was Michael. He had no wings but he glowed. Right there on the battlefield at Gettysburg. A shell grazed me, but the angel looked in my eyes."

Myrtle blushed, twisting the napkin in her lap. Joseph almost reached to settle her hands. He wanted to touch her.

"Those are nasty gashes," the man said. "Have you been to war?"

Now Myrtle was perfectly still.

❖ ❖ ❖

The sun had begun its drop among the smoke stacks to the west. Horses whinnied in coach houses, and the knife sharpener walked by, pushing a cart and ringing his bell. Myrtle's hair came free of the pins. She pulled her shawl tight as a gust of wind sent snowflakes, defiant and insubstantial, whirling flimsy insults at the new buds and grasses.

"Let me take your hand."

Joseph's words blew loose with the snow, and he couldn't take them back. Swirls of language broke out in his mind, spinning, though he said nothing. He felt at once afraid and captivated. He held her cold hand and hers gripped back. They walked past the paperboys. The tavern windows glowed, but Joseph looked past the taverns now, to the row house on Widmer Street where Myrtle's oval upper window looked like it might wink.

She said goodnight. He said: "I could walk you next week to your choir."

❖ ❖ ❖

Later that evening, Cho waited for Joseph in the alley with the cards lined up by number and face, reluctant to shuffle the ordered deck; but Joseph knew that a story could mix Cho's cards up again. When he told of an old saint chasing snakes, the words came from a place within Joseph that he'd almost forgotten. He relished the place. With the child, Joseph's voice was free.

"Scar Man," Cho whispered. "I want to hear the story of the boy who killed the hound."

"Ah, Cuchulainn," Joseph said, shuffling the deck. "Again? I've told you that story. Are you sure that you want to hear it?"

"Coo-hoo-lan," Cho repeated, as though the name had magic powers.

"Cuchulainn didn't always have his name. He had to earn it. But before that, he had to be born — which was ..." Joseph paused, choosing his words carefully, " ... tricky, since his father, Lugh, was god of the sun."

Cho's eyes twinkled in the lamplight.

Joseph paused slightly in order to recall more details. "Lugh fancied a maid called Dechtire, but she was engaged to marry someone else. At her wedding, Dechtire drank wine, and the sun god, clever as he was, turned himself into a fly and she swallowed him."

"Ah ha!" Cho exclaimed. "But what happened to the sun?"

"Oh the sun still shone — Lugh made sure of that, and he also made sure that Dechtire could escape the wedding."

"Why?"

"To bear his child."

"I thought he was a fly.

"He was."

"Did my sister swallow a fly? Is that how she got hers?"

"Most certainly not."

Uncle Seamus' old story of Cuchulainn's birth did not provide the answer. "You're to be an uncle, then?" Joseph asked, avoiding Cho's question.

Cho drew the ace of hearts and grumbled: "Jing's going to have a baby." He discarded the ace with a thump.

"Well, that's different. When a husband and a wife come together ..."

"Their bedsprings make a lot of noise."

"Exactly." Relieved, Joseph settled back into the tale. He told Cho that Lugh turned Dechtire and fifty other maidens into birds, and that eventually the magic flock flew to King Conchobar at Navan Fort. "The king and his knights heard a baby crying."

"I don't like babies much."

"But this baby was no ordinary baby."

"He was Coo-hoo-lan."

"But he didn't have that name yet. He had to earn that name, remember?"

"By doing something brave." Cho wriggled forward, forgetting about the maw game. "Tell me, Scar Man."

Joseph did his best to give Cho an adventure, even if the details were sketchy. Joseph remembered that Cuchulainn's original name was Setanta, that he was King Conchobar's nephew and stronger than all the other boys at Navan Fort. "So strong that he fought the blacksmith's dog, the fiercest hound in Ireland — and *won*."

Cho growled and flailed about on the ground, jabbing at the air and clawing at the earth, until Joseph said: "King Conchobar was impressed." Cho sat up, looking pleased with himself. "But Culann, the blacksmith, had lost the best guard dog in Ireland, and he wasn't happy. Setanta promised Culann to be his watchdog until another fierce beast was found. And so, Cuchulainn got his name which means 'Culann's hound.'"

"How old was he?"

"How old are you?"

"Seven."

"The very age of Cuchulainn when he earned his name."

"Cho!" William called from the window. "Let Mr. Joseph go home now. Time for you to go to bed."

"How do you know those stories, Scar Man?" Cho asked quietly, as he gathered up the cards.

"I..." Joseph cleared his throat. "An uncle back in Ireland told them."

"Was he a good uncle?"

"I never met him."

"Then how did you hear the stories?"

"He told them to someone who told them to me."

Cho waited.

"To Mam. My mother."

"I don't remember my mother." Cho stood silently for a moment. "Have you been to Navan Fort?"

"I have."

"Is it magic?"

"Some people say so." Joseph looked down at his boots.

"Cho!" both Jing and William called.

"I think the Monkey King went to Navan Fort once," Cho whispered, mostly to himself, then shouted: "I'm coming!" As they walked to the house, Cho asked quietly: "King Conchobar, the uncle. Did he ever have to change baby Setanta's dirty nappies?"

"I'm sure he did." Joseph tried not to smile.

Cho sighed and hung his head. "Good night, Scar Man."

"Good night Cho, Brave and Mighty."

As Joseph walked home, he thought about Cuchulainn and his love, Emer. And of Myrtle. And of Deary.

❖ ❖ ❖

On Wednesday nights, Joseph accompanied Myrtle to her choir practice, waited for her in a nearby tavern, and walked her home.

"Perhaps you'll hear us sing sometime," she said.

"I'd like to."

On Thursday evenings, while Myrtle worked her shift in the soup kitchen on Sheppard Street, Joseph waited in a tavern of plants and pipe smoke, and a waitress with a rouged face. He wanted badly to unhook the waitress's blouse, but she only sold spirits, so he drank a single shot of whiskey. By the time the Sheppard Street soup was gone, the sun was a copper disc. Myrtle's buttons might have been copper too. "They paint it on," she said. The buttons cost half a week's wages. "Soon will come the summer hats."

He kept thinking of the waitress's blouse and what her breasts were like beneath it. The thoughts distracted him from imagining Myrtle naked, which he wanted to do, but didn't feel he ought to, as she chatted so ardently about her work. He heard very little.

Suddenly Myrtle smiled, and he forgot both his troubles and his craving for more whiskey.

She was allowed to entertain guests in the parlour of the spinsters' house. The tea was hot and black, and Myrtle drank the first cup quickly, but not as fast as Joseph. The two old women sat sentinel in the dining room, plainly visible through an archway. On the mantel an iron lion stood poised to pounce. Beside it, candies had hardened and stuck together in a dish.

When he said goodnight, he did not go to a prostitute.

The next Wednesday evening, Joseph waited out choir practice in a different location, a tavern of red carpets and Queen Victoria, ornately framed. "She keeps the rabble out," the owner announced, pointing across the street to the Catholic Church. "The last thing I want is a shebeen. No RCs, thank you very much. The Fenians can go elsewhere."

"They can go to hell," a patron said, swigging on his beer. "Bloody taigs."

Inured to their words and to his own inability to call himself an "RC," much less a turned Catholic who didn't pray — not even for salvation from himself — Joseph sat down to his pint where the voices were lost in other conversations. When the clock struck eight, the moon shone like a moth's white wing and he took comfort in it. When Myrtle stepped from the church, they walked east instead of west along Shuter Street. "I want to show you something," she said.

Before they'd walked half a block, a red setter bounded out from between two houses, panting eagerly, and licking Myrtle's outstretched hand.

"The dogs still like you, then?"

"I haven't a clue why. I don't know the first thing about them — apart from that we get along." She bent to stroke the red fellow's ears and rubbed noses with him. Then the dog stood his two front paws on her waist and licked her cheek. His nose sniffed each brass button on her jacket. "All right, enough," she said, giggling. "I take it back. Go on now!" Myrtle brushed herself off. "Sometimes I imagine having a little dog. Do you?"

"No. Being Irish, I'd have a great, walloping hound."

She laughed, and the sound of her voice made him smile.

They came to a block of red-brick row houses with picket fences and small gardens. They stopped before one with a lamp in the window.

"I used to live in that house. A long time ago, before you knew me." For a moment, they were quiet.

"Did you ever come here when you lived on Leader Lane?"

"No. Beatrice wouldn't let me. I wasn't allowed to even talk about this place. As far as I know she's never been back here." Myrtle sighed. "I helped my mother with her sewing here when I was very little. She worked for the old dressmaker who had the shop Beatrice and I moved into after our parents died. The dressmaker was long gone long by then.

"My father worked down at Gooderham's distillery, but he'd been laid off because of the pain in his back and hips. I don't know what my parents did for money then. Once, I remember my father walked to meet me at school on Trinity Street. He smelled of pipe smoke and factory oil when he came home from work. After my mother poured his bath he smelled like soap. 'Little girl,' he called me. And he'd point to the hollow of his cheek and I'd kiss it. My mother smelled of rosewater and tea biscuits.

"The water must have been what got them, Beatrice said. The typhoid. You live your life and then one day it's upside down. Fever's like that. You don't see it coming. And even if you do, it comes anyway.

"Beatrice kept me shut in my room after Father came home sick. When Mother took ill tending him, Beatrice ordered me not to leave our bedroom. I used to beg to see my parents, but Bea only opened the door to pass me bread and butter, jars of cider or small beer. Never water.

"My sister fought with God. I'd hear her swearing through the walls, through the window when she went out to the yard. I heard my parents, too, in their delirium. For three weeks I stayed in our room." Myrtle led Joseph to the back of the house. "There." She pointed up to a window where moonlight gleamed on the glass. "I never saw my parents again. One night Beatrice opened my door when I was half asleep and let me out. I awoke in another life."

"Where's Beatrice now?" Joseph clung to the moment, holding up his end of the conversation, however tenuously. Being with Myrtle kept him awake to the world, if only he could let himself stay. He recalled her look of betrayal years ago when he'd gone to Beatrice. Now that look of jealousy, of hurt and confusion, was gone, or well hidden.

"On the Esplanade."

His question had been rhetorical, though he couldn't admit that he'd crossed paths with Beatrice several times; she'd neither recognized nor noticed him. He knew she'd stayed in the same business.

Myrtle smiled and looked at him squarely. "People never were much good at getting Beatrice to change her mind." Her smile faded. "She's living harder, now."

"Did she see you in the years when you were in Sunnyside?"

"She always finds me." Myrtle paused. "Do you remember the old man at the strawberry social? The one who said he'd seen an angel?"

"Yes."

"I've prayed for an angel to help me." Myrtle blushed, looking down as they continued walking. "I've tried to see one, to feel the presence of an angel. I close my eyes and concentrate. The face I always see is Beatrice's. The nuns say people can't be such things, but I don't know what to believe. Do you believe in angels, Joseph?"

"Annie!" a woman called into the street from her front door. "Annie, come inside. It's late." A little girl emerged from her front garden and stared at Joseph. He couldn't help but gaze back at her moonlit face. He might never have moved had the mother not shooed the girl inside. Up the steps she went like a spectre in her white dress, her hands full of flowers.

"Joseph?"

Angels. "I believe in the painted ones. As for others, I'm not sure." They were walking again. "When I was a boy back in Ireland, I think I might have imagined one once — an angel, or a fairy — or something else. Maybe nothing at all."

The words surprised him. Annie's name repeated itself, again and again, in his mind.

"I can't imagine you as a small boy. Tell me about you, then."

Surprise became alarm. "There's not much to tell." Liar. Annie.

"No parents? No brothers or sisters?"

Annie sank to the bottom of the sea. Colleen was taken, too. And Mam ... "Not by the time I came here."

Joseph hated that he had lied; more precisely, he hated that his relief in lying didn't last. He couldn't begin to tell his childhood. He'd never told anyone — except for Deary, and even then, he hadn't told her all.

Joseph admired Myrtle — for telling him about her past, for many reasons. She was strong in a way that he couldn't see himself being, any more than he could see the details of his life, which he kept hidden in his own murky depths.

Finally, they arrived at the spinsters' home. Behind the open window of the house next door, an old Labrador let out a single bark.

Before a memory could interrupt, Joseph kissed Myrtle.

26

"*How* many years have you been living here, Joseph?" Nanny asked with a wink. "And why don't you bring your girl to Mr. Ramsey's birthday supper?"

"Would he want me to?"

"Ay," Nanny said, slightly ruffled by the question. "He told me to ask you."

That day, alone with Joseph, James Ramsey burned his rush cross. "You're not to bury them, not here, away from country," he confided. "Only for you and me to see, Joe." When it was ash the old man shuffled towards the dahlia bulbs that Nanny pulled up each fall and reburied in spring, a squirrel of industry, smoking her pipe to keep the *sidhe* in their place. Ashes of Ireland fell from James Ramsey's palms. "My last birthday," he said, eyes wet and slightly red, "and such a fuss." Then he smiled. "I do like a fuss."

That evening Joseph stood at the back of the Catholic church. When Myrtle stepped forward for her solo, Joseph fancied that the eyes of the saints on the south wall opened wider.

Later, he met Myrtle at the door. "This Saturday is a birthday party for James Ramsey, my employer. We'll have a large group gathered. I'd be glad if you'd come with me."

The words hung in the air and Joseph felt the blood rising to his face. Finally Myrtle said: "All right." She smiled, but looked uncertain. "They're fine people, the Ramseys. But what if I say the wrong thing?"

❖ ❖ ❖

Under Nanny Polk's direction, three eating areas were established: the long dining room table for James and Maud Ramsey, adult Ramsey children, spouses, and guests; two kitchen tables on the covered back porch for grown grandchildren; blankets on the lawn for small and medium-sized children, including Cho Pei. Today, Cho carried the Monkey King, King Conchobar, Tripitaka the monk, Lord Buddha and Cuchulainn. The boy immediately enacted dramas with his figures; occasionally, when Quan Yin or a dangerous beast was needed, Lord Buddha allowed himself to be transformed. Kenneth and Pamela Ramsey's small boy and girl watched Cho intently. Every so often, little Olivia seized a toy with her chubby hand and tried to thrust it into her mouth. Despite the boys' interventions, she successfully bit Cuchulainn's head and licked the equanimous Lord Buddha.

In the dining room, Joseph introduced Myrtle, who complimented Maud Ramsey on her beautiful home and cameo brooch, and complimented Nanny Polk on the chicken. She wished James Ramsey a happy birthday, to which the florid-faced old man responded: "Eh? What did she say?" from the other end of the table. When asked, she described her work at Crutchfield's: "I make hats and sew patterns. I've always liked fine suits and dresses — to help people feel happy about the way they look. Of course, we're not meant to care about appearance. Clothes aren't deeply important — not like kindness or one's soul — but when clothes can bring joy I'm content."

Dermott Ramsey smiled at Myrtle. "I understand," he said. "A church is similar. Inside, a church doesn't need to be well dressed, but how lovely to adorn it. I sew banners."

"Oh, I've seen the extraordinary work you do — and your family's windows. I've seen Joseph's drawings, his art, and been amazed. I could never be such an artist."

Joseph didn't know what made him blush more, the embarrassment of being singled out at a table of his teachers, whose work was more than equal to his, or the strange, unfamiliar delight in Myrtle's compliment. The awkward silence that followed gave him time to think; he got nowhere.

"Tell us about your family, Myrtle," Bette said, eyes a-twinkle.

"My parents died when I was young," Myrtle said, carefully dabbing her lips with her napkin. "My sister Beatrice raised me, and ..." Her voice trailed off in the wake of words crashing loudly at the other end of the table.

"The man had a vision for the city!" Mr. Jimmy railed. "I don't agree with his evangelism or his temperance, but people are entitled to their religious views. He was charitable. He made progressive changes."

"Like what?" Kenneth said. "Rousing the whole damn street railway crew to strike? Supporting the notion of unions? Siding with Irish nationalists like William O'Brien?"

"He didn't overtly side with O'Brien."

"He certainly did! He let the man stir the pot and the riots followed."

James Ramsey fixed a pale and once-immobilizing blue eye on his heated son. "I'm talking about *Canadian* nationalism. We need to invest in our own systems, businesses and people — and our people need to work and eat. They have a right to do so safely. Am I a protectionist? When it comes to protecting decent working people's rights, yes I am. Produce in Canada, buy and sell in Canada, take care of people in Canada. I'm not talking about England, Kenneth. Or America. I'm talking about Toronto — right here."

"Well of course I'm all for decency in the work place," Kenneth said, "but I believe that people should have the right to decide how they live and shape this outpost of a place. Howland imposed his own morality and used public funds to do it. He made bad choices, wasted money. Straightening a river — for God's sake!"

"*Kenneth*," Maud said. "We're at table."

"As for vision —"

"As for vision he cleaned up the streets," the old man said.

"Ha! But not the government. Unprecedented fraud — thievery in the city's waterworks. How did he clean the city, Father?"

"Howland took a tough stance on crime. Inspector Archibald, for example."

"Inspector Archibald?" Myrtle was visibly surprised and embarrassed by her interjection. For a moment the whole table was silent.

"Inspector David Archibald," Mr. Jimmy said, gaining volume steadily, "clamped down on saloons. He targeted the gamblers who wasted their family's money and the alcoholics who drank it. I'm an Anglican, Kenneth, but I see eye to eye with the Presbyterians, the Methodists, and the like: the fine people we work for in this 'outpost,' as you call it. I am *not* a proselytizing evangelist, but I am happy that Howland targeted disease when he went after the lowest elements in this city. His aim was not to punish, but to reform. To catch and rehabilitate thieves and to stop prostitutes. Look at his aid organizations and prison reform." James Ramsey stopped, out of breath and perspiring.

Kenneth sighed. "Nobody's ever going to stop gambling, alcoholism and prostitution," he said quietly, spearing his last radish. He cast a weary glance at Joseph, who read it as a tacit indictment — or at the very least, a gesture to living proof.

"Well, it's a shame Howland died," Bette said, conclusively. "There you have it, Myrtle. A typical Ramsey supper of political arguments."

"Hear, hear!" several older Ramseys said, raising their glasses.

Bette turned back to Myrtle. "You were speaking of your sister. You said she raised you. However did she manage?"

"Well ..." For a moment, Myrtle looked nervously at Joseph, who could provide nothing more than a concerned smile. "She worked."

"What kind of work?"

"Oh, piece work. A little of this, a little of—"

"Daaaa ..." Cora moaned, shaking her head, smiling. "Heee daaaa tisss ..."

"I beg your pardon?" Myrtle asked, as flustered by Cora's sudden participation as she had been by Bette's question.

"Heee daaaa tis wi taot ..." Cora repeated, drooling. Once again, Cora opened her mouth into a wide, wet grin: "seeennnn ..." She spat. "... Leh t-heeem fffuuuh st caaaa st ..."

Nanny Polk swooped in, wiping Cora's face and neck. Maud patted Cora's hand. "Yes, Cora dear. Very good. 'He that is without sin *among you*, let him first cast a stone at her.'" Maud turned to the company. "We have been reading the Book of John."

Dermott Ramsey raised his glass. "To Cora!" he said. "She says the darnedest things."

"To Cora!" the others shouted, and the table erupted into a peal of laughter and the sound of ringing crystal. Cora laughed too. She clapped her hands, rocking vigorously and nodding. Mrs. Jimmy added proudly: "I told you my Cora has gifts."

As the subject of Beatrice was forgotten, Myrtle relaxed and allowed her glass to be filled for a third time.

"And where were your parents from, Myrtle?" Bette asked.

"England. My mother was from London. My father's people were from Yorkshire, but they came down to London for work when he was a boy. So London, mostly."

"London!" Maud exclaimed. "Our Pamela is from London. What a small world."

"London is not small," Kenneth said, sawing his meat.

Danny Abrahms said, smiling: "'O town of townes, patron and not compare, London, thou art the flower of Cities all'."

"Dan," Mrs. Jimmy said, "they call you the people of the book and I see why."

"Thank you, Maud."

Bette broke into giggles that she half-suppressed, making for a slightly convulsive, brief episode as Danny grinned and whispered: "She meant it as a compliment, Bette."

"Pamela is a model parent," Maud said. "Look at how she keeps that baby sleeping." They peered at the infant who clearly had no interest in being awake. "And she manages to volunteer as well."

"Oh! What kind of volunteer work do you do?" Myrtle asked, visibly relieved to no longer be fielding questions about her past. She looked dangerously at ease. Joseph felt enough worry for both of them.

"She makes charity baskets."

"That's wonderful," Myrtle said, caught slightly off guard by a hiccup.

"Do you volunteer?"

"Yes I do," she said, hiccupping again.

"For your church?"

"Yes."

"And which is that?" Maud asked, buoyed by the success of the new topic.

Now Joseph knew why he was nervous.

"St. Michael's Cathedral. Bond Street."

"I see," Maud said gravely.

Fortunately, Nanny Polk entered the room and announced: "The cake is ready in the yard." Joseph breathed a sigh of relief. As Myrtle rose, wavering slightly on Joseph's arm, she seemed blissfully oblivious to the notion that being Catholic might be considered as unfortunate as being raised in an asylum or a house of prostitution.

James Ramsey shuffled beside his wife to a massive slab of candle-festooned layer cake. "Well, well," he said, chuckling. "This is just marvellous. A marvellous party. Thank you, Maud." He kissed Maud's flushed cheek. "You and Nanny worked hard to produce all this finery. Thank you, Nanny. Thank you, everyone, for coming to see an old man grow even older. Now, forgive this Irishman a moment of sentimentality. You make me proud. May God keep you all in the palm of His hand." The assembly applauded and cheered.

Moments later, Dermott invited Myrtle inside to look at fabrics. When they'd gone, Bette said: "She's lovely, Joseph."

"Yes," he answered, agreeing fully. She *was* lovely to behold, but more than that, her presence filled him with something new and frightening. Hope.

Before Bette and Danny could say more, Cho arrived, tugging on Joseph's arm. "Scar Man," Cho implored, crestfallen, pointing at Nanny. "She took my men. She took Coo-hoo-lan."

Joseph's nerves settled as he sipped tea and told Cho: "Don't worry. Nanny can't hurt Cuchulainn. You'll get him back, Cho. Cuchulainn can be counted on to return. Did I ever tell you the story of the time he went away from Ireland?"

"Tell me, Scar Man." Joseph and Cho sat down on a bench amidst the irises.

"Well," Joseph said. "He loved Emer, you see."

"Who's E-vair?"

"Emer was ..." Joseph paused for a moment in thought. "She was beautiful," he said, stealing a glance at Myrtle. "Emer promised to marry Cuchulainn if he would take her away from her family — a rough lot. But first he had to complete a quest that carried him to the most dangerous places."

"Where?"

"To the island of a cunning warrior-woman, Scáthach, who taught him all her craft." Cho nodded soberly and gazed across the yard at Nanny Polk. "To the Plain of Ill-luck, where men's feet became stuck — but not Cuchulainn's. To the Perilous Glen, where he survived the wild beasts. To a bridge that tricked people by springing up straight when they stepped on it. Each time Cuchulainn tried to cross the bridge he failed. Then he grew angry. Do you know what happened when Cuchulainn became angry?"

"What?"

"He got his hero light. When Cuchulainn fought, he shone. He jumped to the middle of the bridge and slid down the far end as the other rose up. He made his way across — and back to Ireland."

"Did he marry Emer?"

When Myrtle saw him looking, he averted his eyes, smiling.

"Ay, so he did. Cuchulainn married Emer."

"Well, well," came an old man's voice. "I haven't heard about that fellow in a while." Mr. Jimmy limped to the bench and settled himself beside them. "Joseph's turning you Irish, I think, boy — filling your head with Cuchulainn. Next you'll be talking about the Brown Bull of Cooley! My goodness it's a warm evening. And look at what a delightful young lady, Miss Myrtle, gave me for my birthday." He reached into his shirt pocket and pulled a white handkerchief embroidered with the letter 'J.' "Nanny!" he called. "Here's the boy you were looking for." Across the lawn Nanny held up Cho's toys.

"My men!" Cho ran towards the old woman, no longer a formidable adversary. "Goodbye, Scar Man!"

Old Mr. Jimmy chuckled. "What story were you telling him?"

"The story of Cuchulainn and Emer."

"Was she his wife, or did he marry Fand? It's been so long ..."

"Emer was his wife. Fand, I think, was *sidhe*."

"Ah yes. A fairy." James Ramsey dabbed at his brow and the back of his neck with the handkerchief. "But didn't Cuchulainn also love Fand?"

"I think he did, yes."

"And what happened?"

"I don't remember much, except that Fand went into the water. Cuchulainn and Emer went to Navan Fort and drank the drink of forgetting."

"Navan Fort!" Jimmy Ramsey smiled. "I went there as a child, at Easter, with my brothers. We rolled eggs down the hill. I wasn't any bigger than Cho. Good little lad, that Cho."

"He is."

"And you, Joe. I must say that I've enjoyed your being with us. I don't just mean tonight." James Ramsey paused. "My company did you an injury once, Joe," he added, more seriously. "I hope that we've made amends and that you'll stay with us as long as you like. You've got a promising life ahead of you, Joe. A fine life."

Joseph thanked James Ramsey and left him sitting by the purple iris flowers. "Fand," Joseph said under his breath, blinking the image of Deary away.

When Myrtle found him, he was truly glad for her return.

27

That night, in a surprisingly empty Widmer Street house, two candles glowed in Myrtle's window. One, a tall white taper beside a metal Saint Anthony, was for finding what was lost; the other, a red votive, burned for the Lady whose porcelain face was turned to the street.

Joseph took Myrtle's wrist and pulled her close. Her kiss was fluttery, and he lingered in her mouth as long as he could before she backed away, twirling slowly, smiling softly in the candlelight. Myrtle leaned against the wall and he followed. Then she led him to her bed where his scars faded, and he forgot the details of his life beyond her touch. Joseph welcomed Myrtle with every fibre of his being. On the blouse she'd sewn, the buttons finally opened. Nothing mattered but to get to her.

And he did.

Joseph buried his face in Myrtle's neck, as she gripped his back, pressing into him fully, rhythmically as he entered her, and everything became her taste, her touch, her smell, her blood.

After, in her arms he fell asleep, not to escape, but to remain.

When Joseph returned the next night, Myrtle opened the door and led him back upstairs. They sank onto her bed in all the fragrant, warm, deliciously wet undoing.

"Come here," she whispered, taking his hand and guiding it beneath the silken folds of her skirt. "I'll show you what I'd like."

❖ ❖ ❖

James Ramsey's last real estate purchase was a house in the workers' lanes off Wellesley Street, to be leased inexpensively to Joseph and Myrtle, his bride. To Maud Ramsey's great relief, the Anglican Church had been quick to accommodate the couple one Saturday late in August. No questions were asked about the urgency surrounding the wedding; Myrtle wore a store-bought dress that Bette and Danny Abrahms gave her. "The only white wedding dress I'll ever buy," Bette said, having married in taupe and teal at City Hall. "I think I'm safe in saying this is the last time I'll be a bridesmaid." William stood up as Joseph's best man, and various Ramseys happily looked on.

In the Don River valley, Joseph walked home past boys swimming and willow trees bending, and people drifting by in boats. Late evenings, the birds' chatter lulled him into remembering his tarpaulin days. High grasses and goldenrod rustled in the moonlight. Joseph wanted to share the twilight walks with Myrtle, to hold her hand and feel her hardening belly beside the river; yet part of him clung to solitude. While he wanted to believe in the new life she offered, part of him was terrified to let go of the old one, despite its miseries.

At home, he did his best to take her in — as much of her as he could. Joseph took refuge in their sex, abandoning himself to their pleasure, the exquisite scent remaining on his skin. Yet by day, during their routine interactions, he found himself growing distant from Myrtle. Often subtle, the distance bewildered him. He felt edgy, impatient, constrained.

Sometimes, on his way home, Joseph stepped into the water upstream of "Ireland," relieved to feel un-witnessed. But the relief never lasted. He would arrive at his door to find that his wife had kept his supper warm, knitted baby gowns and embroidered blankets folded on the couch where she rested. Joseph poured a measure of gin and sipped as the moon climbed.

❖ ❖ ❖

In late September, a month after Joseph married Myrtle, she no longer felt tingling in her breasts. A day after the tingling stopped, she
awoke in waves of pain until something asleep in blood slipped away
from her. On the floor beside their bloodied bed, Myrtle bowed her
head onto Joseph's chest as he held her.

Eventually she wrapped something tiny and grey in a baby blanket with embroidered edges. Joseph dug a hole in the small yard as
Myrtle whispered: "Whither shall I go from thy spirit? Or whither
shall I flee from thy face? If I ascend into heaven …" She broke into
sobs. "Do you think we're being punished, Joseph?"

Joseph kissed the top of her head. He breathed the sweet smell of
her hair as she trembled.

"If I ascend into heaven, thou art there; if I descend …" Myrtle
paused, staring at the blanket: "… If I descend into hell, thou art
present. If I take my wings early in the morning, and dwell in the
uttermost parts of the sea, even there also shall thy hand lead me: and
thy right hand shall hold me." Myrtle touched the blanket. "… Darkness shall not be dark to thee …"

"And night shall be light as the day," Joseph said.

❖ ❖ ❖

When James Ramsey collapsed on the floor beside his mound of
paper, he died facing east.

In St. James Cemetery, in a black crepe dress, Cora frowned as
her brother Andrew pushed her wheelchair along the wet path. Maud
Ramsey held onto Kenneth. Nanny Polk's procession was solitary,
smokeless, and unusually silent. Danny and Bette linked arms and
walked between two sets of Ramseys, heads bowed, to a stone that
bore the first Mrs. Jimmy's name and dates in pale grey granite. There,
William stood beside Cho and Jing, who gripped her infant daughter

in a bunting that Myrtle had sewn. Myrtle stood beside Joseph, expressionless.

Weeks later, when Maud Ramsey determined that a second family stone would be erected, a little higher than the first, Joseph and William accompanied her to the mason works. There, Joseph found Myrtle's gift: an angel, made affordable due to a slightly discernible crack through her jaw. Joseph set her by their front door where Myrtle acknowledged the statue with a faint smile.

❖ ❖ ❖

James Ramsey left the house in the lane to Joseph and Myrtle. While they were shocked — and very grateful — Joseph felt bound more than ever. His walks grew longer.

One evening, Joseph saw a woman by the river in a white gown, her face in profile, her thin cheek and her hair slipping from combs at the back of her neck. Deary. He blinked. The woman turned and walked back up to the street. She was not Deary. He was not prepared for the sadness that followed.

Overwhelmed, he sat at the river's edge in reverie for a part of his past he dared to miss. He missed Deary. He missed longing for Deary. In a moment that could only change his new life irrevocably, he decided that he still longed for her. That way, some of the missing went away. The unrest he experienced was familiar and welcome. And he hated it.

He felt responsible for Myrtle's despair.

Myrtle had left her job at Crutchfield's when they married and had purchased her own sewing machine, though Joseph seldom saw her use it after the miscarriage. Myrtle was without her church, her choir, the soup kitchen, and the nuns who ran it. She put away her statues and rosary beads. As inclined as Joseph was to evening wanders, Myrtle was inclined to sleep, so deeply that Joseph couldn't find her. He knew that he didn't try hard enough. Not only did he feel responsible for her pain, he feared it. And it repelled him; yet he wanted the reassurance of her embrace.

In the months following their secret loss, Joseph felt his own solitude most acutely in Myrtle's arms. He felt Myrtle's absence and missed feeling cherished. He missed the sense of hope she'd given him. Joseph blamed himself for her listless state, but blaming didn't help. Joseph searched Myrtle's face for someone familiar; he could not see a child in her. Even when she became pregnant again, though briefly lifted from malaise, Myrtle remained childless in spirit. The blood that followed confirmed her fears.

❖ ❖ ❖

"Your work has become astonishingly good," Bette said, "despite everything." He knew she saw the circles under his eyes after an almost sleepless night. She saw his shakiness. Sometimes, when he arrived, Joseph still tasted late-night whiskey under his morning cigarettes; she must have smelled it on him, before coffee sharpened hand and mind. Something in Joseph knew that Bette had seen his weakness all along, and that marriage hadn't changed him. But she'd also seen his progress as a painter, and he couldn't deny the surge of joy her praise brought him.

Drawing and painting became Joseph's life. He took on more difficult projects with the Ramseys. At home, Joseph drew on the many nights when he couldn't sleep. He sketched the chairs and the curtains, bowls of fruit, wilting flowers, and his own hands. The drawings usually found their way to the fire — he was his own toughest critic. Occasionally, Joseph left a sketch on the table for Myrtle to see, but she passed by without noticing, or if she did, without response. He wished for her praise again, which seemed ridiculous and self-centred, knowing he should have wished for so much else for her.

In the yard on a late winter night Joseph stared at the scrubland leading to the cemetery. His and Myrtle's unnamed children were too small, too unknown to merit marking. They were simply dug in earth under a blanket of snow that Joseph found solace in.

Somewhere beyond the yard was a woman whose face Joseph tried in vain to picture. Later, in the dark house, Joseph sketched what he recalled of Cyrena Ayre: cobweb lines and fairy wings. She was easy to burn; he never got the picture right.

Blood

***

1900–1904

28

"The perils!" Cho called delightedly, pulling Joseph by the hand through the fairground gates. Since their trip to the Bijou Theatre where the waxworks, menagerie, and chamber of horrors had coalesced in the boy's mind with the dangers of Scáthach's island, he'd begged Joseph to bring him to the Exhibition. Cho's persistent reminders, the possibilities he imagined and described all summer, were impossible for Joseph to resist. Like Myrtle had been, years earlier, Cho was elated when Joseph promised to take him for a day of magic — an escape from Jing and William's new-baby house.

This time, when Joseph asked Myrtle if she wanted to come along, she declined. "I'm a little busy at the moment," she said, threading the needle on her machine. Myrtle had begun to sew again. Her return to work appeared to restore a sense of purpose in her, slightly easing Joseph's concern; yet it did little to bring them together. The girl in the yellow dress, her frayed cuffs and sparkling eyes, was just a memory. The woman who stood before him was someone else.

But Cho's lively presence kept Joseph focused on the fair, marvelling at how everything had become mechanized — a whole midway of rides that whirled and chugged, roared and rolled electrically. Cho rode a red chariot on a roundabout of painted monsters. He led Joseph past ornate calliopes, grinding and hooting in three-four time. They walked through the Crystal Maze of mirrors where Cho, ecstatically misshapen, multiplied into an army. "More perils!" he said giggling at the fun house, and Joseph couldn't help but smile. Their happiness was as electric as the rides.

Only as the two rose up on the Big Wheel did Joseph glimpse a face that caused his heart to skip a beat. He strained to keep the woman in view, yet she inevitably disappeared in the crowd. The wheel kept turning. Later, as he and Cho stood in line for the daredevil's feat, Joseph looked around for her until Cho's excitement brought Joseph's attention back to the death-defying show: a man rode his bicycle along a high wooden track, soared into the air, and somer-saulted into a pool far below. "The Salmon Leap!" Cho shrieked, caus-ing several heads to turn. He beamed up at Joseph. "Like the Bridge of the Cliff, Scar Man. Cuchulainn."

Joseph put his arm around the boy's shoulders and gave a squeeze. They walked through Day and Night in the Palace of Illusion, and saw the Queens of Fire and Air. For several spellbound moments Joseph watched the magic lantern show play out against the Fire Queen's fluttering dress and legs. Then he put Cho on a swing to turn in circles while Joseph searched the crowd. Three times he paid for Cho to ride the swings, and smirked at his own folly. Of course the woman he'd seen had not been her; it was ridiculous thinking she might be.

Cho searched in vain for a tiger at the animal show, growling keenly at the leopards and wolves, instead. Joseph and Cho watched a magician make a woman disappear. At the Vardo wagon, Madame Ava offered to tell fortunes for seven cents. Without judgment, but with a pang of sadness, Joseph recalled Tim's long-ago warning to avoid soothsayers. Seldom had Joseph shared his old friend's opin-ions; even so, he missed Tim. Joseph looked into the lady's eyes and smiled. "Not today." He didn't want to know his future.

Cho took Joseph's hand again and directed him to the Grand-stand where Kelly's Big Top Circus had pitched its tents. "Can we go in? Please?"

"Oh ay," Joseph said, suddenly weary, but still content, emptying his pockets for yet another world. Tight-rope walkers, trapeze flyers, clowns — "More perils," Cho whispered, as a dancer on horseback galloped past the lion cage, eliciting real growls. An abruptly quiet, frightened Cho gripped Joseph's hand more tightly. An hour later, as man and boy approached the exit, they passed posters pinned to a red velvet curtain. A moustached man held out his two palms. The left palm read, "Spanish seer sees" and the right, "your soul." Cho led Joseph to a table with a densely labelled ceramic head. Behind the table with the phrenology sign sat a pale, thin woman with shadows in the hollows of her eyes.

Joseph didn't recognize her at first, even when she stood, wincing slightly, gripping her ribs for a moment before opening her arms to Joseph.

She was not the woman he'd seen in the crowd. Transformed as she was, she could only be one person.

"Deary."

❖ ❖ ❖

"My name is Madame Delphine Paradis," she said, hugging Joseph carefully. He kissed her cheek and paused to breathe the sweet smell of her skin. Cho tugged on Joseph's sleeve.

"This is Cho." Joseph gestured to the boy. Deary nodded, grinned, and shook Cho's hand.

"I fell from my horse. At a show in Rochester," she explained, "a thunder clap spooked Monty. I'd danced on his back a thousand times. Now I feed him extra sugar. I let him nuzzle my neck. I love that horse! You'll both have to see him — when I 'have leave' from this table." She winked.

Deary. Joseph's mind whirled. The sudden lightness of elation thrilled him beyond anything electric at the fair. "We'll wait."

In the stables beyond the horse ring, Deary brushed the beast with vigorous strokes despite her bandaged ribs, then handed the brush to Cho, who proudly imitated her movements. She planned to ride the horse again after the show in St. Thomas. "It could have been worse. We could have been struck by lightning."

Phrenology, a sideshow attraction, was a temporary kindness bestowed on her by the circus owner, Jack Kelly, Deary said. Kelly's "distinguished phrenologist," Emilio Cortez of Milwaukee, could use assistance now that his drinking habit was in full flower. Cortez often snored behind the curtain under a blue sombrero while Deary worked. Phrenology was almost a thing of the past; so she adopted a French name to elevate her art: "Delphine Paradis in place of the Latin Luminary," she said, smiling wryly.

"What happened to theatre?" Joseph asked. Then, upon seeing her expression falter for a moment, he regretted it.

Yet Deary had no regrets, she said, recovering a bright countenance, despite her pallor. She'd taught herself French after Agnes Tripp fired her many years before — "for misbehaviour with Hamlet. No Ibsen after that."

Euphoric as he was, beside her again, Joseph found it hard to speak to her. Cho chattered in his stead.

"Our circus wagons travelled to Toronto on flatbed trains to put on our show here for thirteen days," Delphine Paradise explained to the boy after his fifteenth question. On the sides of the wagons were mirrors. When standing in the gap between the wagons, a person was reflected in lines without end. The mirror on Deary's wagon was plain, but she urged Cho to try the others. Cho spent several minutes delighting at becoming thin and tall, wide and short, and upsidedown — "Like the Crystal Maze!" The boy made a ferocious face, a leering smile, and giggled.

"This circus only has one ring," Deary said. "We feature showmanship, *not* spectacle. The newspapers vilify us for offering sideshows, but crowds pay for sideshows and we performers have to eat.

Some people are complaining that the circus has taken over the fair this year. The newspapers want more stoves and farm implements and industrial machinery." She chuckled. "The Crystal Palace is a disappointment, they say. Men and women in tights are decadent and tawdry." Deary smiled. "The word tawdry was mine." As she gazed into Joseph's eyes her smile faded. "Can't we simply entertain?" Then her expression hardened. Joseph wasn't sure if Deary's face betrayed indignation or regret; he knew she wasn't looking for an answer.

At the end of their visit Deary did not say: "Come back tomorrow." But she did not say: "Don't come back tomorrow." She reached and lightly touched Joseph's face when the boy wasn't looking. "I'm glad to see you." Then she looked away.

Cho was delighted to return with Joseph the next day. Cho's head shape indicated a strong leader, Madame Paradis confirmed, from certain bumps at the base of his skull where the long, black hair was tied. Cho liked phrenology, and the monkeys, and the clowns who shot water at each other on horseback. "For now, the men on stilts and the freak show draw crowds; but I tell you," she told them, "gymnastics are an art form. I'm going to fly trapeze."

Delicate lines from the corners of Deary's eyes radiated outward —because she smiled so often at her audiences, she said. "Meaningless," she said, taking Joseph into her bed long after he'd seen Cho home, returned, and the crowds had gone. The Exhibition grounds were quiet and dark, and the late August air was cool. Alone with her, naked, he gave himself fully to her body. Elation became ecstasy, and a kind of oblivion. He didn't care what became of him. Joseph touched Deary's breasts and the bandage beneath them. He touched the lines beside her eyes. He touched the soft, wet place between her legs where he would enter, and kissed her neck. So close, he was, to losing himself.

"Nothing here anymore," Deary said.

"What do you mean?" Pulling up, he saw her smile, faintly, but not at him.

"Sometimes I think I'm an empty vessel."

"That's not true." Gently, Joseph set his ear to her chest. "I can hear it."

"What?"

"Your heart."

◆ ◆ ◆

At home, Joseph fell asleep and dreamed about the disappearing woman: the blue hem above her feet, vanishing up the side of a hill. "Where are you?" he cried out, unsure to whom he was calling.

"I'm here," Myrtle answered.

Awake, he felt her hand squeeze his. In the dark, she couldn't see his silent tears.

If she could see him as he really was, she'd be horrified, ashamed. He hated himself for all the comfort her hand should have brought and how he couldn't squeeze it back.

◆ ◆ ◆

On the third day, Joseph visited Deary at twilight, as the crowds were leaving. She walked among the horses, feeding them sugar and stroking their backs. Joseph led her back to the wagons, where they stood for a moment beside hers, reflected in the darkening outer mirror. He stared hard to keep the image of the moment with him: the two of them together on the surface of the glass, sacred and forbidden. If Joseph followed Deary into her wagon, he could touch her again; yet if they stayed reflected in the glass, Joseph almost believed that they would last together.

Always, Joseph would remember walking out of the mirror.

◆ ◆ ◆

Deary's face glowed in the dim interior light of the circus wagon. "You used to tell me a fairy tale about children who were turned to swans." She looked like a girl again and she smelled like cinnamon. He brushed her dark blonde hair from where it had fallen across her face. She turned her face into his hand and kissed it.

"Deary."

"Madame Paradis to you, sir, if you please," she whispered, pulling a sheet across her shoulders and wrapping his naked body inside it, too. He breathed the spices in her hair; he kissed her ear.

"Tell me a story," she said, grinning. She kissed his open mouth, long and languorously. "Like you used to do when we were children."

"I want to ask a question first."

"How daring." She traced a cross on his chest and then pretended to erase it.

"What is your real name, Deary Avery?"

"I don't know." Deary's smile faded. "Of course, I could be lying."

"Would you lie to me, Deary?"

"Maybe."

"Pretty lies, then," Joseph whispered, pulling her back close to him. "Would you really lie to me, Deary?"

She slid out from under the sheet and stepped naked across the wagon to a wooden box in the corner. She opened the hinged top. She wound a handle and suddenly waltz music filled the room.

"May I have this dance?" Joseph bent to kiss her breasts, the bandaged ribs and her belly and the narrow bones of her hips. Joseph embraced her on his knees and she knelt with him.

"I meant it."

"What?"

"Tell the story about the swans, like you did once at Grenadier Pond."

"Where those poor grenadiers fell through the ice so long ago? And you dove in. I thought you'd vanished. You terrified me."

"Yes, my sweet Irishman." Deary cupped his face with her hands.

"Are you making fun of me?"

"Ay." She kissed his forehead. "But I hadn't vanished. I told you I could swim under water, remember? Then you gave me the white feather."

"What am I to do about you, Deary?"

"Just tell me about those swans again."

"You could stay."

For a long time neither of them spoke. The gramophone music finished. Finally Joseph's voice broke quietly through the silence. "They were the children of Lir, an old god of the sea."

"They were under a glamour," she whispered back to him.

"You're under a glamour," he said, rocking her back to the floor in his arms. He lay gently with her, careful not to put his weight on her ribs. She was so thin.

Deary stared up at him, wide-eyed as he lifted her left hand to his lips, kissing her fingers. "Lir's wife turned the children into swans."

"And they were beautiful," she said, tracing the lines on his face.

"They flew for hundreds of years. They flew across the sea until finally ..."

"They awoke as from a dream."

"Madame Paradis —"

"I remember! They changed back into people. You had me looking for a spirit called Annie. Was she one of them?"

"Tomorrow's your last day here."

"You used to tell me how the swans turned back into children, but they were old and wizened and about to die. I wanted them to be real children again. Or better — to be like real children. I wanted them to be free. Well, perhaps they were."

"What do you mean?"

"So much here isn't seen."

❖ ❖ ❖

By the light of a kerosene lamp, Joseph drew Deary. He learned the contours of her face in partial shadow. He memorized her mouth. He mastered the strokes of her hair. Joseph studied how the lamplight fell across her naked body. He made each drawing better than the last before they returned, inevitably, to her bed.

"I'm glad we met again," Deary said on the last afternoon of the show.

Joseph could not speak.

If he quit his job, Joseph could follow Deary's circus to Hamilton, Brantford, Guelph; he could see her ride each day — the wheels and the horses, the steam and the track. But his hands organized pages that he tied between leather covers.

She took Joseph's face in her hands, lightly tracing his forehead with her fingertips. "You are always sincere," she said softly, "and sometimes wrong. Go to your wife, Joseph. Go home."

"How long must I wait?" he asked, finally.

Deary kissed his closed eyes.

❖ ❖ ❖

Myrtle waited for Joseph on the horsehair settee. As Joseph entered the parlour, he was aware of how heavy the drawn curtains looked, additionally weighed down, it seemed, by the stale air in the house. Laid out across a wing-back chair was a new suit Myrtle had made for him.

"I hope you like it. I've been gone so much lately," she told him, studying his face. "In part, I've been making this for you. Also I've been working." She paused, searching his face, which remained blank. "I've accepted a position with Robert Raymond, a tailor on Spadina Avenue. He's expanding his business. I'll be a dressmaker, not a seamstress. He says he wants me to sew from fashion plates but also from my own patterns. He liked the samples I showed him. My hours will be long. Sometimes I'll need to be at the shop, sometimes here. I hope you don't mind. Joseph? The vest is old-fashioned, but it's my favourite. Prince of Wales."

Joseph stared at the suit, unable to speak to her.

"I wanted to make something for you," she whispered. "Something useful. Something beautiful." She looked at the leather portfolio of drawings under Joseph's arm. He looked away. "Say something, Joseph. I won't ask where you've been."

That night, Myrtle moved out of their bedroom and into the work room. They hadn't called it a nursery for a long time. When Joseph walked by her closed door shortly after one o'clock, he heard the sewing machine, smelled cigarette smoke, and thought he heard Myrtle sobbing, then realized she was humming.

29

*T*he twentieth century moved through wires, and early in 1901, the K.J. Ramsey Decorative Glass Painting Establishment moved into larger offices on Richmond Street. William's small, stone Buddha disappeared and re-emerged, as did William, in a new suite of rooms, beside a new oven, sitting silently in the early morning. Cho went to a new school; on most days he came to help at the shop after school was over. Cho and Joseph still played cards. William still poured tea. But Kenneth Ramsey seldom drew anymore. On the telephone, he took orders. Winter days on Richmond were dark and long and full.

Another Church of England was scheduled to be built, on Piper Street across from the Queen's Hotel. St. John's would take several years to complete, Kenneth explained, but already the Ramseys had been commissioned to design and build the windows: mostly three-light gothic with tall centre lights. "Not exactly original," Bette said, chuckling after her brother Kenneth's predictable sigh, "but elegant. Ever pleasing." The east wall window above the sanctuary would comprise five lights and elaborate tracery.

"The ascension," she said. "Kenneth's domain. Unfortunately, ecclesiastical east is really north in this church. I wish, for Kenneth's sake, that it could be better lit." The other five-light window, on the west wall, would feature the baptism of Jesus. Bette and Simon would design it. Plans for the ecclesiastical north wall of the nave included the annunciation, nativity, and good shepherd windows. The north wall of the sanctuary would also show the last supper and Christ carrying the cross. Across the chancel, the crucifixion and empty tomb would be set in place. For the first time, Kenneth invited Joseph to design a series of three windows to span the south wall of the nave.

"For a growing city, the committee is dedicating the nave's south wall to stories of Christ and the multitudes," Kenneth said. "I'd like to see what you can do with that."

Joseph's assignment was to create multitudes and miracles — the wedding at Cana, one or more of the healings, the loaves and the fishes, Jesus walking on the Sea of Galilee, and finally, the children's window.

Thus, when Joseph found himself between more pressing jobs, which was rarely, he made sketches for the Piper Street window project. He saw the multitudes each day: in the streets, on the trolleys, in the taverns. In the furnace that Cho learned to stoke, Joseph imagined the brightening glaze, molten heat and colours setting. Figures emerged, one by one, in line drawings that he filed away as winter turned into spring. He looked for her everywhere; but he could only imagine Deary's smile.

Often after work, Joseph was lulled by the ready camaraderie, the clink of glasses, and buzz of the taverns. After more than a few drinks, he walked home feeling comfort like sweat on a cool glass as the spring nights grew warmer. For him, as for Bette Abrahms, work had become a kind of church. He no longer questioned it and was faithful. As he passed St. Peter's Anglican Church on Bleecker Street, he noted that, three years after being married there, and childless, he and Myrtle had stopped receiving letters from the minister inviting them to return. On the wall of an abandoned apothecary shop across the street, someone had painted three words: "I am here."

Joseph chuckled wryly. Nonetheless, the words drew him. He peered through the grimy window at rows of dusty bottles once arranged with care; they seemed to gaze at him. One lay shattered on the floor beside a dead geranium. "I am here," he whispered, touching the letters on the brick. The details took him back. He thought of the lady in pink flowers peeking at him from his mother's hand at Navan Fort. He thought of the multitudes.

And he wished he wasn't drunk.

Some evenings, instead of drinking, he walked down into the ravines. In the tangle of willows, black locust and sumac trees, the words, "I am here," repeated in his mind. Joseph became aware of his own footsteps then, and of his breath. He noticed the terns' songs. He noticed sparrows, crows, and osprey, and occasionally caught a glimpse of a heron in flight.

As the summer unfolded, Joseph allowed his work-blackened fingers to graze sweet clover and yarrow. The river valley eased the place inside him that ached when he searched the crowded sidewalks for Deary, fully aware of the futility.

In the crowd scenes he envisioned for the Piper Street church project, Joseph wished that he could depict Jing carrying her baby on her back; a clown washing away his painted face; a woman dancing on a horse; a man playing cello on the street outside the Rossin House; a patch-eyed boy selling papers; Myrtle singing. He remembered Myrtle's voice at play in the Cathedral, spiralling up and out beyond him. He thought of her skin, her embrace, and how he wished that he could reach for her again — impossible — gripped by shame that he wished he could depict Deary holding hands with him in a mirrored moment. Then wishing became unbearable. He went back to drawing strangers in the Holy Land.

❖ ❖ ❖

Cho rarely asked for Joseph's stories anymore, until the bruises came. On Cho's arms and on his shins. Occasionally, a bruise darkened one of Cho's eyes.

"Tell me about the bulls," he said to Joseph, as they sat out behind the shop, after Cho's day at the new school was done. He carved the ground with a piece of broken glass.

"The bulls," Joseph said, inhaling pipe smoke and studying the black eye that didn't look back at him. "It's been a while since I've thought about those two."

"They were *sidhe*," Cho said, twisting the fragment deeper.

"They were indeed."

Honestly, Joseph could not remember all the shape-shifting details of the two magical beings that became the most famous bulls in Ireland. Each time he'd told Cho the story, Joseph had made parts up, but Cho never minded when the details changed. Joseph invented a series of wild beasts that fought endlessly. When he needed to think, Joseph blew a smoke ring, which kept the boy's interest as closely as the litany of battling brutes. More beasts sprang forth, and then two warriors. Eventually the story always came around to the warriors becoming maggots.

"The maggots dropped into two rivers," the boy said, urging Joseph out of a pause. "And two cows drank the maggots."

"Right. Then two magnificent bulls were born: one in Cooley—a fine, brown bull for Ulster; the other in Connaught—a white-horned bull. Connaught's Queen Maeve wanted both for herself. She sent her army to fight the Red Branch Knights of Ulster."

"The white-horned bull's body was red like blood," Cho said, "because of all the bleeding that came after."

"The bleeding that came after was a waste," Joseph said softly. "Here's a better piece of glass for you." Joseph reached into his tobacco pouch and handed Cho a beach-smoothed piece that wouldn't cut the boy's fingers.

"But the Cuchulainn stories—so many wouldn't have happened if there hadn't been bulls to fight for."

"All because of an insult and a jealous queen and king. Foolishness." Joseph refilled his pipe.

"You never said that about Cuchulainn. You never said he was foolish."

"The war for the bulls was foolish. No use blaming Cuchulainn. In the end, after our hero defeated Queen Maeve's army and won the bulls for Ulster — even after all that, those bulls tore each other apart. You see the waste of it. All of those men dead."

Sad endings seemed to satisfy Cho the most.

On another day, Cho returned limping after his latest schoolyard encounter. One black eye had faded to a yellowish-green; the other was faintly purple. Cho asked for the story of when Cuchulainn killed his own son.

"That's a terrible story!" Joseph exclaimed, shaking his head and producing a new pipe which he filled, lit, started, and handed to Cho. Cho's eyes sparkled through the bruises. The boy took the pipe and inhaled. Then he gagged.

"Go easy."

Another try produced several partially suppressed coughs. Instead of telling the story of Connla, Joseph taught Cho to smoke. "You've had some battles yourself, I see."

The boy said nothing, but stared hard at the ground he'd scored. Then, a small voice followed. "I don't want to talk about it."

"All right," Joseph said. But it wasn't all right.

When William called, they hid the boy's new pipe under the steps. Joseph put his hand on Cho's shoulder. "Until next time, then."

❖ ❖ ❖

When the next time came, they removed the boy's pipe from its hiding place and lit it. Once again, Cho coughed until he gagged, and Joseph reminded him to go easy. He asked about the injuries. Once again, the boy refused to talk. He wanted to hear the story of how Cuchulainn killed his own son, Connla.

Connla's story was shrouded in secrecy, somewhat like Cho's bruises. Joseph recounted that during Cuchulainn's quest to win Emer, he tricked a warrior-woman who had the power to grant wishes. One of Cuchulainn's wishes was to stay with her that very night.

"Did she ride horses?" Cho asked.

In the silence that followed, Cho unsuccessfully tried to blow a smoke ring.

"Cuchulainn wished that she would bear him a son," Joseph said.

"But he was in love with Emer."

For a moment, Joseph remembered Myrtle on a late spring night, moving gracefully across the Ramseys' lawn. Then he blinked her image away, as he did so many that came when he told Cho the stories.

"Yes he was. The magic warrior-woman demanded that Cuchulainn name his infant son before leaving. 'Connla,' Cuchulainn said. He placed a gold thumb ring in the palm of the lady's right hand. 'When the boy grows up big enough to wear this ring, you must send him across the sea to me.' Cuchulainn added that Connla must never reveal his name or refuse a fight. Connla's mother cast a spell to ensure it."

"Why did Cuchulainn kill him?"

Joseph stared at the boy's bruised face, and for a moment saw a man at Keady mill, handing his son three coins. To the son, now, Ireland was as tenuous as a story. Did the old man ever wish for his children to return from their faraway land? Joseph pictured the gold ring on the man's left hand. And what of Mam? Had he missed her? Did he miss her still? What did any of it matter? The questions didn't make things better; they only wearied him.

He blinked the man and the coins away, but discomfort lingered. "I beg your pardon?"

"Why did he kill him?"

"He didn't mean to." Joseph sifted carefully through memory now, intent upon finding only pieces that he wanted. "Cuchulainn killed him by accident. By the time the baby grew into a boy and found his father, Cuchulainn didn't recognize him. They fought because they had to. Cuchulainn demanded to know the boy's name; of course, Connla wouldn't tell."

"And a sad thing happened." Cho was almost smiling.

"Yes," Joseph said. "Before Cuchulainn fought Connla, the boy said: 'If I wasn't under a spell, you're the person I'd tell my name to.'"

"Why?"

Unavoidably, Joseph's father smiled down in his memory, the man's warm hand on Joseph's head.

"'Because I love your face,' Connla said. When they fought, the hero light shone around Cuchulainn. When the boy saw that light, he knew who he was dealing with. Connla thrust his sword in such a way that it wouldn't hit his father; but before Cuchulainn understood, he'd already thrown his most powerful weapon."

"The *gae bolge*!"

"Ay," Joseph replied. "The *gae bolge*, his magic sword."

"I want you to draw it for me."

"I will," Joseph said. "As Connla lay dying he revealed his name."

"That's sad," Cho said, rocking and puffing and smiling slightly, almost satisfied. "What did Cuchulainn do?"

"Cuchulainn's sorrow was fearsome. To distract him, an old wizard made the waves of the sea stand up straight, like armed warriors. Cuchulainn fought them with his sword until he dropped from exhaustion."

"I want you to draw that, too," Cho said. From his satchel he took a sharpened lead pencil and his elementary-school notebook.

"May I draw the pictures here?"

"Yes," Cho said, carefully turning the pages. "Here." He pointed. Cho supervised the drawing until the *gae bolge* appeared before him and the waves stood on end. Then William called, and Cho crawled under the back steps to hide the pipe.

Joseph roughed in a warrior's figure. Ink had bled through the other side of the page and he turned it over to where the words "I AM

A DIRTY CHINK" had been scrawled in another child's pen. "Cho," Joseph said, tearing out the sheet of paper and crumpling it. "I can do a better one. I'll have to finish at home."

"Let me see."

"Too late." Joseph struck a match, and lit the page.

That night Joseph drew three pictures for Cho: the *gae bolge*, the fight with the standing waves, and the man and boy staring eye to eye above the caption: "Because I love your face."

"What are you drawing?" Myrtle asked as she passed by him at the dining room table.

"Just Irish stories."

She disappeared into her room and Joseph disappeared into the whiskey bottle, and once again, the waves of the sea stood on end. Later, when he opened his eyes and lifted his head from the table, Joseph realized her sewing machine had stopped. He ascended the stairs, paused at Myrtle's door as he did every night, and listened for a moment. Nothing. She must be sleeping. He touched the wood lightly and kept walking.

❖ ❖ ❖

Cold water. Coffee. Smoke. In line for the tram, unshaven, but alert, he could walk straight and, more importantly, draw. But first he paid a visit.

After Joseph delivered Cho the pictures, privately he told William about the message in Cho's book and his concern about the schoolyard fights. William nodded. He and Jing had been to the school. They'd spoken to the teacher and hoped for change, though it hadn't happened yet. "Difficult to learn," he said, wistful.

"What is that?"

"Feeling separate and knowing you are not."

"But does he have to be beaten to learn that?"

William smiled, but his eyes looked sad. "Do you?"

30

*S*ometimes, when Joseph came home early in the evening, he heard Myrtle singing before she knew he was in the house. Joseph closed his eyes, listening. Myrtle often sang verses from the St. Michael's choir hymns. Eventually, "Lead kindly light, amid encircling gloom," gave way to "Casey would waltz with a strawberry blonde, and the band played on. He'd glide across the floor with the girl he adored ..." Then, over the course of several minutes, "Just Another Fatal Wedding" became, "East side, west side, all around the town — the tots sang 'ring-around rosie' London Bridge is falling down." When a knock came at the front door, Myrtle hurried down the stairs as she sang. Upon seeing Joseph, she let the music fade. Myrtle opened the door to the first of her evening customers.

Women or their husbands frequently knocked at the door to take receipt of packages. Even on Sunday afternoons, Sherbourne Street ladies arrived to be fitted.

"Your wife makes the best bell-bottomed skirts," one told Joseph. "And her blouses! The lace! She knows where to draw the eye and how to make me look slender."

Another customer informed Joseph that she'd come for Myrtle's *sans ventre* corset. "No stomach," she insisted in a heavy Italian accent. "No stomach. She promise *me*. To*day!*"

In the dry weather, Myrtle rode her bicycle to Robert Raymond's shop on Spadina Avenue. Her divided cycling skirt elicited more knocks at the door.

"Truly, Mr. Conlon, your wife Myrtle is something. She's an emancipated woman."

Robert Raymond found her reputation good for business. He put a sign in his storefront: "Featuring the work of Mrs. Myrtle Conlon." Soon Raymond dropped the "Mrs." and the "Conlon." The sign simply read "Clothes by Myrtle" beside a silhouette of a woman on a bicycle. A small, round-brimmed hat completed the woman's forward-looking profile.

While Myrtle's daytime work at Raymond's remained steady, she showed no sign of limiting her home business. The only evenings that Myrtle didn't take customers were Tuesdays, when she took lessons from an experienced songstress on Parliament Street. Miss Dorothea Small taught her art songs. As far as Joseph could tell, the statues lately resurrected on her windowsill, and the dressmaker's form, were her only audience apart from him, and then only when his arrival went unnoticed.

Among the advantages of studying with Miss Small were her theatrical connections. Myrtle's dressmaking talents became known to a Rosedale children's dance school, and Myrtle found herself designing and sewing costumes for a children's ballet. Over the course of one week in early December, a troupe of tiny dancers arrived, one by one, with their elegant mothers, to be fitted for a January church-basement show. Joseph heard Myrtle and the children in her sewing room making plans.

"I'm going to be a dancing fairy," one distinctively pale child announced to Joseph as she entered the parlour. Shadows encircled her eyes.

"She's lost weight," Myrtle whispered to the girl's mother.

"Yes," the mother answered, faintly.

"You're going to be a magic ballerina," Myrtle said to the girl. "Come with me, Effie. I'll find your wings."

Joseph remained on his parlour chair, reading a day-old *Telegram*. He heard the child's small squeal of delight: her wings, half-finished, had been revealed. "Hold the railing on your way down," he heard Myrtle call after the child. Myrtle and the mother remained upstairs, speaking in hushed tones.

For a moment, Joseph saw the dressmaker's shop on Leader Lane — the old bolts of fabric and a twelve-year-old Myrtle perched upon a stack of dusty cloth. Then Effie Douglas, the spectral ballerina, descended in a loosely pinned dress, holding out her wand. "I'm magic," she told Joseph.

He put his finger to his lips in a motion for them both to whisper. "May I make a picture of you, Miss Marvellous Fairy?"

"Oh yes," she said solemnly. "Of course."

"Thank you."

Effie approached him to see the drawing. She stared at it for several seconds, breathing slowly and audibly. Then she regarded Joseph, looking satisfied.

When Myrtle and Mrs. Douglas descended, Joseph tucked Effie's picture away beneath the chair.

Myrtle carefully removed the wings for beading. "So you'll shine in the lights."

"May I stand with the angel?" the child asked.

"The angel?"

"Beside your door. My mother told me we were coming to a house with an angel."

Joseph couldn't help but gaze at Myrtle then. He missed her tenderness, which he didn't deserve. He missed her touch. When her eyes met his, he looked away.

"I think you must be magic to make my dress so beautiful," the girl said.

"I'm not magic, Effie."

"Then maybe the angel helps you."

Myrtle paused. "When you come back, your dress and fairy wings will be ready."

"Mind you don't work too hard, Myrtle," Joseph said before he could stop himself.

She looked pale and tired, yet somehow charged with fiery energy. "You're one to talk."

"I'm just concerned."

"Please don't be." She closed the wings and went upstairs.

For the first time Joseph wondered about the long hours Myrtle kept — not at home, but at Raymond's. That night Myrtle sang without words. By dawn she was gone.

The next evening, after supper was over, Joseph called up the stairs to say that he was going for a walk and opened the front door to leave, but something caused him to pull the door closed again. He walked quietly to where he had tucked away the drawing of Effie and began to fill in the picture. The more he worked, the more clearly the child seemed to be trying to tell him something.

After a few minutes, Myrtle began to sing. This time, not only the sound of her voice but her words held him in the house. He wanted to be held. He stared at the figure on the page, listening:

Sea-birds are asleep,
The world forgets to weep,
Sea murmurs her soft slumber-song
On the shadowy sand ...

Joseph set his drawing of the dancer down upon the stair, wiped his hands on a towel, and wandered silently to the sideboard. He opened the bottom drawer and lifted the edge of a never-used linen table cloth that Bette and Danny Abrahms had given them for a wedding present. Joseph pulled the cloth from the drawer and pressed it lightly to his face. He inhaled the scent of wood. Joseph set it on a chair using his left hand to be sure not to smudge it.

I, the Mother mild,
Hush thee, O my child,
Forget the voices wild!
Hush thee, O my child,
Hush thee ...

Beneath the cloth, his sack had remained undisturbed. Carefully, he pulled it from the drawer and set it on the table, aware that the pieces inside had become more fragile than they once were. The Brigid's cross of woven rushes was brittle. He touched the crumbling edges. He dared not open the walnut shell, round and cool in his palm. He removed the leather-wrapped shard of glass that bore an image of Mary's face painted by a young James Ramsey, still darkened with Joseph's blood. Two hair ribbons had faded long ago: one pale green, one black. They were soft and veined. Beside them he set a series of unsent letters written in a child's hand. The scrawled characters seemed to want free of the paper, slanting urgently toward the edges.

Foam glimmers faintly white
Upon the shelly sand ...

"Deary," Joseph whispered, pausing to touch a letter's closing line. He pulled out the speller that the nuns had given him to replace the one he'd brought from Darkley. The new-world speller contained none of Joseph's old-world prayers; those had vanished with the animals that had gazed serenely. "Rat, Rabbit, Badger, Dog ..." He opened the back page of the Our Lady speller to a single name penned in ink: Annie. Then he realized that he did still pray; his prayers were the names he whispered. Joseph read the question written beneath: "Where are you?"

I murmur my soft slumber-song,
My slumber-song,
Leave woes, and wails, and sins ...

Joseph gathered the items back into the sack, gently placing it at the bottom of the drawer, under the linen cloth.

> *Ocean's shadowy might*
> *Breathes good-night,*
> *Good-night ...*

"Goodnight, Myrtle," Joseph whispered.

Quietly, he opened the door and stepped into the darkness.

31

The early December air was unseasonably mild. He could imagine sleeping in the ravine tonight. He felt safe exposed to the night air, the breezes through the willow branches and brittle grasses, the stars, as he had been when he'd lived in the valley under a tarpaulin. On his meanderings now, if he was too late for the last streetcar, Joseph found the valley setting more reassuring than a house, even when the house belonged to him.

Tonight's wandering took him south to Queen Street and east. Much of the land was still in small pastures and rough plots of tangled brush. To the north and immediately east of the river, brick homes were being built on what some city dwellers still considered wilderness. At the bottom of a tiny, unlit lane was a tavern, and Joseph immediately felt relief in a dram of whiskey. He sat at a thick chopping block of a table, above which was a shelf displaying several stoutly bound editions of *The Leisure Hour* and a pile of magazines. Joseph reached inside his pocket and found a pencil stub. He wished that he'd brought paper.

"Fine journals, there," the proprietor, a large man crowned with a shock of white hair, said. His wild eyes were decked by wiry, grey brows appropriate for someone railing on a heath. Instead of railing, he introduced himself: "I'm Tommy Blunt," held out a set of stubby fingers and firmly shook Joseph's hand. "I haven't seen you at my place before."

"I haven't come this far east."

"Enjoy your drink, then."

Joseph had a sense of something occurring that he wasn't privy to. He also had the feeling of being watched, but he settled heartily into his whiskey. On his second glass, Joseph pulled a *Christian Herald* down from the shelf and identified it as the Thanksgiving issue of 1898 — already four years old. He flipped open to a section titled, "Remarkable Conversions" and read the stories beneath the captions: "Saved from Suicide," "A Brand for the Burning," and "She Prayed to the Devil." Joseph longed to draw again, and would have done so happily over the newsprint columns, but Tommy Blunt continued to stare from his station behind the counter. "You're holding the real thing, there," he called. "My wife keeps every issue."

As Joseph flipped past the articles to the ads, several men entered with bulky satchels. One carried a bureau drawer covered over with a sheet. "Deliveries," the man told Tommy, walking to the back and disappearing downstairs with the others.

Joseph settled into the advertisements. Allcock's Porous Plasters, Gold Dust Washing Powder, Dr. Worst's Famous Catarrh Treatment, a cure for varicose veins with patented seamless heel elastic stockings — nothing to inspire thoughts about what to get Myrtle for Christmas. In spite of everything that had, and had not, gone on between them in the past two years, they still trimmed a tree and exchanged gifts. He finished the second whiskey, and before he knew it, Tommy Blunt came by with a third. On the house. A double.

"Thanks."

"Don't mention it. What do you do and who are you? If you don't mind my asking."

Joseph provided Tommy with a few basic facts.

"You're a long way from home."

"I felt like the trip."

"I like your style, Joseph. 'I felt like the trip.'" He chuckled and shook his head back to the bar.

On his way outside to the privy, Joseph heard several men speaking in low voices, until a patch-eyed white shepherd dog barked, causing the men to stop their talk. The dog wagged his tail and barked again, scampering up to Joseph and licking his hands.

Joseph returned to his table, preparing to leave, when Tommy asked him: "What are your thoughts on gaming?"

"Gaming?" The third whiskey had struck its mark. Joseph was aware of slurring his words and feeling slightly unsteady on his feet. "Do you mean cards, then? Do you have a rummy table here, somewhere?"

"More or less. I'd say more," Tommy said, once again eyeing the magazine. "My wife wouldn't mind if you took that issue. You seem to like it. Are you a regular reader of the *Herald*?"

"No. Not at all."

"When you play at cards, do you ever sweeten the deal?"

Joseph stared.

"Do you bet?"

"I did a lot when I was young."

"So you like that sort of thing then."

"Sure."

"I like you, Joe Conlon. I've always said the Irish are a fine lot. Times were when people — no offence intended, Joe, but folks here wanted to run your kind out. Ignorance: plain and simple. No Christian decency. No sir. I want you to feel welcome. Come back tomorrow night. We're having an event. You'll enjoy yourself." Tommy paused. "But come alone. Keep it hush. And please, take the magazine. My wife would want you to have it."

The dog was gone when Joseph left the tavern. Outside, in the dim window-light, Joseph paused and flipped the magazine pages. When he found an ad for gramophones, he knew what he would buy Myrtle for Christmas.

Joseph stumbled westward. He crossed the bridge and found a path down to the river. He walked north as far as he could go before collapsing under a willow tree. "Not cold enough to freeze." He slept.

❖ ❖ ❖

A familiar voice spoke Joseph's name very clearly into his left ear. "Tim!" he replied, suddenly awake and bolt upright in the freezing, pre-dawn air. "Where are you?" Joseph's hands and lips were going numb. He wrapped his scarf around his face and readjusted his oil-cloth coat, which had served as both a blanket and a ground sheet. A white-tailed deer bounded out of the high, dead grass, and away up river at the sound. "Thanks," Joseph said, and headed to work.

❖ ❖ ❖

At his desk, Joseph left the magazine open to the ad for "Gram-o-phone as Home Entertainer: All natural as life itself—these perform-ances being nothing less than ACTUAL REPRODUCTIONS." After finishing the paint on another Christ knocking at the door, he head-ed for a store on Spadina. He and Myrtle didn't have the money or the training for a piano, but she might find a gramophone useful to accompany her singing. He would try not to think about dancing with Deary to the sound of a gramophone waltz.

Joseph stopped at the bank to withdraw money. Going by the 1898 advertisement, he estimated the current cost to be roughly twenty-six dollars. He took out twice that amount, just in case. The man behind the counter took thirty—the machines had been im-proved—and threw in several records.

The box was heavy, but not difficult to carry. Something sud-denly possessed Joseph to surprise Myrtle with the present. Very rarely had Joseph visited her at work, but this seemed as good a time as any. As he walked, found himself smiling at passers-by.

The large window of Robert Raymond's Fine Tailoring and Dressmaking Establishment bore signs for services rendered to perfection — one need only step inside. A houndstooth coat and several crisply starched shirts hung on hangers in the men's display area. On the dressmaker form in the ladies' window was a two-piece emerald suit. Hats adorned the ladies' display case, each one intricately stiff and feathered. Several hats were veiled in puffs of dark net.

"No fairy wings here," Joseph said, noticing Myrtle's sign, and Myrtle herself standing at work on a wedding dress. He leaned on the building wall to alleviate the weight of the box and, from the edge of the window, allowed himself to watch her work. Myrtle appeared content, pinning delicate pieces of lace and satin onto the form, staring intently at the lines she'd cut and carefully stitched together, setting her pearl-headed pins on the counter and smoothing the torso lightly. Myrtle's hands moved with ease along the waistline, adjusting the ribbon. When she was satisfied, she moved to the back of the figure, threaded one of many needles, and from a tin box drew the first eye to stitch at the back of the collar. Joseph imagined her humming. The dress itself was a presence; somehow Myrtle's touch enlivened it. Joseph could imagine the sleeves reaching out, perhaps to him.

The mood was broken by the entrance of Raymond to examine the neckline. Myrtle stepped back and wiped her brow with the back of her wrist. Raymond spoke and Myrtle smiled; then she laughed. Raymond turned his gaze from the dress to Myrtle, placing his hand on her shoulder. The hand travelled from Myrtle's shoulder, down her arm, to her waist. He leaned into her, and Myrtle whispered in Raymond's ear. Joseph couldn't watch any longer.

Outrage cut like sharp scissors through his ribs, yanking open a cage that held no serene, sacred heart — but jealousy, shame, fury.

He returned his gift for a refund. With the money, Joseph bought time in an Esplanade apartment. He didn't care that Beatrice Wren watched him enter the building from her fourth-floor window. He didn't care about the stranger he was with — didn't hear or speak her name. He just fucked her. On the street again, Joseph resolved that he'd return to Tommy Blunt's that night.

32

*J*oseph worked late and took the Queen tram east as far as it went. He soldiered on briskly, past the Christmas carollers at Moss Park, pausing only once to light a cigarette. His storefront reflection — expressionless, scar-faced, a man standing tall in an oilcloth duster. Soon smoke obscured the face. Kicking in the glass would do nothing to change what he was.

When he arrived, the tavern was almost empty. A solitary old customer sat in back-corner shadows washing down mashed potatoes with his ale. At the bar stood a tall, lanky youth with hollow cheeks, a hooked nose, and a bulging Adam's apple.

"Good evening to you. Do you know where Tommy is?" Joseph asked.

"Dunno."

"Do you know when to expect him then?"

"Not sure," came the monotone reply. "Supper for ya?"

Joseph's mash soon arrived, along with his ale. He returned the rumpled copy of the *Christian Herald*, exchanging it for *The Leisure Hour* of 1901. Joseph started on his mash as he turned pages in the hefty volume, trying to distract himself from thoughts of Myrtle and Raymond. Joseph stared at the stern-faced Maharaja of Travancore. He skimmed "The Trade Guilds of Turkey," "Gold-mining in New Guinea," and "The Advance of German Shipping." Joseph read about Boer prisoners of war and bird-life on the veldt. Anything.

From outside, he heard a familiar bark. Then Joseph carried his bowl of potato mash outside to the patch-eyed shepherd dog that wagged his tail in greeting. "You'll take your chances with this," Joseph said, setting down the half-full bowl, which the dog lapped at, eagerly at first, then less eagerly, yet still determined.

Joseph read about the future in "Telephones without Connecting Wires." He read about "The Death of Queen Victoria," and was about to peruse "The Siege of Shanghai," when several men entered, carrying bags, crates and covered drawers. All went downstairs.

"Is the game in the cellar, then?" Joseph finally asked the youth who appeared, in his own dull way, marginally alarmed at being spoken to.

"You have to ask Tommy."

"Tommy's not here."

"He will be."

The second ale eased Joseph's impatience. Even "Electric Lamps and How They are Made" became vaguely compelling. He found a chalk drawing of a little girl with wings entitled, "Peace." The model reminded him of the pale child, Effie, who in turn reminded him of Myrtle singing. Joseph swallowed again, quickly lighting upon photographic plates of California redwoods. An advertisement featuring a lady in a suit reminded him of Robert Raymond's window. He pictured Raymond's hand on Myrtle's waist, her face looking up at him, her whispering lips, almost a kiss. In a painting called "The Bird's Nest," three girls on a beach approached the viewer; the one on the left, paying no attention at all to the nest, looked like Myrtle.

In the end, only the Irish sections provided Joseph faint distraction from his still-roiling jealousy. He couldn't hate what Myrtle had done if he didn't care about her, he knew. Of course he knew. And knowing only made things worse, because she couldn't care for him now. He'd seen to that. Outside he patted the dog again and went to the privy, banging his forehead sharply, deliberately, on the makeshift wooden wall. That and the first dram of the night made things better.

Joseph gazed at photographic plates of Ireland's High Crosses. On the stones he saw hares and goats, wild boars, stags, dogs, and an eagle with a fish in its talons. The long-ago carver had portrayed the human multitude in the form of eight circles. Joseph gave himself over to the page: "Carrickfergus, Ballycastle ..."

He closed his eyes and pictured Navan Fort.

"They can take the man out of Ireland, but they can't take — "

"Hello, Tommy," Joseph said. Now the tavern was abuzz with chatter.

"My son Alfie tells me you're anxious to get started."

"I don't even know what I'm playing at," Joseph said, feeling for the remaining Christmas money, which had become a kind of weight upon him.

"Come and see."

As he descended the cellar stairs, Joseph entered another world. The air was thick with smoke, but a stronger stench overpowered that of the pipes and cigarettes, the mustiness, and even the men's sweat. The men formed a circle in the centre of the room, almost silent. The dim room's edges were lit by flickering sconces, but in the centre, a single gas lamp hung low.

"You've found the inner circle, Joseph. At the end of this round, I'll set you up with Alfie. He'll take your wagers. You'll make money here. You'll meet rich men tonight."

Joseph heard scuffling. A thin shriek pierced the air, followed by clucks and the beating of wings on wood. Chickens — that was the smell.

"Yes!" several of the men hollered, frenetic with back-slapping and handshakes, while the others slouched and shook their heads. As Joseph stepped into the light, his eyes discerned a low platform covered in blood. In the centre lay a dead rooster, its feathers splayed, one eye missing, its breast torn open.

"Punctured lung. Poor Phelps," the old man said, removing two silver spurs from the rooster's legs. Then the old man lifted the animal and stared into its dangling face. "Over there, then, Tommy?"

"Sure."

The handler discarded the bird on a pile of several others at the dark edge of the room. One of the animals still twitched, cooing faintly.

"Between you and me," Tommy told Joseph, "Phelps didn't stand a chance. You see Firebird, the winner over there?" A grey-haired man in an oilcloth coat set down an almost unruffled bird. "That cock-a-doodle-doo was born to wear the gaffs. He'll fight him again tonight. You'll see." The bird's owner lit a cigarette and grinned a gold-tooth grin. Joseph saw a metal bracelet on the man's left wrist. He looked into the man's scarred face and remembered a ship's hull and the queen of diamonds.

Gerry.

All at once Joseph's head ached terribly. He raised the back of his arm to wipe his brow. His coat sleeve smelled of ashes. Suddenly nauseous, Joseph stared at the scar-faced old gambler standing tall across from him.

Tommy's words became background noise. "See Alfie now, Joseph, to get in on the round. The next two up are — hold on. Alfie! Who's up this round?"

"Red Ralph and the Gay Blade."

"There you go, Joe. Take your pick. Do your best and do it fast. I've got to go back upstairs or we'll have hookers drinking from the taps. Good luck tonight. And Joe," Tommy leaned in close, lowering his voice. "Between you and me, the Gay Blade's just come off the moult — behind schedule. He's won his share, don't get me wrong, but when he's still raw with the new feathers ..." Tommy tipped his head back and laughed: "I didn't say anything!" He slapped Joseph on the back and disappeared upstairs.

How clearly Joseph remembered the game.

Ignoring Tommy's advice, Joseph bet on the Gay Blade and won. He bet on Frankie Boy against the Rookie and won again. In fact, he won five rounds in a row. Joseph's pocket bulged with money, but he didn't feel glad, just driven. He ordered a double shot of gin to overpower the reek of blood and excrement, and to stay lightly numb as waves of memory rolled through him: Gerry's scarred face in the darkness, the gleam of grease on his coat, the smell of whiskey, oil-cloth and ashes in the warm space beneath the man's arm. And his empty words as he passed two children on a bench in Union Station almost twenty years ago. "Not goodbye, boy; good luck! And I'll see you ..." With the words came the little girl who'd sat beside him on that bench, about to be taken to a better life. The fleeting thought of her pulled Joseph's arm across his eyes. Ashes. He felt sick.

Before the sixth round, the only birds left, apart from Firebird, were injured. Gerry fastened his rooster's crate, as any combat with Firebird would be no contest. He held his head high, limping slightly as he crossed the room to leave. Then the older man paused, exchanging glances with Joseph, the other big winner of the night. The two didn't speak, but stared into the lines of each other's faces. Joseph realized that with his scars, his bearing and his heavy coat, he had come to resemble Gerry. They were almost mirror images, though their age difference was obvious and Joseph's left wrist lacked a metal band. On Gerry's bracelet, years ago, a woman's name had been melted over. If Joseph were to try to complete the mirror, whose name would he destroy?

He couldn't answer. He didn't want to look like Gerry.

When the two of them nodded, Joseph's heart raced, and he looked away resolutely, tensed to keep the gin down.

By the time he reached the top of the stairs, the tavern was empty except for Tommy. Joseph ordered a cup of black tea, put *The Leisure Hour* away, and sat sipping quietly for several minutes in an attempt to clear his throbbing head. Then other men came up grumbling that the night was young and there should have been more fowl.

"There, there," Tommy said. "Next Tuesday's a big one. Bring your birds." Alfie emerged, carrying a large, misshapen bundle tied in a bloodied sheet, and a cash box that his father took. "Straight out the back, now, Alfie."

Almost immediately after Alfie left, he returned, still carrying the sack, but invigorated. "They're fighting in the back!" he exclaimed. "They've got a goat."

Tommy thrust the metal box back at his son. "Take their bets, Alfie. Run!"

Alfie ran, and his father followed.

For a few moments, Joseph settled into the tea and the relative quiet of the room. Men's fervent voices outside didn't induce him to move, but a familiar bark did. Joseph found himself hurrying out to where the men stood around a fenced paddock, taunting a goat and the patch-eyed dog. The goat reared and trembled, wild-eyed — bucking. The dog barked, growled, and yelped. Its side bled, where someone had whipped it, trying to force a shepherd to fight a herd animal.

"Stop!" Joseph cried. "He's my dog!"

"What?" Tommy said.

"He's my dog. I don't fight him."

The men closed in.

"We placed bets on these animals," a deep voice said.

"Here." Joseph thrust his winnings at Tommy.

A minute later, Joseph carried the dog west along Queen Street. "Cu," he whispered in the dog's limp ear, "we'll fix you."

❖ ❖ ❖

Joseph and Cu spent the night on the steps of a Broadview house with a shingle advertising veterinary services. In the morning when the vet found the two on his doorstep he etherized the animal, stitched his side, and told Joseph: "He's just a pup." Joseph paid for the procedure with the emergency cash he kept in his shoe, a habit since his newsboy days. Joseph also paid for a collar and a leash. He carried the sleeping dog to work; the animal awakened on a blanket near the soldering table.

When Cho arrived at the shop after school, Joseph introduced him to Cu, who lifted his head, wagged his tail twice, and licked the boy's hand.

"When he gets better," Joseph told Cho, "you can borrow him. You can walk him on the leash wherever you want to go. And Cho" — he looked steadily into the boy's astonished face — "the dog will be good protection. If you need more, talk to me."

"Scar Dog," Cho said, stroking the fur above the stitches.

❖ ❖ ❖

On his way home, Joseph wrapped the borrowed blanket around Cu and tied him to a pole half a block from the house. When he arrived at his gate, he saw Myrtle at the door, and a familiar woman heading towards him. She wore a fine hat — Myrtle's work — the veil partially concealing her face. Her fur cape closed over a faded, and slightly muddy black dress. A crocheted black purse dangled on the wrist of the bare hand she extended to him.

"Joseph," Beatrice said in a voice lower than he remembered, "it's been some time." At a loss for what to do, he shook her hand. She raised her veil and leaned into him, kissing his mouth hard and standing back, a little unsteadily. "Sorry I couldn't make it to the wedding." Her face was still young and pretty, yet very old. Joseph smelled the rum on her breath.

"Good to see you, Beatrice."

Beatrice's smile faded as she lowered the veil and pressed his chest with an index finger. "Liar. I came to see my sister." Then she pushed by him through the gate and headed south. "Stop lying," she called without turning.

Suddenly, Joseph felt remarkably dirty. He had lived in the same clothes for two nights and three days, he realized. He needed a bath, a shave, and a clean bed. He needed to lose the taste of Beatrice's lips.

"She came for money," Myrtle said. "Why did you come?"

"Because I live here."

"Really?" Then she turned her back and entered the house.

"Myrtle," he called, following her.

"Don't worry. I'm not crying," Myrtle said. "I won't give you that discomfort — or the satisfaction. I'm beyond both."

"Myrtle, I'm sorry," Joseph said, his chest and throat tightening, his hands hanging uselessly at his sides. Where to begin? The Esplanade woman didn't mean anything — they never did. The money he could win back. His mind raced.

"Where have you been?" she said.

"I've been at the shop. I've been working, Myrtle."

"For two nights? I don't know why I bother to ask. You're a drunkard, Joseph. I suppose I should be grateful that it's you and not a police officer at the door to tell me you're dead in a ditch." Her back still turned, she stared out the kitchen window.

Joseph felt immobilized. This was the closest thing to a conversation they'd had in recent memory. Myrtle could have said anything and he would have been dumbfounded. He was too shocked by her rage and anguish even to wish that he were elsewhere. Then the gravity of her words struck. A drunkard. Well, she was wrong there.

Fleetingly Beatrice's voice flashed through his mind: "Stop lying."

"Did Beatrice upset you?" he asked, struggling to dispel his panic.

Myrtle laughed. "Beatrice always upsets me, Joseph. It's like breathing."

"Because she came here?"

"Of course she came here. She knows where to find me — she always has. I'm sorry if you're bothered that she can find you, too. After all, you know where to find her — and her friends. More especially her friends, I think. Am I right, Joseph?"

Beatrice must have recognized him the day before. She must have told Myrtle about the woman in the tenement. He should have gone to the brothel on Pembroke Street instead. But he'd been so angry, so hungry for relief and yes, revenge, that he hadn't been careful. Looking at Myrtle now, he couldn't imagine wanting to hurt her for anything — even for her moment with Raymond.

A mere moment, after all. Surely.

He wanted to reach out and touch her, but he couldn't move. "I haven't seen Beatrice since we were ... not since Leader Lane."

"I suppose you haven't needed to." Myrtle stepped past him, and up the stairs. Her move unfroze him and he followed, past the door of her sewing room, to the end of the hall. She entered their bedroom where he hadn't seen her in a very long time. Myrtle lifted the mattress and withdrew a leather portfolio. Then she scattered his sketches of Deary across the spread.

Joseph swallowed.

"Beatrice saved my life once," Myrtle said, staring at the nude figure drawings. "Sometimes I'm not sure why. When you stay out at night, would you mind not bringing home pictures of the women you go to bed with?"

He took a breath. "Nothing — " He hadn't opened that portfolio in weeks.

"Nothing," Myrtle said. "Nothing what? Nothing happened? Nothing to be done. Or nothing worth keeping — but these, perhaps." She gestured to the drawings. "For you. Nothing more to be said, Joseph."

"Nothing here," he said, touching his chest. Joseph gathered up each sketch, folding the pile once, then again, firmly. He stared at his hands as they gripped the creased pages. "I will burn these," he said quietly. "She was a friend from my childhood. We knew each other. The things you think — of this woman and me. Of me. They're true, Myrtle. They *were* true; but I haven't seen her in more than two years."

Myrtle stood composed in the momentary silence.

"Well," she said at last. "What do we have? People call this 'a marriage of convenience,' I believe."

He folded the pages once more in his clenched fingers. "We have a marriage."

"Only because you felt you had to marry me. Or maybe the whiskey decided."

"I was not drunk!" He kicked the open door — and a chunk of plaster crumbled. She pushed past him down the hall.

Joseph followed to the sewing room and stood on her threshold, breathing hard.

"She was a friend from your childhood," Myrtle said, making a small cut in a bolt of ashes-of-roses cotton and tearing. She smoothed the fabric across the table. "What was I? A curiosity? A nobody living in abandoned rooms? Someone safe? You could throw away pictures of me easily, Joseph. I felt sorry for myself once; but I've taken a leaf from your book. Do you understand?"

"I —"

"I'm talking about my heart. Everything is simpler when there's only passion — or none. An old flame, Joseph, is what she was — *is* — to you. I understand. My flame burns now and I don't apologize. You know what I mean, or would, if you were listening."

Joseph stood for several seconds in silence. "I'll not see her again." He couldn't swallow, as he realized that the words he'd just spoken were true.

Cu was barking miserably by the time Joseph reached him. He stroked the animal's snowy head and untied him. When Joseph carried Cu upstairs, Myrtle's door was still open and she stood, pinning pattern cut-outs to what would become another Rosedale woman's blouse. Cu limped across the floor and buried his nose in the bottom of her skirt.

"Merry Christmas, Myrtle."

33

*J*oseph worked at not drinking. Mostly, he just worked — at the shop, and at home. Discussion of the dog's injury and care requirements were the last words that he and Myrtle spoke to each other for many days. Instead they wrote practical notes:

> *Joseph,*
> *I'm working late downtown. Pickled turnips, beets, and salt pork in the pantry. Please clean up after the dog.*
> *— Myrtle*

> *Dear Myrtle,*
> *Have cleaned up and taken Cu for a walk through the lanes. Now have gone on my own walk. Don't wait up. You can turn out the lamps.*
> *— J.*

He knew she'd snicker at that one. Joseph crossed out the last sentence. "Please leave a lamp burning," he added. Too much. He crumpled the paper and tossed it into the stove. "Gone walking," he scrawled on an ad for the Universal Food Chopper. Only later did he think about the ad's illustration: a ring of exuberant, soon-to-be chopped animals and vegetables. Joseph had written in a space beside a pig headfirst in the bowl with the whirling blade.

He hated when Myrtle worked late at Raymond's, but he refused to discuss it, preferring instead to think the relationship would pass. He thought the same about the whiskey cravings.

Most of Myrtle and Joseph's messages concerned the dog. Apart from consuming sizeable dishes of minced stewing beef, Cu had an affinity for beet soup and stuffed potatoes. He also enjoyed ham fritters, which he gobbled while Joseph and Myrtle ate in silence. Joseph was able to see Myrtle smile, because she wasn't looking at him but at Cu.

The dog was not averse to desserts, as his ingestion of an entire pan of apple crisp the next night confirmed. Most of Cu's gastronomic affections were discovered by accident, as were his preferred "accoutrements," in abundant supply in Myrtle's sewing room. Joseph arrived home one day to find the dog's playthings strewn about the parlour: a very wet black lace mantilla, a tooth-marked tatting shuttle, four well-bitten bobbins, a whitework bed jacket — no longer white, a Honiton lace wedding veil which — "Oh, thank God!" Myrtle exclaimed upon returning — had merely been fun to drag, a leg-of-mutton sleeve, and a heavily boned S-bend corset mauled into an almost perfect letter C.

Dear Myrtle,
I'm so sorry about your things.
— Joseph.

His note received no reply.

Myrtle usually arrived home first, and when Joseph entered quietly he heard her singing, the dog accompanying her — howling through English translations of the Schubert and Schumann lieder. Elgar's "Sea Pictures" elicited particularly earnest yelps; Dvorak's "Gypsy Songs" inspired wails. Every so often Joseph heard Myrtle patting the animal's side and whispering, then the sound of Cu crunching on a biscuit while she won several paid-for seconds of solo time. By the end of his first week at their house, scrawny Cu had gained three pounds.

Dear Joseph,
Cu seems to like the old blacking factory grounds. A good place
to take him walking when you're home. Please.
— Myrtle

Joseph called the dog down and took him to the wild, abandoned grounds of the burnt-out glue and penny stove-blacking enterprise. Though little remained of the P.R. Lamb Manufactory, several surviving posts were attractive enough to satisfy Cu's needs. Each night, as Cu grew stronger, their walks grew longer. Eventually, Joseph walked Cu through the dark Donvale streets, past the Necropolis, to another one of Lamb's enterprises, the Riverdale Zoo. While many of the exotic animals remained in their shelters during the December evenings, Cu barked through the fence in an attempt to gain the interest of the Siberian bear, two ocelots, a pair of arthritic wolves, and a hippo. The pheasants provided a momentary thrill. One night, the single-humped camel went down on her knees in what seemed like an act of supplication. Still Cu barked; defeated, the dromedary rose and walked away.

Wherever he was, Cu tried to herd things, generally unsuccessfully. Black squirrels ran up trees and jeered. Horses, broughams, and the electric street railway car remained steady on their courses. Cu even barked at the angel on the front doorstep.

Sometimes Cu barked at Joseph and Myrtle, too. Myrtle stroked Cu's head and whispered to him, while Joseph watched, wishing to step closer but unable to. He missed the touch of Myrtle's skin, the smell of her hair. Missing Myrtle in her presence was worse than missing her when she was gone. Inevitably he thought of her with the dress shop owner. Joseph walked until his mind emptied of the mess he'd made of his life. After the tavern, he made it back to his empty bed.

During the early days of Cu's residency, the dog stayed fenced in the backyard and, according to the neighbours, barked. The result was a series of friendly knocks on the door.

Dear Joseph,
Mrs. Horner suggests we hire the dog woman.
—Myrtle

"Do you want me to call on her?" penned Joseph in response to Myrtle's note.

"Yes," she replied on the back of a *La Nouvelle Mode* fashion plate. The plate featured an abundant length of red cape worn by a woman whose back was turned, yet her face in profile appeared to see the viewer from the corner of her eye. "Thank you, Joseph," Myrtle had added beside the almost-smiling woman. "— M."

❖ ❖ ❖

The dog woman's name was Nellie Sparks. She lived in a row house on Alpha Avenue, and thus was known as "Alpha Nellie." In her younger years, she reputedly had made her living as a washer woman and, by all accounts, she'd known cleaner days. She also had raised mastiffs and had acquired the reputation for being something of a savant in canine communication. Her present companion was a lap-dog named Puff, a blend of species unknown, that, despite its diminutive size, was as tough as her four-foot-ten mistress. The woman and her dog made a formidable pair. Each time Puff growled at Joseph, Nellie silenced her with a snap of her soil-encrusted fingers.

"You got a barker, eh?" Alpha Nellie said.

"Yes."

"You need dog services."

"We do."

"You need the indoor and the outdoor."

"Yes. Of course, we'll pay you."

"I take money. Or good meat."

Joseph would have offered a side of the Riverdale Zoo buffalo if he could have.

Alpha Nellie not only walked Cu each day at noon, but enrolled him in a full battery of training: hand signals, bones and manoeuvres, and low-pitched vocalizations. Very soon Cu's barking stopped, as Nellie had a calming effect. "Your wife catches on," Nellie told Joseph. "She knows a thing or two." Joseph and Myrtle paid in pork chops, and by the end of seven days of dog services, Cu was markedly more tranquil.

Joseph arrived home on Christmas Eve to find Myrtle writing to him at the dining room table. Upon seeing him, she folded the paper and actually spoke: "Just in case the dog has a setback, we should probably spare his digestion the tree ornaments." Their words were few and transactional, but at least they were talking to each other again.

No tree was trimmed; Christmas passed quietly. Myrtle gave Joseph a pair of carefully creased, cuffed trousers, for which he thanked her sincerely. He felt sad about the gramophone.

"Thank you for Cu," Myrtle said, patting the dog, who gnawed blithely on a ham bone that she'd tied with a red ribbon. "He's good company. And you remembered that dogs liked me."

For a moment Joseph thought that Myrtle might have been blushing, but she left the room quickly to check the meal. They didn't talk much throughout supper, apart from his compliments on her cooking. Myrtle hurried to her sewing room afterward.

Joseph sat for a long while after Myrtle's departure. Then he took a Christmas card from his vest pocket, left it on the dining room table and took the dog for a walk. "In countless ways I've been afraid to hurt you," he'd written. "In spite of my fears, I know that I've done even worse. I am sorry for what happened two years ago, Myrtle."

Joseph knew that Myrtle had brought home a wrapped present from Robert Raymond's shop. He had overheard her opening the paper in her room. He thought he heard Myrtle humming, but she was weeping.

34

*B*y the time the little girls and their mothers returned at the end of the month to collect the completed ballet dresses and wings, Cu was most delighted to lick their hands and their chins, and to burrow his nose into their skirts while they giggled, despite the mothers' nudges.

"Will you come to our ballet?" one child asked.

"I'll try," Joseph said.

The only child who did not arrive for her dress was Effie Douglas. Throughout the New Year's celebrations and resolutions, her wings hung on a hook on the inside of Myrtle's door.

In January, Joseph took Cu with him to work. Inevitably, Cu tried to herd the Belt Line tram; but gracious in defeat, he rode the tram with Joseph, unfazed by the passengers who stroked his head and commented on what a nice dog he was.

At the shop, Cu stretched out on the blanket beneath the soldering table. When Cho came to visit at the lunch hour, he could barely contain his eagerness. For weeks he'd been anticipating the time when he could walk Cu. "You've got to show him who's boss," Joseph said, passing on his recently learned lesson. Cho practised walking Cu on the leash, grinning, calling orders, puffing his chest and looking taller. In Sunlight Park, the boy was allowed to let the dog off the leash and the two of them ran. And ran.

Eventually, by agreement with Myrtle, Jing, and William, Cu was granted overnight visits with Cho. When the dog was away, nights were quiet at the Conlons'. On one such evening, the Conlons received the first call on their new telephone. Effie's father rang with apologies, informing Myrtle that the child wouldn't need the dress, but was asking for the wings.

An hour later a knock at the door startled Joseph, who was working on sketches at the dining room table. Myrtle opened the door to a tall man in a grey herringbone wool topcoat and a black cashmere scarf, who gripped his hat by its stiff brim. He looked too young for his white hair.

"Bill Douglas," the visitor said with a half-smile that betrayed his nervousness.

"You're Effie's father," Myrtle said.

Joseph shook Bill Douglas' kid-gloved hand. "Please come in." Joseph couldn't remember the last time they'd had a guest. Myrtle took Bill Douglas' coat and derby hat, then sat on the horsehair settee. Joseph badly wanted a drink.

"May I offer you something?" he asked. "A whiskey, perhaps?" Douglas politely declined, which made Joseph thirstier. "A cigarette, then?" Still Douglas shook his head. Then Joseph reached for his pipe and filled it, settling onto a wooden dining chair.

"I … I mentioned that Effie won't need her dance costume. Again, we apologize for your efforts, Mrs. Conlon. Of course, we'll pay you in full for the work you've done."

"I've no doubt of that, Mr. Douglas, and it's been my pleasure to make Effie's dress. But wouldn't she like the gown for … when she's recovered?" She returned to the coat stand where she'd hung it. She held the butter-yellow dress with embroidered daisies and a blue sash in the doorway, the place where the child had stood weeks before as Joseph sketched her.

Douglas stole a glance at the little dress, which seemed almost to be dancing.

"For a party perhaps, or a special outing," Myrtle said.

For a moment, Joseph saw Myrtle when they were children at the fair, her look of amazement at the wealthy children's clothing. Now, here she was, so deservedly proud of her work. He was proud of her, too. And he wished that she could be proud of him — of his drawings, at least. She used to like them. Joseph felt ashamed for thinking of himself.

"Effie won't be getting better," Bill Douglas said quietly. "The doctors are conclusive now. Of course, we'd hoped for different news. All the weight loss — we thought maybe a change in diet would help. Then we thought that more movement — the dance lessons. She was always an eager, active little thing. She ..." his voice broke off for a moment. "Effie suffers from diabetes mellitus, Mr. and Mrs. Conlon. She's starving to death. My daughter's dying."

Myrtle remained motionless. "We're terribly sorry."

Douglas rubbed his eyes on his sleeve, smiling through the taut mask of his face. "I'm sorry to share my trouble like this. I wish I'd come with better news. Effie would like to have the wings you made for her, Mrs. Conlon. She talks about them."

"Of course." Myrtle rose and went upstairs. The two men sat in silence until she returned. Tiny beads shimmered in the gaslight.

"May I go with you?" Myrtle asked. "I'd like to give Effie the wings myself."

"I think my daughter would like that. Thank you, Mrs. Conlon. I'll be pleased to bring you. But ... I do warn you that my wife is not herself."

"I understand. Really, I do."

❖ ❖ ❖

Thereafter, quite often, Myrtle took the dog with her for evening walks, west and north into Rosedale to visit Effie. Her work at home slowed, and Joseph rarely heard her singing. Alone in the empty house, Joseph thought about the days when they first moved there — Myrtle's joy as they crossed the threshold into a new life. The sight of her in their bedroom, undressing. Her fine auburn hair brushed out and shining. The softness of her touch, the sureness. Her embrace in their bed where he'd slept alone on so many nights since. Myrtle had swelled with life when they first came here; she'd welcomed it. And he'd wanted to share her joy; but so often he'd felt dread.

Sometimes now, when she returned from walking late in the evening, her face was streaked with tears, and she didn't speak. While he could understand she must have had reason to seek silence after visiting Effie, part of him felt something else was troubling Myrtle.

Joseph followed her one night. She turned right at Parliament, continuing north to the cemetery where a man stood waiting by the gate. Raymond. Joseph watched the two open their arms to each other.

Then he walked south to the first tavern.

The next night neither of them went out. Joseph heard Myrtle tearing fabric behind her sewing-room door. She sang again, but without words. He drank without stopping, then slept. When he awoke, she was gone.

By the time of the children's ballet, Myrtle was exhausted, thin, but unable to settle. She greeted the girls with greenhouse roses. She embraced and congratulated each child after the performance while Joseph watched from the wings. She congratulated the parents, glowing in the presence of her appreciative customers. Turning from them, Myrtle looked cheerless, haggard.

She gave up her singing lessons when Effie died.

Myrtle and Joseph walked with the Douglas family and friends across the frozen cemetery ground to where Effie would rest once the earth had thawed. Myrtle took Joseph's arm and leaned into him as they made their way along the icy path. Suddenly, she pressed her body fully against him and wept, burying her face in his coat.

Though he kept his arm around her, Joseph felt as frozen as the world around them. Myrtle's sorrow immobilized him. She pulled away, clutching her scarf tightly beneath her tear-streaked face. They placed flowers on the snow when the child's coffin was taken to lie in the vault with the other winter dead awaiting burial.

On the night of Effie's funeral, Myrtle took Cu walking. Joseph couldn't blame her. All he could do for her, he realized, was draw, as insufficient as that was.

Joseph worked on his sketch of the child in her special dress and wings, heightening the contrast, and musing as to what message the little girl might have been trying to give him. For the first time, Joseph turned the handle on Myrtle's door and entered. He lit the coal-oil lamp and turned up the flame until the walls glowed in a warm, steady light. Joseph stared in wonder. Fastened to the wall were fashion plates, some intact and some torn, with handwriting scrawled at the edges; sheet music; lace pieces; a ballet dress torso ripped from its skirt; the un-seamed skirt with a string of white feathers loosely pinned, aflutter over the daisies; a photograph of Myrtle's parents; a studio photograph of Beatrice and Myrtle as small children, staring seriously in matching frocks. Dresses hung on hooks, spectral in the dim light. Myrtle's room was art.

Joseph set Effie's picture down where Myrtle would see it, and opened the top drawer, searching for a pen. The drawer was empty but for his Christmas card, a folded page, and the five-cent bracelet, perfectly preserved, that he'd bought for her years ago, at the Industrial Fair. Joseph recalled how begrudgingly he'd purchased that trinket, a way of appeasing Myrtle because he wanted to leave early. Joseph recalled how she had stretched out her arm so that she could admire his gift. He pictured the frayed cuffs on her yellow dress, her joy and obliviousness to his agitation. Suddenly he didn't have to imagine her, because here she was, unfolding on the page he opened — a drawing he'd made long ago. Joseph removed the yellowed paper, gazing at the girl's smiling face: one he'd studied to get the lines right, but hadn't really seen. For all these years she must have saved it. Only now did Joseph see the child Myrtle had been. He found himself shaking with sadness. And something else. Something he couldn't name, but pushed back down with the poison. She should have known better than to place her trust in him. Joseph closed the drawer and the shaking stopped.

In the next one he discovered a pencil and a box tied with a brown satin ribbon with Myrtle's name on it. He'd seen the writing before, on orders from Robert Raymond's shop. He wanted to open it, but didn't. He wanted to throw it out the window, too, but he didn't do that either. Raymond's Christmas present. He set it on the table. With the pencil and a blank page carefully torn from Myrtle's address book, Joseph wrote the short message he'd planned and placed it beside the drawing of Effie.

"What are you doing in here?"

"Myrtle," Joseph said, gasping. "I didn't hear you come in. I —"

"Get out. Please."

"I didn't look at anything," Joseph said, catching himself in his own blundering lie. "I mean … I didn't see …"

Myrtle stared at the box with the brown satin ribbon. Then she gazed at Joseph as he looked away, too embarrassed to speak.

"He pays attention to me."

Joseph pushed the drawer firmly closed. He felt the blood rising in his face as he bolted from the room, from the house, the door slamming behind him.

35

*B*y mid-summer, Joseph found himself working through the weekends in the Ramsey offices. He took solace in sitting alone in the shop, savouring the silence, and in a Saturday ritual — a walk for a four-o'clock pint, which took him through a Catholic section of the city. On several occasions he stepped into St. Mary's church, simply to feel the cool relief of it. He stared at scenes painted by others and remembered the image of St. Brigid staring down at him, long ago, in St. Patrick's, Keady. Roused from memory by birds' shadows beyond the St. Mary's glass, he proceeded down to the Sheaf tavern for a beer with the Irishmen. Joseph sat alone.

On the last Saturday in August, he discovered that the sketch book he'd brought with him was one he'd forgotten about. He hadn't seen it in months. In the back, he found words he'd scrawled, erased, and rewritten several times before setting them down for Myrtle.

> *Dearest M.,*
> *As a child you were my friend. As a woman, you've been so much more to me.*
> *—J.*

That much was true. Then he read the erasures — old words she'd read before: "I've been afraid to hurt you." He'd lied so many times.

He knew that he'd been afraid to hurt himself. Joseph tore out the page and crumpled it. At least he'd spared her that.

As a child when Joseph had stared at St. Brigid he'd felt shame, because he believed she knew him. Now the shame was mixed with nostalgia, dread, and yearning. "The sin of my very being," Joseph muttered, recalling Granny Dolan's words over his second beer. Sometimes St. Brigid and Granny Dolan became one in his mind. He imagined that they had known him, not only as a child with all the wrongs that made up his being, but as an adult too: the sum total of his sins. The barmaid asked if he wanted another beer. He wanted one very badly. He declined.

Outside, people walked west toward the summer's annual fair. Joseph had stopped looking for circuses long ago. Suddenly, without trying to understand why, he needed to be sure that Deary Avery wasn't at the Exhibition. Confirming her absence was now as important as the many years of searching for her had been.

He joined the throng for the perils.

The Manufacturers' Building drew the biggest crowds. Outside, Joseph watched a boy hold his younger sister's hand, leading her through the crowd. The boy pushed on, while the younger one chattered until she fell and cried. When a clown walked by, she chattered again. "Try the two-prize throw!" a man's voice called. "Step up and win two prizes." Joseph stared off at the Ferris wheel, suddenly shaking his head at the futility of coming here.

Near it was the same Vardo wagon that Joseph had seen three years earlier; Madame Ava sat before it at a small table. Before he had time to think, he set a dime on Ava's tin plate.

"Palm or tarot?"

"Palm."

She took his hand in her warm, brown fingers and studied the lines. For much longer she stared into his face. Joseph looked away, but still he let her hold his hand. He felt soothed.

At last Ava said: "You find."

Joseph could scarcely find his own voice. "What?" And then: "Who?"

"The ones you seek."

He thanked her and dropped two more coins onto her plate.

"A winner every time! A prize winner every time!" shouted a man at the Giant Ring Toss. A boy in tights and a jester's cap was juggling. Another clown called: "Mysteries and miracles, curiosities of nature! Giants, monsters, mermaids! Step right up for a ticket! Step up to the circus!"

"Is this Kelly's Big Top?" Joseph asked.

"Kelly's? No, sir," the young promoter answered through his broadly painted grin. "We're Rutherford's — the best show in the province." He shouted: "Mysteries! Miracles!" Then he added: "See for yourself."

Joseph felt lost — then irritated by his own foolishness. Better not to have hoped at all. Nonetheless, he paid his money and walked through the wicket. A parade of elephants elicited laughter and applause. Under smaller tents were the various freak-show stalls, but he couldn't bear to look. Joseph watched the trapeze flyer and a woman dancing on a horse.

He walked away from Rutherford's Circus into the cool evening air, smiling now at his lunacy in thinking that he might find Deary when he knew she was gone. Kelly's show had never returned. Beside the roundabout, Joseph remembered Myrtle's excitement when he'd taken her for that ride so many years ago. The ride had brought a joy that Joseph couldn't understand. For him, the wheel just went in circles.

Joseph sought refuge in the relative quiet of the botanical gardens. At the very least, the day had brought Madame Ava's warm hand and tired, kindly face.

Past the tables with the winning petunias, African violets, and geraniums, Joseph sought the arrangements that had escaped the judges' written comments. Perhaps the fragrance of roses drew him. Maybe he was lured by the bright petals and shining leaves of the hibiscus. The gleam of setting sunlight through the windows was enough to settle him. Joseph sat on a wooden chair with his hands folded in his lap.

"Colleen."

A butterfly fluttered up from among the branches.

A young woman looked at him. Suddenly Joseph saw nothing but her face and the knot of her hair, loosening at the nape of her neck. She smiled and walked towards him, and Joseph's eyes, blurred by tears, lost her details for a moment. A young man walked beside her; an old woman shuffled behind.

"Colleen," the man repeated, "we must be going."

She wanted to stay a minute more, she said.

"We'll wait outside then."

Old Ciara stared too, but the aged woman's whitened eyes were blind.

The hibiscus shone like a red and silent trumpet. "I've never seen this kind before," said the woman who might have invited Joseph to walk in the moonlight on the Black Pad down to Keady. Anyone in Darkley would have recognized her as Nora Conlon's daughter.

"Colleen?" The old woman's voice was the hull of a dark ship, rocking.

"Just a moment, Gran."

She bent to touch one hibiscus petal, ever so lightly, smiling.

"Do I know you?" the young woman asked Joseph.

In the multitude, she was the one missing.

In the dream, she was the one knocking.

She was the one he'd hugged goodbye at Union Station, her tiny hand waving, the warm weight of her lifted, lost. But Joseph's thoughts were not an answer to her question. How long had he wandered?

Joseph saw her as a little child laughing and running to him again beside the Callan River.

"No," he said.

❖ ❖ ❖

No longer could he stop the memories.

❖ ❖ ❖

Joseph was a child once more, on the road to Navan Fort.

"This road has no beginning," Annie whispered to him.

"We'll find it," Mam said. No one knew who'd planted the old trees around the hill. "They're part of the treasures," Mam told him. Her eyes were red from crying.

"Keep walking," Annie said, the breeze said.

The faces of the people in the fields and by their doors were solemn. "Solemn" was a word in Joseph's speller. "I can read," he whispered to the spring soil. Yellow and purple vetch would come and he wouldn't see them because soon he'd be in a new world.

"Read my face," Annie said.

"Where?" He looked at the moon. He looked at the stars and all the tangled branches pointing.

"Sleep now." At Navan Fort, Nora, Joseph and Colleen unrolled their blankets in the cool night air. In the muddy ditch, he fancied he could see the first shoots growing. Hares, newly breathing, wriggled into holes in the sides of the hill. The ground was soft. The stars were bright. Joseph heard Mam whispering through her tears.

"She's praying," Annie said.

On the hill, wrapped in shawls and kneeling, Mam muttered words that Joseph couldn't fully hear. He drifted in and out of sleep, his shivers subsiding in the heat of the Monaghan quilt and Colleen's little body snuggled next to him. He heard Annie say: "You're in a dream."

❖ ❖ ❖

Half-awake, Joseph remembered his father's face in a Keady Mill window: his hand with a white cuff, waving; his clean white collar; his manners. He met them on the lawn behind the mill, well away from the street. Then the four walked together, the secret little family, along a path into the trees. "Joe," Mam said to Joseph's father, not to him, and Joseph hummed a tune for Annie so she'd come and see how miserable he was. When Mam pinched his arm, he stopped humming. His father held Mam's hand, making Joseph more miserable. He patted Joseph's head and said: "You look like a strong boy, Joe. Strong enough to go to sea, then?"

The sound of Mam laughing. How he loved her laugh. Joseph wanted so badly to make her smile at him, too.

"Yes, sir," he replied with manners, as his father reached down and placed three coins in his hand. Joseph buried them in his shoe with a "Thank you." The man's gold ring, his clean hand. It didn't matter if his father came with them. All Joseph wanted was to make Mam smile.

As the coins grew warm, Joseph knew how he'd spend them.

The Bottle Man.

On the Friday before their journey, Joseph ran two miles to Keady Market where the roads came together. He ran splashing along the muddy Black Pad, through the wet fields past countless blackthorn hedges, and into the street, alone. Joseph brought his coins. The Bottle Man waited at his cart of creaks and cures. "I'll take three of the kind with ladies in pink flowers — for my mam," Joseph said, laying down his money for all the medicine Mam would ever need.

Joseph didn't pray for his father to stay behind when they sailed for Canada. He prayed only that the bottles would be safe.

❖ ❖ ❖

Mud got into Joseph's nose while he lay awake, thinking of his father and the bottles, in the ditch at Navan Fort. Joseph's cheek was moist and the quilt was itchy. Giving up on sleep, he crawled up the mound. For a moment the praying woman seemed to glow in the dawn light and Joseph wondered if she was Mother Mary herself. She looked into his eyes. Then Joseph recognized Mam. The magpie circled.

"Where's the other magpie?" He was groggy, but he knew that kind of bird should be seen in a pair. "Not right to see one alone," Granny Dolan had told him; never would he see Granny Dolan again. And Mam wasn't listening. "This is Ireland," Joseph said to the dirt he'd just swallowed. He squeezed the grass that was dead and not quite born again. His eyes were blurry.

When he saw Mam, the only bottle she'd brought with the lady and pink flowers was empty. She'd spilled it, Joseph reasoned. The thought made the secret of his gift all the better. "She spilled it by accident," he whispered.

Joseph took his mother's hand, but he didn't read her face. She was too flushed and wet to look at now. Her skirt was a better place to hide. Mam's skirt was smooth and warm, and when he pressed his face there her hand rubbed his neck.

In Mam's left hand was the letter that she had opened at the house where Joseph's father had never arrived. Joseph's father was a liar. Mam opened and closed the letter many times before putting it away. She buried the empty bottle on the mound.

The three secret bottles in his pack were silent.

He found himself jumping as they walked to the Armagh station. He kicked at the stones. Colleen slapped at the air. On the dock at Derry, he wished his mother's face would dry.

Some time after stepping onto the ship, the words came. "I have a gift," he told Mam. On the morning of the third day he touched Mam's shuddering back. "For you."

36

*I*n the kitchen, Myrtle stood beside the boiling pan in the final stages of ironing a man's dress shirt. She peeled the shirt from the board and hung it behind her on a cupboard knob. From a pile of newly sewn clothes on the table, she pulled a tiny Christening gown and set it before her, studying it for a moment, and then carefully working the steaming iron tip into the folds.

"Joseph, I need to speak with you."

"Myrtle ..."

"Joseph, it's time that we talk about a divorce."

At first her words didn't register. He noticed only the delicate beads of moisture on Myrtle's brow and the way her hair curled in the humid air. She worked in a thin, sleeveless nightdress, her hands moving confidently along the tiny gown.

His words came before he could stop them. "I suppose you'll move to Spadina Avenue, then. Or do you fancy Raymond's Rosedale house? Is he divorcing his wife too?"

"I've quit my job at Raymond's!" Myrtle said. She set the iron down firmly and turned to face him. Joseph wanted to look into her eyes, but couldn't. Instead, he looked at the white gown trailing over the edge of the board; at his empty hands, at hers.

"Why?" he asked quietly.

"Why what? Why a divorce, or why did I quit?" Then, after a

moment Myrtle said: "I'll answer both: because I want my heart back, Joseph. Damaged as it is, I claim it. I vow to live by it. I can't — no — I *won't* — live without it. I can live with the injuries, Joseph. I can live with myself. I'm not sure that I can live with you."

Joseph thought of a thousand things that he should say, but didn't. "Are you pleased with your decision, then?" he asked, finally.

"What decision?" Myrtle replied, bewildered.

"To leave Raymond's."

"Yes." Myrtle lifted the little dress, smoothing the arms and adjusting the lace collar. "I'm looking for my own shop. I'm going into business for myself."

"I thought you had a shop upstairs. I thought you already were in business for yourself."

"Well, yes ... in a manner of speaking."

"Your work is more than a manner of speaking. The things you do for people, the pieces you make — your work is beautiful. People value it. You can do those things," he said, stepping closer. "You could stay in business here, in our house."

Myrtle continued to stare at the little dress. She lifted it onto a hanger and hung it in front of the shirt. In the same moment she reached for a lady's jacket on top of the large heap and lay it along the board. "I want my own shop," she said, pressing the lapel perfectly smooth. "I've saved for this, Joseph. You have no need to worry about my means. I can support myself."

"Myrtle."

"We don't choose our children," she declared quietly.

"I wish you well in your work, Myrtle," Joseph said, wishing that he could brush the fallen strand of hair from her eyes.

"Thank you," she said, faintly. "I'm sorry, Joseph. Things didn't turn out as we planned. I'm not blameless in our marriage. I acknowledge that."

Joseph stood in silence.

"Did you hear what I said to you?" she asked quietly.

"Yes, but you had no need. Don't speak against yourself. Please. You said 'consider' ... Only *consider* a divorce ... Of course. You're right, Myrtle." As usual, he'd said nothing to Myrtle that she'd really wanted to hear.

37

*A*fter Joseph destroyed his initial designs for the three Multitudes windows, Cora's face emerged upon a new page. He drew her searching, her eyes intent upon the blue hydrangea of the foreground that would glow when the sun rose from the east end of Piper Street. Images of the healings of the official's son, the cripple at Bethesda pool, the man born blind, and Lazarus, were watched by a woman in her wheeled chair.

Bette called the south wall project Joseph's Miracle Windows. "A miracle if they get finished at all," Kenneth Ramsey grumbled, too overworked to do anything but wait. The construction of St. John's Anglican Church was almost complete, and Joseph volunteered to work nights in order to make up the time. Each miracle was different; each was witnessed. As usual each patron made requests: an uncle here, a nephew there, a wife, three daughters and a niece, and himself of course — all satisfied by fish and bread and wine. Joseph made sure that the faces were rendered accurately in a biblical village crowd scene with distinctly Torontonian features. The other faces were drawn from memory: the men of the mill on the rocks by the Sea of Galilee; the newsboys scattered on temple steps and empty lots, impossible to marshal. On the ground, a green ribbon. The girls from the Esplanade pushed at the edges of the paper. Joseph placed a young Myrtle far from her sister, in the third panel of the children's window.

She stood in the background, barefoot on cobbles in a frayed yellow dress. In her hands she held an unfinished chain of dandelions.

❖ ❖ ❖

On a separate page, Joseph sketched the old man who had sat painting beside his cottage in the park years ago, when as a boy Joseph followed Deary secretly on her walks to Grenadier Pond after escaping from the orphanage. The old man always sat there with his paint box, ushering things into being: hollyhocks in deep purple, orange, and butter-yellow spears; lilies and feather plants; a twisted log with a serpent face. He seemed content at the edge of his garden, where black squirrels scampered. White-haired and glitter-eyed, he gazed up from designs that could easily blow away, though he didn't seem to worry.

Joseph closed his eyes because the scene was so clear. The old man watched Deary follow the path on her way to the long meadow. She nodded as she passed. People said he was the city's oldest architect. "His wife went mad," the orphanage children said; she'd stared from her bedroom window at the creation of her tomb, his final gift to her. He had loved her, people said. He loved her still.

The old man had another family — children, long grown up, by a woman who lived downtown. The old man loved her, too. "These things happen," Sister Martha said, sighing, though no one was supposed to hear.

In his mind, peering through the hollyhocks, hiding among the rose trees, Joseph followed Deary down towards the tomb of the old man's wife. He tried to go unnoticed, though he suspected that the old man painted him also. Deary finally turned along the bluff leading down to the pond, well past the old man's house and its window ghost.

"You're following me," Deary said. "You have to give me something."

"All I have is this glass."

She put a piece of his beach glass in her mouth and pulled it out again. It glistened. She handed it back. "Nice, but I want something else." They walked towards the pond. "I want your story."

He began to tell of the Brown Bull of Cooley, but she stopped him. "Not an old Irish tale. Your story. What is *your* story, Joseph?"

The pond offered up the sky in countless reflected fragments. The grass was soft and high, and smelled green. Then the words came — released to Deary, to the pond, to the breeze and wild ducks and to the flowers — even to the old man. And for several minutes Joseph's story was a simple vibration with the birdsong.

Only one part remained unspoken. It had broken off and lodged inside him.

"Close your eyes," Deary said. She kissed his closed eyelids. Story time was over.

◊ ◊ ◊

Joseph knew that Deary would not return. He accepted that knowledge now, in the night, by the steady burn of the ovens and a single lamp.

Joseph placed Deary's image beside a dove as it descended in the wrong window. The Holy Spirit belonged in Bette and Simon's baptism of Jesus; but Joseph's people were in need of miracles.

Ramseys who recognized themselves in Joseph's paintings were inclined to shake their heads. "Unusual," Kenneth Ramsey said.

"Glorious," William said.

In the long evenings, the shop took the place of the taverns. The hand moving across paper and glass turned water into wine that Joseph didn't need to drink. Working was shot through with loneliness, but familiar, and welcome. A cloak was crimson, another lavender; haloes shone and hands opened. Grass bent gently on the breeze.

Myrtle accompanied Joseph to the dedication service, though they'd spoken little since their talk of divorce. The Reverend Frank

Wheeler guided the congregation through the renderings from the annunciation and nativity, through St. John's baptism of Jesus and the good shepherd windows, then on to the sanctuary windows depicting the crucifixion story.

Myrtle stared at Joseph's south wall creations, reading his multitudes slowly and carefully. When Wheeler arrived at the south wall in his narrative, Joseph feared that the Toronto details jarred the onlookers, breaking the illusion of the Holy Land, banal anachronisms set amidst much more important images. His work didn't make sense. Kenneth had been wrong to trust him. Panic was followed by shame, familiar and tolerable.

"This is a truly uplifting vision," the minister said heartily above the crowd's applause. Joseph was numbed by the sound. He barely heard the man's words — something about a living God for a living city. Wheeler thanked the committee for its plan. He thanked Joseph Conlon for his vision, and the donors for their generosity.

Myrtle smiled. "Your work is beautiful."

He loved the windows then.

38

$\mathcal{T}$he spring of 1904 was unusually cold. When the city caught fire, the wind from the northwest pushed through Wellington Street in steady brilliancy.

The buildings burned like bodies. The windows: alarmed, stark eyes. Creaking bones collapsed in sprays of spark. Poles toppled. Water froze and melted again, as though the whole world had become one smoking ruin, icicled like an old man's beard. Light was doused and flared again. MacIvor's Flour Mill exploded and sagged in on itself. Much of Front Street had already been incinerated before the crews arrived — from Hamilton, Brantford, London, Niagara Falls, and Buffalo — and would lie in ruins for decades after.

Joseph entered St. John's, unnoticed by the crowd attempting to save the Queen's Hotel across the street. The church was quiet. He bolted the doors behind him.

The east and south wall windows blistered from the heat of neighbouring structures. Thick smoke, enveloping the building's exterior, prevented flames from lighting all of the Sea of Galilee, Capernaum, and the faces in the silent, once-bright crowd. Yet several of Joseph's figures still glowed erratically.

In the window of miraculous healings, a woman in a blue dress knelt beside a pool where an angel troubled the waters. With open palms, the woman glimmered.

Joseph hated her image now — not because she would vanish, but because at last, he would fully see her.

All at once, anger seized him in a way he'd never known. He kicked at the sides of the newly dedicated pews — threw a hymn book at the lectern, where it connected with the eagle's gold wing and crashed down onto the marble. He took aim with the King James and knocked down three silver candlesticks. He picked one up and wielded it again onto the steps of the altar. He swore at Kenneth Ramsey's depiction of Christ's ascension in a sky lit by flames. He swore again at the same figure in a crimson cloak, carrying the lost sheep. Joseph paced the aisle, kicking hymn books as he went, shouting, groaning, terrified.

Beyond resisting, he crawled towards his multitude windows; Joseph raised his gaze to the woman in blue.

✧ ✧ ✧

A scene that had long been submerged finally surfaced. "I have something to tell you," he whispered. Joseph sank to his knees on the tiles; then he lay flat, arms outstretched, feeling the closeness of the earth — all he wanted now. The roof of the church was burning.

Above him on the mound at Navan Fort, Joseph's mother walked across the grass. He watched her blue skirt sway.

From where he lay, Joseph saw her pour the contents of the bottle onto the grass. She wept quietly, knelt, and dug a hole in the damp earth carefully with her fingers. Mam buried the lady in pink flowers. "A healing place," she muttered. "God save us."

She stayed a long time on her knees.

Eventually, Mam returned to Joseph and Colleen, removed her shawl and wrapped it snugly around her children in the shelter of the ditch, shielding them from the chilly night air.

"Finish the story of the children turned to swans," Joseph said.

She smiled and for a moment she didn't look tired or sad. Mam looked calm. She looked safe. "They grew up," she said quietly. "They turned into people."

"Is that all?"

Mam nodded. Joseph didn't question Mam for changing the story, though it puzzled him almost as much as pouring out the contents of the bottle.

Now, years later in the burning church, Joseph realized that he'd known the answer for a long time, but not until this moment had he faced it. She'd tried to save herself that night, and might have, if he had not mistaken poison for medicine.

So proud he was of his gift, on the death ship. He held his head high, showing her how much he cared. He could take care of her. "For you," Joseph said, with his best manners like a grown-up man, handing her the bottles. Because he loved her.

The last picture of Mam's smiling face would not burn. He opened himself to it now, in agony and in relief.

Joseph received the memory like a shawl tucked gently around him.

For a long time he lay listening to the beams creak above him. He crawled to a bench and sat, watching his pictures glow and fade in irregular pulses of firelight. His eyelids grew heavy as he inhaled the thickening vapour.

Three words came through the smoke: "I forgive you."

❖ ❖ ❖

One by one, the windows shattered. The ascension came down in sheets that seemed to shriek as they exploded on the chancel floor. The crucifixion and empty tomb fell next. Joseph's window of miraculous healings disintegrated. Smoke filled the sanctuary and the nave. Flames lapped at the skeletal window frames and licked the pillars that still held the ceiling. Joseph saw the hull of a ship in the groaning roof beams and watched the children's window buckle and slip from its frame, smashing. The ruin of his work was complete.

❖ ❖ ❖

He staggered through the door frame, to a ruined city block. At the bottom of the stairs he doubled over, coughing until he retched. When he could breathe again, Joseph walked through the smoke beneath criss-crossed wires, past ruined columns, burnt-out facades, and alley dogs panting and scuttling. St. John's Church collapsed shortly before dawn. Joseph watched it fall. In the pre-dawn light he walked north, released into a multitude beyond his drawing.

Myrtle Conlon waited with Cu where the damage was greatest. Walls cracked and toppled, but Myrtle knew where Joseph would return from. Joseph reached for her hand and she took his. Cu barked and wagged his tail. Then Joseph pulled her close to him and kissed her neck, her soft cheek, her lips. He breathed in the sweet smell of her skin.

Joseph and Myrtle walked home from the fire.

Epilogue

*U*nion Station survived the Fire of 1904, as did a note addressed to "Mr. Joseph Deary," penned by a stranger's hand. The Circus was coming, and would he please meet the train. "We understand that you are the next of kin."

At the doors to the station's new building, a waif sold newspapers hand over fist and asked Joseph if he'd like a shine. Joseph put a coin in the youngster's cup. Then he made his way through the arcade and down the steps to wait under the old clock tower. The clowns' painted faces didn't seem out of place here. A man juggled apples and caught one in his teeth. Wrappers from factory candy drifted. He heard chatter. He heard bells.

Joseph sat on the bench beneath the station sign's gold letters.

He held a card up so he could be found.

Presently, a young woman wearing a trapeze artist's leotard and skirt under an open coat approached him. "Mr. Deary?"

"Joseph Conlon," he answered. "But I'm the one you're looking for."

The woman held a page signed "Darlene Avery." Miss Paradis had left it before she stepped into the air from a bridge in Grand Rapids, Michigan, she told him. "A passer-by saw her leap. He never saw her surface. They dragged a good deal of the river, but it's deep, and the current's strong. A body could have been washed along for miles. She jumped on the sunniest of days. I'm sorry."

A boy in overalls parted the crowd. Heated, flustered, he kicked the bench before facing Joseph. "I think she swam," the boy said. "I wasn't s'posed to tell, but I can't help it now. She was practising." He looked around at the company of incredulous performers. "That day she told me to meet her on the bridge, but when I got there she was gone."

"She told you lots of things, boy," an old woman said.

"And showed me, too. She was my friend. I saw her jump from high places before, and she could swim under water. Only this time she left her dress folded up under a stone on that bridge. And she left this." He reached into his shirt and pulled out a white feather.

Several troupe members shook their heads.

"It was ... a very high bridge," the trapeze artist said.

The boy studied the feather before handing it to Joseph. "You can have it, I s'pose."

Joseph managed a smile for the lad, whose expression eased as Joseph tucked the feather into a clasp beneath the boy's collar. "Here."

The station clock tolled, and for a moment all the old, invisible wings inside him fluttered.

He let them go.

People stood solemnly, holding their hats, as Joseph stepped forward into the calm and another woman spoke. "In her letter she said the wee girl's yours, sir."

The little child was wrapped in a pale blue cape knitted carefully in measured rows. She rested on an aerialist's hip, sucked the fingers of one hand and held the other out to show the tiny flower that someone had drawn there with her name.

"Hello, Annie," Joseph said.

Acknowledgements

The Shining Fragments began years ago when the spirit of an Irish boy came into my life; I knew I'd have to cross the ocean to find out who he was.

I remain grateful to Maurice Batley for sharing his knowledge of ships and rail history in the 1880s, and for helping to arrange my first trip to Northern Ireland in 2003. Thanks to Roger Weatherup of the Armagh County Museum, and to his wife Anne, who welcomed me and took delight in showing me their country. Thanks to author Trevor Geary for sharing his expertise on Armagh County history, and for taking me to explore 19th century mill sites, including Darkley and Keady. Thanks to Dr. Greer Ramsey and Brenda Collins for discussing regional traditions and industrial history. Thanks to Maureen and Francis Oliver who hosted me at their home near the Lake of Treasures; from there, I walked to Navan Fort and dreamed this book. Thanks to my mother, Gail Blackburn, who made my trips to Northern Ireland possible by creating "Camp Gigi" for my then teenage daughter, Charlotte.

Piecing together Toronto's past was both a passion and a challenge. First and foremost, I am indebted to the Toronto Public Library which offered me a wealth of resources and became, as it had been in my childhood, my home away from home. Thanks to Sister Veronica O'Reilly of the Sisters of St. Joseph and to Linda Wicks, the Toronto

Sisters' Archivist, for resources and insights into the city's early Catholic institutions. A forever thank-you to "Élève Bordeleau," my Tante Monique Bordeleau Blackburn, for her insights into growing up inside a Catholic institution. Thanks to Audrey Borges, Records Analyst at the CNE Archives, for resources on the Toronto Industrial Fair. Thanks to retired miller Anton Pracyk for lessons on grain milling, including a field trip. Thanks to Theodore Hazen, a master miller and mill historian, who put significant efforts into helping me to visualize the interior of a late-1880s commercial flour mill. Ted's detailed e-mails, including ingeniously sleuthed photographs and links, enabled me to write accurately.

Decades ago, I began paying attention to Toronto's stained glass windows, not only in churches, but in the city's Victorian homes. While researching present-day Cabbagetown (formerly Don Vale), I discovered the impressive, five-generation McCausland family stained glass business: in fact, the oldest stained glass company in North America. Thanks to Andrew McCausland for kindly spending time with me, imparting family lore, and teaching me some basics of window making. While the Ramseys of my novel are fictitious, they were inspired, in part, by Andrew McCausland's colourful histories.

Thanks to the Ontario Arts Council for several votes of support in my early days of drafting. Thanks to Samuel Waldner for his insights, astute commentary, and rock-solid encouragement much later in the process.

I am deeply grateful to the literary angels who helped in the creation of this book: to Mary Jo Morris for her readings and valuable encouragement, advice, and friendship; to Wayson Choy for his generous heart and shining words; to editor Charis Wahl, whose wisdom and sensitivity helped to guide and grace my revision process; to Denise Bukowski who believed in the book and worked hard on its behalf; to Mary Morrissey who coached me in turning stumbling blocks into stepping stones on the way to publication; to Julie Roorda who ultimately copyedited this book and helped significantly in making its publication happen. Heartfelt thanks to Michael Mirolla and Guernica Editions for saying yes.

Thanks to my dear family, friends, and colleagues for their dedication and enthusiasm, and their patience. Finally, thanks to my loving and supportive husband, Hugh McBride, whom I met while working on *The Shining Fragments*. As it turned out, I could not have finished this book without him.

About the Author

Robin Blackburn McBride is an author and poet, as well as a teacher, speaker, and coach in human potential. She was born and raised in Toronto, and lived in that city for much of her life.

Robin has a passion for local history, intergenerational family stories, and the hero's journey in its myriad forms. The idea for *The Shining Fragments* came as a call to adventure: to connect with the past and explore the land of her ancestors. Research for the novel led Robin to Northern Ireland twice in the early 2000s.

Robin holds degrees in Drama, English, and Education from the University of Toronto. Her self-help e-book, *Birdlight: Freeing Your Authentic Creativity*, became an Amazon Best Seller in 2016, and has since been released as both a trade paperback and audiobook, read by the author. Robin's volume of poetry, *In Green*, was published by Guernica in 2002.

The Shining Fragments is her first novel.

Robin lives with her husband, Hugh McBride, in Gatineau, Quebec.